BROTHER OF WRATH

The Blackwood Brotherhood
Book 3

Wendy Vella

ARE YOU SIGNED UP FOR DRAGONBLADE'S BLOG?

You'll get the latest news and information on exclusive giveaways, exclusive excerpts, coming releases, sales, free books, cover reveals and more.

Check out our complete list of authors, too!

No spam, no junk. That's a promise!

Sign Up Here

www.dragonbladepublishing.com

Dearest Reader;

Thank you for your support of a small press. At Dragonblade Publishing, we strive to bring you the highest quality Historical Romance from some of the best authors in the business. Without your support, there is no 'us', so we sincerely hope you adore these stories and find some new favorite authors along the way.

Happy Reading!

CEO, Dragonblade Publishing

CHAPTER ONE

THE MARQUESS OF Stafford stood before the old stone house, its looming façade as forbidding as the memories it held. Blackwood Hall. The name alone left a sour taste in his mouth. Built from dark gray stone, the right wing smothered in thick coils of ivy, it sprawled wide enough to swallow five London townhouses whole. Time had passed, yet the place remained unchanged—cold and unyielding as the day he'd left it. Merely setting eyes upon it again stirred the old anger Jamie could never bury, a reminder that some stains upon the soul could never be washed away.

He'd lost part of himself within these walls. He might appear to be everything his lineage suggested, a man of consequence with one of the oldest titles in England, with wealth, estates, two sisters, and friends who loved him, but none of it had erased the demons Blackwood Hall had left him with, nor the numbness he still carried.

Jamie had learned to hide it. People saw a man who was amiable enough when required, a gentleman who walked in society alongside those of similar birth. His civility was a façade, and one he knew he would wear until he drew his last breath.

"I will find you," he vowed, eyes fixed on the building. "I will hunt you like the animal you are and end you."

Turning his horse on that vow, he headed back along the road as if the dogs of hell were at his heels. Bent low over the long black neck, he let the cold wind lash his face, gulping in air—anything to rid himself of the furious rage.

The wind slapped him hard, accompanied by the rustle of leaves on the trees lining both sides of the road. Dark, cold, and alone.

"Fight it, Jamie." Closing his eyes briefly, he tried to shake the memories and emotions the hellish years he'd spent boarding at Blackwood Hall still made him feel. Opening them, he saw a figure before him.

"Move!" Jamie roared. He was going too fast to stop.

At the last minute, the person leapt aside, diving into the trees.

"Whoa!" He reined in the horse and dismounted. "Stand, Archie!"

Sprinting back down the road, he searched for the figure. The cursing gave him his first clue as to where she was. He'd nearly run down a woman. This was a new low, even for him.

"Are you hurt?" He stepped into the bushes and reached for her. Gripping her waist, he pulled her out and back onto her feet. "Are you all right?" Jamie stepped back, not wanting to intimidate.

The moon allowed him to see her—well, the top of her bonnet—as she was busy slapping at her skirts.

"Why are you out here, madam, at this time of night, alone?"

Her hands stilled, and she looked up at him.

"Lady Alice?"

"Lord Stafford," she snapped. "What the bloody hell did you think you were doing, riding down a country road at such breakneck speed at this time of day, sir?"

"It's the middle of the night, my lady. What better time is there?" He'd never heard her swear before, which was also true for most people he encountered in society. Jamie rarely swore in company. Even so, it was a surprise to hear the words come from her mouth. Lady Alice Smythe was everything that was proper.

"You nearly ran me down, my lord! While that may be amusing to you, I assure you, it is not for me!" She snapped the words at him.

"Forgive me, but I did not expect to see someone wandering along as if out for a stroll at such an hour." His tone now matched her clipped one.

Jamie did not know Lady Alice well, though he had admired her from afar on the few occasions he'd seen her at society gatherings. There was a quiet refinement to her beauty that drew the eye. A serenity the ladies of the ton strove for but few possessed. She had a soft, pale complexion and hair the color of midnight. He didn't know her exact age but knew the ton considered her well past marriageable.

Since her brother's passing two years earlier, she had largely withdrawn from society, but even before that, she'd made only a few appearances each season. Jamie also knew that, like him, her brother had been a Blackwood boy.

"I have every right to wander where I wish, when I wish it, and I assure you I am no fool for doing so." Her chin rose as he studied her face.

Her father, Lord Smythe, lived in France now, leaving Lady Alice with only her aunt for company.

"You're out here alone, my lady, at night."

"As you see." The words were coated in ice.

"A woman walking in solitude at such a time is folly, Lady Alice. Any rogue could have chanced upon you."

"As you are the only person I have encountered, and society often views you as a rogue, perhaps you are correct. However, your opinion carries no weight with me, Lord Stafford, and I do not care for it. Good evening."

With those words, she turned and walked away, leaving him speechless for several seconds. It took a lot to set Jamie back on his heels. *She'd just called him a rogue.*

"I can't let you walk home alone, my lady," he called when he'd found his voice.

"Go about your business, Lord Stafford," she said over her

shoulder, "and leave me to mine."

"And what business would I have at such an hour?" he muttered.

Walking back to Archie, still smarting from the rogue comment, even if he knew it was a valid one, he sighed. Society had often called him and his two friends that, though not anymore, as Anthony and Toby were now respectably married.

He mounted and started after the woman striding away from him. Jamie weighed his options. He could follow, which would take some time at her current pace, even with long, angry strides, or he could seek out a brandy, which sounded far preferable. But he couldn't, in good conscience, leave her alone.

He had two sisters; if one of them were doing something so reckless, he would hope that whoever encountered them would come to their aid.

Sighing, he nudged Archie forward, watching as she stepped to the side of the road to allow him to pass. He doubted she'd listen to reason, so Jamie bent, caught her around the waist, and lifted her up before him. She already thought him a rogue so he may as well live up to his reputation. Her shriek nearly pierced an eardrum as he settled her on the saddle.

"Put me down at once!" She wriggled furiously—and in that moment, he realized Lady Alice Smythe had a deliciously rounded bottom.

"The gentleman in me cannot, I'm afraid, in good conscience allow you to walk about alone, to fall prey to any unscrupulous individual."

She struggled, so he simply tightened his grip. With one hand on the reins and his thighs controlling the horse, he nudged Archie into a slow canter.

"If you attempt to jump from this height, you will harm yourself."

"How dare you handle me in such a manner!"

"I am looking out for your welfare, madam, which clearly you are not capable of doing for yourself."

She cursed loudly—a string of words any salty sailor would be proud to have in their repertoire.

"Tut-tut, Lady Alice. What will society think of your vocabulary, considering the prim façade you portray?" Jamie said, slowing his horse to a walk.

"I don't give a fig about society," she snapped. "Fools, the lot of them, and that includes you."

"I do believe that hurt." Her body felt lovely pressed to his, even as she tried to put distance between them. Jamie had to admit he was enjoying holding her far more than he should—a surprise, given how rarely he felt anything at all. He was cold inside, and yet, with Lady Alice Smythe in his arms, he felt warm.

"Surely not all of society are fools?" Even as he spoke, Jamie knew he agreed with her. There were good people among them, but many were idiots, whose sole focus was to be seen, and in the best light.

"Put me down, Lord Stafford." Her tone was calmer now, and like his sisters, she was attempting to reason with him, having understood that rage would not work. A lesson, he thought, some men would do well to learn.

"Not until I have you home."

"And I have no say in the matter?"

"None."

They rode in silence for several minutes as Jamie searched for a topic to ease the tension. "Your brother was younger than I, therefore I did not know him well, but we went to the same school, my lady. Please accept my condolences on your loss."

Her breath hitched, and he was sure that a soft sob escaped her lips. Idiot. Clearly, she was still struggling with her brother's death.

"Are you all right?" Jamie asked. He often felt as though he were walking barefoot over broken glass at the bottom of a bog when confronted with tears, especially those of his sisters. He was woefully ill-equipped to comfort anyone.

Jamie had no empathy left inside him.

"I am well," she said in a steady voice that made him wonder if he'd imagined the sob. "My brother was a good man."

"I'm sure he was."

He'd often thought someone should have written a manual about women. One solely for the purpose of helping men navigate the treacherous waters of their moods. Not that men were much better, but at least with them, what you saw was what you got. If they were angry, they roared or hit something. But a woman could slice you to ribbons with a single cutting word or look, and you'd have no idea why.

"Why are you on this road alone, Lady Alice?"

"I like to walk when I cannot sleep."

"I can't fault that, as I do the same. Why can't you sleep?"

He didn't think she would answer such a personal question, but then she said quietly, "I believe you also lodged at Blackwood Hall like my brother, my lord?"

This time it was Jamie who had no wish to answer, but he did, with just one word. "Yes." Suddenly, he was tense again.

"And did you have… was Mr. Kenneth Jackson your housemaster, Lord Stafford?"

Hearing that name always sent him back there, to the screams, the pain, he and his friends begging for mercy as they were plunged into hell. It had been prolonged and vicious, orchestrated by a man who took pleasure in it.

"Yes," Jamie rasped.

She turned then, twisting her body to look at him. "My lord, are you all right?"

"We are here," Jamie said, urging his horse down the drive and into the courtyard of her father's estate. "Good evening, Lady Alice," he added, lowering her to the ground. "Don't walk again at such an hour. Next time, the man you come across may not be a gentleman."

She opened her mouth to speak, but before she could, Jamie had turned his horse and fled into the night.

CHAPTER TWO

H E REACHED HIS estate and rode into the stables. It was as he dismounted that he saw the flutter of white. Bending, he picked up the handkerchief. Raising it to his lips, he caught Lady Alice's scent—soft and subtle, with a hint of rose. Tucking it into his pocket, he went through the motions of removing Archie's saddle and rubbing him down. After ensuring the horse was fed and watered, Jamie left the stables and headed back to the house.

His boots crunched on the shells his youngest sister, Briar, had insisted would be "just the thing" to lay there. Jamie had given in, because that particular sister was not one who took no for an answer.

Landerly, his estate, was large and built of pale cream stone. To the left and right of the grand columned entrance stretched two wings. The right reserved for his sisters, their husbands, and children when they visited, and the left for him. Jamie walked along his side to the rear and found the door leading into his library. It was the easiest way in and out without alerting anyone—not that anyone but he was in residence at present.

Taking the stairs up, he passed portraits of his ancestors and the treasures his mother had once collected before she died and headed for his rooms. Opening the door, he closed it behind him and leaned against the solid wood.

Safe. The thought came as the soft lamplight reached every corner of the room. Here, he could be himself, though if he were honest, he had been himself on that road as well, at least until he'd encountered Lady Alice Smythe.

Taking out the handkerchief, he studied it. The top right corner bore her initials in elegant lettering, the thread a soft lilac.

Placing it on his bedside table, Jamie went to the brandy decanter and poured himself a measure. He swallowed it in a single gulp, and then another. As the liquor burned its way down his throat, he stripped off his clothes and washed in the cold water his valet had left. He extinguished the lamp and climbed into bed. He loathed wearing nightshirts; any restriction could have him waking in a cold sweat, or worse, in the throes of a nightmare.

I let it define me, but no more, Jamie. You have to free yourself.

Those words had come from one of the only two men he respected in England. The two who had entered Blackwood Hall alongside him. Peers who had not been protected by the power of their birth when the doors to that place had shut. Toby and Anthony were his brothers in every way but blood. Unlike him, they'd found love, and peace from the demons that had once chased them.

Good women too, whom Jamie now called friends.

Rolling onto his side, he stared into the darkness. The flash of white returned to his mind, and he reached for the handkerchief. Pressing it to his lips, he closed his eyes.

A WEEK LATER, Jamie entered the Barrington ballroom, every inch the gentleman he had been raised to be. Cool smile in place, and clothing exquisitely tailored to fit his broad frame.

"My lord," Lady Blanchard said with a smile. "How lovely to see you back with us."

Her husband had recently taken another mistress, which left her free to do as she pleased. Society, Jamie thought, liked to present itself as proper and its members titled, noble, and dignified. Men and women whose greatest daily challenges were what to eat or what to wear. Yet beneath that polished veneer simmered an underbelly of affairs and secrets. Most acted with impunity, confident their birth would shield them from consequence.

"Thank you, my lady." Jamie walked in the opposite direction.

"That's a happy look on your face," a familiar voice said moments later.

Smiling, Jamie turned to find one of his oldest friends. Holding out his hand to Lord Tobias Corbyn, they shook.

"Where have you been? I know you've been back in London a week, yet neither Anthony nor I have seen you," Toby demanded.

Not quite as tall as Jamie, though close, Toby had recently married Lady Liberty Talbot. His friends were happy, and while Jamie found joy in that, there was also a twinge of sadness, knowing such contentment would never be his. The tender touches and secret smiles would not be for him. Of course, there had been plenty of women who smiled at him, just not with love.

"Busy," Jamie said. In truth, he'd been hunting Jackson, but his friends didn't know about that, and he wouldn't tell them. They had lives to live and wives to care for. He would see this through alone.

Toby moved to stand directly before him, blocking Jamie's view of the receiving line.

"Doing what?"

"Where is your wife?" Jamie asked.

"She has a sniffle and decided it best to stay home, though she insisted I attend. Apparently, she believes I need time in your company. Anthony, too, is coming alone as Evie is visiting friends."

"And you feel as though you've had a limb severed?" Jamie asked.

"Of course not," Toby lied too quickly.

"You're pathetic," Jamie said, ignoring the stab of envy.

"I say, Corbyn, the line is moving!" Captain Dibley roared from behind them.

Jamie smirked as Toby ignored the man.

"God, the traffic is dreadful out there." Anthony, Lord Hamilton, joined them.

"There's a line, Hamilton!" Dibley bellowed.

"My friends are holding my place, Captain," Anthony said smoothly. "How are you, Jamie?"

"Good. And you?"

"Good. How come we haven't seen you for weeks?" Anthony asked.

"He won't tell," Toby said. "But something isn't right with him."

Thankfully, the line began to move again, and after greeting the hosts with elegant bows, they stepped into the ballroom.

"So what aren't you telling us, Jamie?" Anthony asked.

"Nothing. Now, you two, tell me your news."

Toby and Anthony exchanged a look, and it was Toby who spoke. "How does he know we have news?"

"I haven't seen you in weeks so surely something's happened in your mundane lives during that time?"

"Aww, did you miss us?" Anthony teased.

As Jamie glanced toward the dancers, he caught sight of a couple parting, and Lady Alice stepped into view. What was she doing here?

"Jamie!" Anthony snapped his fingers before his face.

"What?"

His friends stood watching him, brows raised.

"What's going on, Jamie?" Toby asked.

"Nothing."

"Oh, very well. If you've no wish to tell your best friends, then fine. We'll tell you our news instead," Anthony said.

Dragging his gaze from the dance floor, Jamie forced his attention back to them. "What news?"

"You tell him," Toby nudged Anthony.

"No, you—"

"For pity's sake, someone speak," Jamie snapped.

"Evie and Liberty are with child," Anthony said, grinning.

"Both?" His friends nodded, and Jamie pulled them into an embrace right there in the ballroom. "That is wonderful news. Congratulations." He meant it. He might never have his own happy ending, but he was glad his friends had found theirs.

"It's both terrifying and exciting," Toby admitted, looking slightly pale.

"I should imagine so. But don't look now because your three aunts are approaching from the right, Anthony," Jamie said.

The three women bearing down on them were important to them all. Though Anthony's relations, it had been their intervention that had transformed Blackwood from hell into something bearable.

"Ah, look at this, sisters, three of the most handsome men in all of society," Aunt Petunia declared. She always wore lavender.

"They are indeed," Aunt Agatha said, her peach gown glowing under the chandeliers.

"Your necktie is crooked, Anthony," Aunt Lavinia added. She favored shades of green. "Honestly, what was your valet thinking to let you leave the house in such disarray?"

Lavinia fussed over her nephew's necktie right there in the middle of the ballroom, surrounded by the loftiest members of society.

"Jamie, how are you?" Agatha asked.

Suddenly, he was the focus of three pairs of eyes.

"Well, thank you. And you?" he said.

"Excellent, excellent," Lavinia said. "Now, dear, we've been thinking."

Three words that never boded well for anyone, Jamie thought as the hair on the back of his neck rose. They were up to something. One glance at his smirking friends confirmed it.

"Must go. I promised this next dance to Lady Alice Smythe," Jamie said, escaping.

"Oh, but we have something to give you!" Agatha called after him.

Jamie raised a hand and fled in the opposite direction. Looking back to ensure they weren't following, he didn't see the woman stepping directly into his path. Rather than knock her over, he caught her around the waist and kept walking. Stopping a few steps later, he set her down.

"Sorry…" The word died as he looked into the amber eyes of Lady Alice.

"Why are you constantly trying to knock me off my feet, my lord?" she hissed, smoothing her skirts.

Around them, onlookers who had paused now turned back to their conversations.

"My apologies, my lady. I did not see you."

"Again?" she snapped. "Perhaps you should look where you're going, Lord Stafford."

"I shall take your words under advisement. Are you free for this dance, my lady?"

She looked startled, so much so that her mouth fell open.

"Dance?" he prompted.

"I—ah—"

"Excellent." Jamie took her hand, placed it on his arm, and led her to the dance floor. As the waltz began, he drew her into his arms.

"I did not agree to this, nor am I sure I wish to, considering how intent you seem on harming me, Lord Stafford."

"I shall endeavor not to step on your toes, my lady."

Since the night she had asked if Kenneth Jackson had been his housemaster, Jamie had been unable to think of much else. His leads in the search for the man had gone cold, and if the woman now in his arms had any clue as to Jackson's whereabouts, he wanted it.

Looking down at her, Jamie noted the delicate lines of her face, the soft curve of her upper lip. A faint flush warmed her cheeks. Whether it came from his imperious behavior or the heat of the room, he couldn't tell. Her dark hair was swept up and pinned with tiny diamonds that caught the light above. She truly was beautiful, and he wondered how she had remained unwed for so long.

"Are you always so presumptuous when you want to dance, my lord?"

"No. And if I say I'm sorry, will that suffice?" Jamie asked. "I wished to speak with you."

"About what? Because the last time I was in your company—reluctantly—you failed to answer the question I posed. I'm unsure why you think I'll answer yours."

She wore deep sapphire blue. The neckline was modest compared to others, but he could still see the faint swell of her breasts, and that single glance made his blood heat. He didn't know much about her, only what others said, but since that night, he'd wanted to know more. Still, he would be cautious. If anyone suspected he was interested in an unmarried lady, gossip would spread.

"Why did you ask whether Mr. Kenneth Jackson was my housemaster?"

"Why didn't you answer me when I asked it?" she countered.

They moved through several steps in silence while Jamie considered his reply.

"If you must know," she said, "since you've no wish to speak, Lord Stafford, I want to know his whereabouts."

Jamie took a deep, steadying breath, something he was accustomed to doing whenever that man's name was spoken. Her scent filled his senses, the same scent that lingered on the handkerchief he had no right to keep beneath his pillow.

"Why?" he managed, keeping his voice even, though his heart was pounding. Few names could evoke such fury, but Kenneth Jackson's could.

"I need to find him, obviously," she said, looking up at Jamie. He saw the turmoil in her eyes. She sounded calm, but she was anything but.

"Yes," he said quietly. "He was my housemaster."

Her expression softened into sympathy before she blinked it away, the cool society lady once more.

"He is not a man for the likes of you to have dealings with, Lady Alice."

"I can look after myself," she replied. "I've been doing so since my brother passed away."

Jamie knew then why she sought Kenneth Jackson, because the man had harmed her brother. It was the only explanation.

"Don't do it, my lady."

"What?" Their eyes locked.

"Revenge is not something to be taken lightly, especially with a man such as he."

"You want it, my lord, yet I cannot have the same for my brother?"

"I have more reasons than my own for seeking revenge, my lady."

"What reasons?" she demanded.

Thankfully, the music ended then. They glared at one another for several heartbeats before she turned and walked away without another word. He went in the opposite direction, making for his friends.

Anthony held out a piece of paper as he approached.

"What is this?"

"Your list."

Jamie actually stepped back. "No."

"Not getting away from it, old chap. The aunts have decided. We manfully refrained from looking at the names," Toby said.

"I'm not touching that," Jamie protested, holding up both hands.

Anthony lunged forward and tucked it into his pocket. "Excellent. Supper now, I think."

He and Toby wandered off, leaving Jamie with two options. Throw the list away without looking, or look.

The note felt as though it burned through his pocket.

"For pity's sake," he muttered. Taking it out, he unfolded the paper and read the three names. When he reached the last, he tore it to shreds and dropped them at his feet. Then he headed for the door. Jamie knew exactly where he was going, and that by the time he reached his bed in the early hours of the morning, he'd be calmer and sporting bruises.

CHAPTER THREE

Alice felt as though her body had been clenched for the two years since her brother's death. Charles had been the only person she'd loved without reservation—besides Aunt Gwen—and the only one who had loved her back, even if at the end he had been too broken to show it.

Looking around the Barringtons' ballroom, Alice wondered how soon she could leave as she had no wish to be here, or to encounter Lord Stafford again. It had been folly to dance with him, and yet she'd wanted desperately to see if he could help her locate Kenneth Jackson.

Revenge is not something to be taken lightly with a man such as he.

He'd spoken those words to her in a deep, solemn voice, and she'd known they'd come from the experience he'd had dealing with Kenneth Jackson.

Alice made a conscious effort to unclench her fists and breathe calmly. She'd stepped back into society in the hope that someone would know something about Jackson. She'd found that someone, but Alice knew it would not be easy to get him to talk to her.

How can I feel so alone surrounded by so many people, she wondered.

The air shimmered with heat, candles flickering in gilt sconces, their flames reflected in the huge mirrors that lined the walls. The scents of orange blossom, rose attar, lavender water, and others, mingled with the sharper tang of beeswax polish and sweat in the air. The chatter of a hundred voices rose and fell, punctuated by the scrape of bows against strings as the musicians prepared to play another set. Silk rustled, jewels sparkled, and every guest was looking their best.

She ought to feel part of it. Her parents had loved society events before her mother passed and her father had fled to France, but since losing Charles, and what they'd endured before the end, Alice was a different person.

His life had not been the same since he returned home from Blackwood Hall, where he stayed during his short school years. Alice could still see him that last day he'd been alive. For the first time in a long while, he'd been rational. There had been no anger or need to hurt her for the pain he was suffering. He'd asked her to make him tea to help him sleep. When she returned, his lips were still, his eyes open but empty, and the silence in the room had been louder than any society event. Charles had been dead at his own hand from an overdose of laudanum she hadn't even known he'd been collecting.

Alice felt like her life had ended that night too. Or rather, she had become someone else entirely. A person desperate for vengeance.

Kenneth Jackson. The name burned inside her, etched into her memory by the pages of Charles's diary, which she'd found when she had gone through his things. Page after page of rambling pain, always circling back to that man. If she thought too long on what had happened inside Blackwood Hall, she felt ill. To know her beloved brother had suffered the horrors he had, made her alternate between rage and weeping.

She'd known he'd suffered, as some of his story had come out, but not all—not the worst parts, and not the name of the man who ultimately had been responsible.

A ripple of laughter pulled her back from her memories, and her eyes went to the dance floor, but did not see the tall figure of Lord Stafford.

Alice was constantly hearing whispers about how handsome and charming he was. But she also knew there was another side to the marquess.

He didn't care overly what society thought of him according to her aunt, who was a font of knowledge when it came to the ton. Lord Stafford didn't step over the invisible line into impropriety, or that anyone knew of, but her aunt said he was close to it a time or two. Aunt Gwen said he had a rakish air to him, and Alice had to agree. There was something a little wild about that man.

She had heard the emotion in his words the night she'd sat before him on his horse. The night she'd asked if Kenneth Jackson was his housemaster too. Something dark and dangerous had been in his gaze when she'd looked at him. Had he too lived through what Charles had not survived? It now seemed likely that was indeed the case after the two conversations she'd recently had with him. Unlike her brother, however, it had not affected his mind, or was he just better at hiding it?

Could he help her find answers to the questions she had? Help her find Jackson?

"Alice!"

The hiss sliced through the hum of conversation, startling her out of her thoughts. She turned, scanning the room.

There, half-hidden behind a potted palm, two familiar faces grinned at her.

"Why on earth are you whispering at me from behind a plant?" Alice asked, eyebrows arching.

"It is a Kentia palm," Thaddeus Thomas declared, emerging with a flourish that made the plant wobble in its pot. "A most resilient species, imported from the South Pacific. Quite adaptable, you know. Thrives even in poor soil—"

"Oh, for heaven's sake," Eloise Thomas groaned, dragging her brother back by his sleeve. "We are not here to bore Alice with a botany lesson. I for one wish to know what she talked about while dancing with the handsome marquess."

Alice's lips twitched despite herself. She had met the Thomas twins upon her first season in London many years ago. Inseparable, they were closer than any siblings she had ever known, though they seemed to thrive on arguing. Their quarrels were legendary, so much so that some people often placed bets on who would win their latest spat.

Even when she'd not returned to society for many years, Eloise and Thaddeus—mainly Eloise—had continued to write to her weekly. Filling her in on scandals and gossip.

"I'll have you know," Thaddeus continued stubbornly, "that the Kentia palm is an exceedingly elegant plant. Strong roots, graceful fronds, rather like myself, don't you think?

"Graceful?" Eloise scoffed. "You trip over carpets."

"I was bowing," he said stiffly.

"You were sprawling."

Alice pressed a hand to her mouth to hide her laughter. For the first time that evening, she felt lighter, and she'd take that relief from her dark thoughts for as long as it lasted.

"Now," Eloise said, turning her sharp eyes back on Alice, "you are cornered. Tell us first what you talked about with Lord Stafford?"

Alice smoothed her skirts, carefully arranging her expression. "We didn't touch on anything really, just the usual. How the weather has been in London the last few days, and how lovely the ballroom is decorated."

"Well, that's dreadfully boring," Eloise said, looking deflated.

"Where is your aunt?" Thaddeus asked.

"Seated with her friends. Discussing novels, no doubt."

Eloise softened slightly. "A delightful woman, your Aunt Gwen. If a trifle… consumed."

In truth, Aunt Gwen's devotion to her books was Alice's saving grace. While her aunt debated fictional heroes, Alice could pursue a real monster.

"I think," Thaddeus interrupted solemnly, "that our dear Alice has acquired a secret lover. That explains her absence these past few days. She avoids us to spend time in some man's arms."

Suppressing guilt, Alice forced a light laugh. "Alas, no lover. I simply prefer quiet evenings to endless balls. But I am here tonight, am I not? To see you both."

Not a lie, exactly. She loved them dearly. But her true reason for being away from London had been yet again following more leads to find Jackson. Unfortunately, that too had led to a dead end.

Thaddeus narrowed his eyes. "You are lying."

"I would never lie to you." She fluttered her lashes with exaggerated sweetness.

He snorted. Eloise rolled her eyes.

"Good Lord," Eloise whispered suddenly, "Miss Ellington is wearing mustard."

Thaddeus followed her gaze, grimacing. "Positively ghastly. She looks like a cautionary tale against overcooked vegetables."

And just like that, the siblings were off—debating the merits of color, cut, and whether the poor young lady ought to be pitied or scorned. They never spoke loud enough for anyone to overhear, except Alice. The twins were not mean spirited, but like many, they just loved to gossip.

Alice let their chatter wash over her. Yet the guilt pressed back in. They thought her absence from society was simply because she preferred to be elsewhere. If only they knew she spent her days chasing trails that might lead her to Kenneth Jackson, and thus far hadn't.

"Tomorrow," Thaddeus declared abruptly, "we are driving in the park, and you shall join us, Alice."

"Do I get a choice?" she asked.

"No," Eloise said.

"We will return, Alice, but right now we need to dance, or Mother will have stern words for us. Unlike your aunt, she watches our every move," Thaddeus said.

She had barely escaped the whirlwind of the twins when another obstacle appeared—three ladies advancing with the determination of a cavalry charge.

"Lady Alice!" Lady Petunia boomed, feathers quivering from the violent flutter of her fan. At her side was Lady Agatha, equally formidable, encased in apricot satin. Lastly was the youngest, Mrs. Lavinia Williams. She seemed to favor different shades of green.

"My dear girl, how delightful to see you," Lady Petunia said. "We were quite certain you had abandoned society altogether."

Alice dropped a curtsy, her smile fixed. "I have been in the country, ma'am. I find it soothing."

"Of course it is," Mrs. Williams said. "But you are far too young to be hiding there, my dear."

"Indeed. You will never find a husband if you continue to do so," Lady Agatha added.

Alice kept her tone mild. "Marriage is not my fondest wish."

The women exchanged a look before speaking again.

"Oh? Then what is, child?" Lady Petunia asked, a gentle smile on her lips.

"To live my life as I choose," Alice said calmly. She rarely spoke like this in public, but perhaps it was time she did, then people would know marriage was not of interest to her. Of course, that was scandalous considering she was a young woman, and they were usually raised with the single goal of finding a wealthy man to wed.

The ladies smiled, like she'd done something that made them proud.

"How refreshing, and I like that you have your own mind, dear, but of course there are plenty of wonderful men who would be just brilliant for you to marry. In fact, we know of one who would be perfect. He is a friend of our nephew's," Lady Petunia said.

Surely not?

"Yes, plenty of wonderful gentlemen in London society, but the one we have selected would be an excellent choice for you."

"Thank you, but no. I have no interest in a husband. Now, if you will excuse me, I am due to dance with Lord Taylor."

She didn't exactly run, but it was close. Skirting the guests, she headed in the opposite direction to where the three meddling women stood.

Over the next few hours, Alice danced, smiled when required, and allowed the Thomas twins to chatter at her until her head spun. She avoided Lord Hamilton's aunts, and of Lord Stafford there was no further sign. It seemed he'd left the ballroom, and she told herself she was happy about that.

He'd warned her to stay away from Kenneth Jackson, and while she understood why—the man was dangerous—she didn't like it and would be ignoring his direction. Alice had made her brother a promise that she would not be breaking.

As yet, she had no idea what she'd do when she found Kenneth Jackson, but she'd think about that when the time came.

After saying good night to the twins when she thought she'd been here long enough to please gossips and her aunt, Alice went in search of her relative.

Mrs. Gwendoline Patterson was her late mother's elder sister and had come to live with Alice after Charles's death. Aunt Gwen's gentle nature and innate kindness had soothed much of Alice's early grief. She liked everyone, and within days had charmed the household staff. Her white hair framed a round, sweet face that always seemed slightly flushed. She loved to stitch, to read, and to spend long afternoons with her friends discussing whichever novel currently absorbed her. Alice adored her.

"Hello, darling," Aunt Gwen said warmly as Alice approached. "Are you ready to leave?"

"Not yet," she said. "I am to take the Thomas twins home." The lie slid from her tongue easily now. Deception had become a second language. She used it to escape the house, and to protect her aunt from worry.

"I wondered if Lady Cecil might drop you home instead, Aunt. It could be a late night."

Lady Cecil, perched to Gwen's right, adjusted the tall black feather in her hair and fixed Alice with hawk-like eyes. Terrifyingly direct, she could cut a man to ribbons with a single phrase. Alice, perversely, adored sparring with her.

"I will drop your aunt home," Lady Cecil declared, voice like a steel blade. "But you'll have a care, Lady Alice."

"They live not far from our townhouse," Alice replied mildly. She leaned down, kissed her aunt's cheek, and then pressed another kiss against Lady Cecil's surprisingly soft one. With her farewells complete, she drifted away, and only when she saw them depart, did she take her own leave.

CHAPTER FOUR

ALICE WALKED INTO the cool night air. The ballroom's heat and perfume clung to her skin, but London's smog swept it aside. The city was a different creature after dark. Dangerous for anyone who did not have a care.

Her driver straightened as she approached. Ezra Samson was as solid as an oak, his blond hair dulled in the lamplight, his broad shoulders filling the space between the carriage and horse.

"Where is your aunt?" he asked immediately.

"She left earlier with Lady Cecil. I have a stop—"

"Not alone you don't," Ezra interrupted flatly.

Alice's mouth tightened. He had once been Charles's footman, employed when her brother's health declined. Ezra and his wife Maggie, Alice's maid, had stood beside the family until the very end. On Charles's last lucid night, he had grasped Ezra's arm and rasped, *Take care of Alice.* It was a vow Ezra had taken seriously.

"This is important," Alice insisted.

"And all part of your revenge, I suppose?"

"Yes."

Ezra's thick brows lowered, shadowing eyes that missed nothing. "Very well, but you'll not go anywhere alone."

She blew out a sharp breath. "Ezra—"

"I made him a promise. But even had I not, I would keep you safe. Your aunt is kind and sweet-natured, and oblivious to the fact you're not the well-behaved young lady you portray yourself to be, content with books and embroidery. I know better. Therefore, I am watching over you."

Her throat constricted. She hated and loved him for his perception. "I'm quite sure Aunt Gwen would take you to task for that statement."

"Likely. But she would not thank me for telling her what you truly do." His deep voice rolled like approaching thunder.

Alice's lips pressed into a line. He knew too much, and always had. She had let him and Maggie close once, when her grief was overwhelming, and they had seen everything. The fury, the tears, the vow for vengeance. Now they watched her every move, especially Ezra.

"I will go to the address and make my inquiries, then return," she said. "That is all."

He grunted but yielded, knowing that if he forbade it, which he had no right to do, she would find another way.

The carriage rattled through narrow streets, and Alice wrapped her evening cloak tighter around her body. She was shivering not from cold but anticipation.

When they stopped, Ezra climbed from the driver's seat.

"I am going in there." Alice pointed toward a tall, dark building. "If I am not back in thirty minutes, find me."

"I said not alone."

Alice made a show of looking around. "And who will hold the horses while you accompany me?" She was already walking away before he delivered the last word and attempted to stop her.

"Lady Alice!"

She ignored the bellow and made for the old stone building. She had several people who were making enquiries on her behalf about Kenneth Jackson, and one had sent her word that tonight, here at this building, he would be here.

She'd been to Blackwood Hall twice. The first time had been to collect her brother with Ezra, after he'd sent word he was coming home. Her father had been in France at the time, supposedly on a holiday. Later Alice had realized it was to visit his mistress. He'd only returned for a few days before leaving to take up residence there.

The day she'd collected Charles, she'd seen him talking to a man as he left the building. Her brother had shaken his head vehemently, and pointed to the carriage Alice sat in. She'd opened the door and stepped down. The man had stared at her and then gone back inside. Her brother had told her his name was Kenneth Jackson, but it was not until later she'd known what he'd done to Charles.

Alice had run through many things she would do to the man, and one of them was to make him suffer. As yet, she was unsure how. She was very good with numbers and investments, and had thought long and hard about destroying the man financially, but until she knew what his situation was, she couldn't do that. Ezra just wanted to beat him senseless, which Alice was not completely discarding.

Walking to the right-hand side of the building, Alice found the door that her informant had told her about, and entered. A young boy stood there as if waiting for someone. Tall, thin, his face was gaunt, and his red hair stood off his head in dirty spikes.

"Hello."

He nodded at Alice's greeting.

"I wouldn't go in there were I you, miss," he said before she could speak again.

"Do you come here often?" Alice asked, and he nodded.

"It's a warm place." He shrugged, and Alice knew then that he either lived on the streets or in a house that was small and cold. Her heart ached for the boy, but he was like many she saw every day.

Dare she ask him about Jackson? Would he tell anyone she was here?

"I am looking for a man, and his name is Kenneth Jackson," Alice said, deciding to take a chance. "I need to find him urgently."

The boy nodded, his eyes big in his thin face as they studied her. His clothes were worn, and she doubted they offered much protection against the colder weather that gripped London in the winter months.

"If I give you his description and some money, would you come to me if you locate him?"

"I can find out where he is," the boy said solemnly.

She wanted to ask how he could do that when he was just a child, but knew that many had to grow up fast if they lived in poverty. Alice pulled money out of her reticule and handed it to him. More money than he had likely ever seen.

"This man is dangerous and mean, so do not approach him as he likes to hurt people, but if you find out where he is then come to the rear door of my townhouse and say you have information for Lady Alice."

He nodded, his eyes on the money clutched in his hand. She gave him her address and then he fled out the door she'd just entered and disappeared into the night.

It was a risk, but one she'd been willing to take.

Exhaling slowly, Alice headed right to a staircase. The deeper she descended, the colder the air grew, until the walls sweated with damp. Then came the sound—a muffled roar.

Alice tugged her hood lower over her face and then pressed a hand to the final door and pushed.

The stench of sweat and ale hit her as she stepped into a cavernous room thick with smoke. Men were pressed shoulder to shoulder, their voices raised in cheers. She moved to the wall, heart pounding, and tried blending into the shadows.

"Lord Stafford is holding his own!"

Her head turned toward the voice. *Lord Stafford?* No. It couldn't be. She moved, slipping between men, all of whom were focused on the ring and thankfully not her, until she found a crate and climbed upon it. The breath caught in Alice's throat as she looked to the ring. Stripped to the waist, and glistening with sweat, was Lord Stafford.

His muscles flexed as he dodged his massive, bearded opponent. Fists swung, as their bodies collided. The crowd roared, but Alice heard nothing except the furious hammer of her own heart.

What in God's name was he doing here?

And why did she feel as though fate had brought her here to find him in the last place she could ever have imagined?

Lord Stafford's opponent swung again, a meaty fist that would have felled most men. He ducked, the movement swift, almost graceful. His counterpunch cracked against the man's ribs. The crowd erupted, stamping their boots, and howling for more.

Alice's stomach twisted. This was no gentleman's sport. This was brutality disguised as entertainment.

She pressed to the wall behind her to steady herself. Part of her wanted to look away, yet Alice could not.

Stafford took a blow to the jaw, his head snapping to the side. For one terrible instant she thought he would fall. But he straightened, spat blood, and gave a grim smile that sent the crowd into fresh cheers.

Why was he here?

Her heart pounded harder then, not from the spectacle but from the sudden realization that this man, so composed in the ballroom, was likely as broken as her brother had been. Did he seek a release from what he'd suffered through violence here with his fists?

Charles...

A memory hit her hard then. Her brother's broken voice whispering, *"I can't stop the hell inside my head, Alice..."* She knew it was likely the same hell burning in Stafford's eyes now as he drove his fist into his opponent's gut.

The larger man staggered and bellowed. He then charged at Stafford like a bull. He met him head-on. They grappled, bodies straining as the crowd pressed closer, the roar now deafening. Men cursed and cheered, as wagers were shouted into the smoky air. Someone bumped Alice's crate and she nearly toppled, but pressed harder into the wall at her back, determined not to miss a second.

And then Lord Stafford broke free. Alice watched as, with ruthless precision, he landed a final, devastating blow. His opponent collapsed, hitting the ground with a dull thud. Silence struck for half a heartbeat before the room exploded into chaos.

The victor's name was bellowed again and again. Coins exchanged hands as shouts rang out.

"Stafford! Stafford! Stafford!"

He stood in the ring with his chest heaving, blood streaking his mouth, and sweat running in rivulets down his back. He lifted his fists once, briefly in victory, then let them fall.

Alice could not breathe. The sight of him, powerful, wounded, and unmasked, tore at something deep inside her. This was no reckless rake amusing himself. This was a man fighting to survive.

Her pulse hammered as he turned, and for one wild moment she thought his gaze would find hers in the crowd. She shrank into the shadows. He could not see her here. He must not.

Alice stayed on top of the crate as the crowd surged forward to celebrate the victory. Her chest felt tight as she struggled to draw in a deep, steadying breath.

She had come here seeking Kenneth Jackson, not to find Lord Stafford stripped bare, fighting his demons his way.

For an instant, she wanted to weep for him and Charles. Instead, she tried to slip from the crate, but her way was barred. Two men stood smiling up at her.

"Hello, sweetheart, not often we get a lovely like you in this place."

"Excuse me. I wish to leave," Alice said, her tone rising above those around them.

"I think not. You may talk like a lady, but no way could you be one coming here," one of them said. "Now, why don't you come down and we'll get acquainted."

Her rash actions, coming here alone, slapped her hard in the face then. No one would help her if these men decided to grab her. Her eyes turned to the ring. *He would help.*

CHAPTER FIVE

JAMIE FELT THE rage ease from his body, replaced by fatigue and the dull ache of pain from the boxing match he'd just finished. His knuckles throbbed and he thanked God for the gloves he would wear when he walked in society tomorrow.

The roar of the crowd faded as he leaned over his opponent. He had no wish to kill a man, nor maim one for life. This was simply another way to leash the demons that sometimes overcame him. The eyes beneath him opened, and Jamie extended a hand. The man took it, and he hauled him upright.

"Thank you for the fight," Jamie said. The man grunted in reply.

"Well done, my lord."

"Thank you, Phillip." He accepted the cloth his man handed him when he'd returned to his corner and began to towel the sweat from his body.

He'd left the ball after dancing with Lady Alice for two reasons. First, there was that damned list given to him by Anthony's aunts. And then there was her. Lady Alice Smythe, with her beauty and the haunted look in her eyes.

A close friend once told me that some of us are forced to survive things others cannot imagine.

Of all the things he could have said to her, why had he chosen those words?

She unsettled him, and no woman ever had. She had also

declared she wanted justice for her brother, and that Kenneth Jackson would pay. He'd assured her he would see it done, but he doubted that would stop her. Jackson was not a man for a woman like Lady Alice to face. He was a savage animal.

Letting his eyes sweep the crowd, Jamie searched. While he'd come here to fight, he also knew that Kenneth Jackson had been seen in the area before. Starting with the back row of spectators, he scanned the gathered men. To his right, he noticed a woman standing on a box set out for those struggling to see. Rare to see a lady here, but not unheard of. Some came with their men; others—ladies of the night—sought their next client. It wouldn't be hard to find one in a room full of men fueled by excitement.

Something about this particular woman caught his attention. As he pulled on his shirt and jacket, he found himself watching her. Jamie couldn't make out her features because her hood was drawn forward, but a strange anticipation stirred in him as she turned.

Why do I suddenly need to know who she is? No woman of his acquaintance would be seen in such a place.

Two men approached her, and Jamie watched as she shook her head. One reached out, and she pushed his hand away. The other gripped her waist, and she struggled. Her hood fell back.

You bloody little fool.

Climbing through the ropes, Jamie jumped down and strode toward her. Men slapped his back and called out to him, but he ignored them all. He had one purpose, and that was to reach Lady Alice before anyone realized who she was.

"Back off!" she shouted, still wrestling with the two men. To his surprise, one stumbled back as she kicked him.

"Now!" Jamie barked when the men hesitated.

They turned. Recognition dawned in their eyes, and then both disappeared into the crowd.

Jamie didn't wait for permission. Instead, he grabbed her by the waist and lifted her down. Taking one of her gloved hands, he began forcing a path through the throng, ignoring her protests.

Reaching the door, he opened it and pulled her through.

"What are you doing?"

Ignoring her demand, Jamie towed her toward the stairs. When she tried to stop him, he turned, bent, and hoisted her over his shoulder. Lady Alice pummeled his back with her fists the entire way up, but he didn't stop until he reached the outer door at the rear of the building. Only once they were outside and in the shadows did he set her down.

"Are you mad?" Jamie thundered. "What possible reason could you have for being in such a place surrounded by men?" He rarely raised his voice, but he was roaring at her now. "Explain yourself at once, Lady Alice!"

"What I am doing there is no concern of yours, Lord Stafford. The better question is why you were conducting yourself in such a barbaric manner."

He had to give her credit. Most people would have fled from his anger, but Lady Alice stood her ground, her voice calm.

"Think again," he said, leaning closer, deliberately intimidating her. "If you came here to find Jackson, you're a fool. I warned you to stay away from him."

Jamie respected women. His sisters would never forgive him should he not behave around them as the gentleman he'd been raised to be. But right now his restraint was gone. The thrill of the fight still coursed through him. Usually, he would walk home and let the night air cool his temper. Not this time.

"You have no say in what I do!" she snarled.

He couldn't help admiring her courage. Minutes ago, she'd been terrified, and likely still was, but there was no sign of it on her face.

She was still dressed as she had been at the ball, and once again, he felt that sudden surge of heat when he was near her. Awareness. He had not experienced it often, if ever. Combined with the aftereffects of the fight, it was a dangerous mix. His senses felt sharpened, every breath charged.

She pressed her lips into a hard line and glared at him, defiant when any sensible person would have quailed.

"This is no game." Jamie gripped her shoulders and shook her once.

"Unhand me!"

"Why are you here?" He pulled her closer until only inches separated them. Her soft floral scent washed over him, stealing his reason.

"Damn you," he muttered, and before he could stop himself, he was kissing her.

He had no right to take such liberties, yet in that moment, stopping was impossible. Her lips were soft, and when her hand clenched in his shirt instead of striking him, the world narrowed to nothing but her.

Jamie slid a hand down her arm to her back, pressing her closer. A low sound escaped him as her curves met his chest. His other hand cupped her head, angling it so he could deepen the contact. She arched into him, and he swallowed her soft moan.

Need pounded through Jamie, driving out rational thought. One kiss led to another. He should stop, but he couldn't, not when she tasted like this.

What's so special about her?

That thought broke through the haze, and Jamie drew back.

"Dear Lord," she whispered. Her eyes were dark with passion. Then, slowly, clarity returned, and shock replaced the heat. He was certain it mirrored his own.

"Why did you kiss me?"

Jamie had no answer. His body still ached with need, as anger and lust warred inside him.

"Why were you in that room, my lady?" he asked.

She stared up at him for several seconds, then released his shirt and shoved him hard in the chest. He stepped back.

"I want an answer, Lady Alice."

Her chin lifted. The cool, composed Lady Alice was back—haughty, beautiful, untouchable. But he knew better now. He'd touched her and felt her tremble. She had wanted that kiss as much as he had.

"I will give you no answer." Her tone was ice.

"Do you understand the danger you put yourself in by stepping into that room? Any of those men could have ruined you had they known who you were. If anyone found out you were here tonight watching a bare-knuckle fight, you would be an outcast, and never able to frequent society again."

"I wore my cloak," she said, her voice husky enough to heat his blood all over again. "And I care little about society."

He snorted. "Spoken like a woman who has never been outside it."

"And you have?"

Jamie remained silent, watching her.

"It's all right for you to do that, is it? To strip to the waist and fight in such a barbaric manner? I fail to see why that would not ruin you also."

"We are not talking about me, but you. I am a man who can look after himself," Jamie snapped.

Behind them came a shout, followed by laughter and footsteps. He turned, positioning himself between her and the noise. Three men were relieving themselves against a fence.

The sound of running feet made him glance back, just in time to see Lady Alice fleeing.

"Damn it."

He followed. Reaching the street, he watched her climb into a carriage. It lurched away before he could stop it. Jamie stood there until it vanished from sight, then turned and walked in the opposite direction toward his townhouse.

There could be only one reason Lady Alice Smythe had been in that room tonight, Kenneth Jackson. But how had she known he might be there? Jamie had found her once on that road, and now this. The woman was deliberately courting danger. The question was, what was he going to do about it?

Kissing her had been a mistake. Now he knew what she tasted like, and that knowledge would haunt him. The night he'd carried her before him on his horse should have warned him how she affected him. It hadn't. Tonight, he'd pressed her soft body to his and kissed her until all sense deserted him.

Idiot.

Jamie didn't need this kind of complication. He could pull back, he was good at that, but he couldn't recall a time when a woman had filled him with such heat and want.

He couldn't offer her anything, ever, and that alone should tell him to keep away from her. But would he? She intrigued him. And if she truly was searching for Jackson—what other reason could there be?—he had to make her see sense before she was hurt.

Her brother had been a Blackwood boy like Jamie, and she wanted vengeance. But that was a path he didn't want her to walk, even if she was nothing to him.

Jamie would need to speak with her and find out what she knew. And then convince her to stop throwing herself into danger. Then he could avoid her.

He broke into a run as the first drops of rain fell. By the time he reached his townhouse, he was soaked through. After washing and changing into his dressing gown, he poured a brandy and sat before the fire, replaying every moment of the night.

After his last two encounters with Lady Alice, he no longer believed that the cool, proper woman society thought they knew was the real Lady Alice Smythe.

"Who are you?" Jamie muttered into the empty room.

CHAPTER SIX

ALICE HAD SLEPT little the previous night. She'd woken with tired eyes and a less-than-sunny nature. Maggie had taken a single look at her and had a bath drawn, believing a soak in hot water cured a great many things. It had not.

"Your aunt has yet to rise, my lady," Maggie said after finishing with Alice's hair.

"Thank you, Maggie. Go to the kitchen now and take your tea with that bossy man of yours."

Her maid smiled. "I'll do just that, thank you, my lady."

After she'd left, Alice wandered the halls of her father's townhouse. He hadn't set foot inside it for many years—not even to attend his son's funeral—which had only confirmed in her mind that he was a weak, immoral, horrid beast of a man.

Yes, he had left Alice and her aunt to live as they pleased in his estate and townhouse, but she would never forgive him for choosing his mistress over burying his child.

Alice returned to her room and sat at the desk. She was the one who ran the family's finances, and who ensured he had money to lavish on his mistress. She sent it through his trusted servant, a man who arrived on her doorstep with notes that never asked after her, only for funds.

"Coward," she muttered.

She had spent the night thinking about Lord Stafford. Alice saw him over and over, shirtless, his big body glistening with sweat. Seeing his power unleashed should have been terrifying. It was not, instead awakening something she'd never felt before. A need for a man she neither wanted nor had room for in her life.

Alice had long ago accepted that she would never marry or bind herself to a man. It had been her choice because she refused to be dictated to, as her father once had. Then there were her memories of her brother, and of the pain he had endured. No, she would never allow a man control over her again.

Until last night, she had believed herself content with that decision. But now Lord Stafford had kissed and held her pressed to the hard wall of his chest. What shocked her was the fierce surge of want she'd felt. She might be innocent, but she was not ignorant. Alice had read books and spoken to Maggie about what occurred between a man and a woman. And in that moment, had he stripped her bare, she would have let him.

Blind need, that was how she'd named it. Blind to everything but the man kissing and touching her.

Alice liked control. Last night, she'd had none. He had taken it from her. It was a terrifying thought for a woman who survived through strength and self-possession.

She turned back to the papers Mr. Bradley, her father's man of affairs, had brought her. Thankfully, he was no fool. He had soon realized that Alice was far more capable than Lord Smythe and had accepted that he would now take direction from her.

When the work was done, she sat back and thought about the new dilemma—Lord Stafford. He knew Kenneth Jackson and had warned her to stay away, to abandon thoughts of revenge. But she could not because she had promised Charles. Even without that promise, she would have wanted to destroy the man who had taken her brother's life long before his heart stopped beating.

"What do I do now?" Alice whispered.

Short of avoiding Lord Stafford, he always would be in her sphere. That kiss would lie unspoken but present between them.

She knew little about the man, other than women adored him and that he was polite and pleasant in society. His two close friends, Lords Hamilton and Corbyn, were both married. Alice had seen him speaking often with Lord Hamilton's three aunts, who were Aunt Gwen's friends. They were strong-minded women who never hesitated to say what they thought.

She was certain Lord Stafford had suffered as Charles had. What Alice didn't know was what she ought to do about it. Perhaps she would write a list. That usually helped her find the right path forward.

A knock on her door interrupted her thoughts.

"Enter."

"Lord Stafford has called, my lady."

Shock held her silent for several seconds as she stared at Phipps, her butler. "Ah—"

"I can send him away if you wish, my lady?"

Phipps looked every inch the proper butler, regal and unflappable. He had also been there for her, along with Maggie and Ezra, when Charles had died.

"Put him in the parlor, and I will be there shortly. Tea too, I think."

"I will see to it at once. Shall I call your aunt to join you?"

"She is still sleeping, so please do not wake her."

"Maggie—"

"We'll leave the door open, so there's no need to worry. Thank you, Phipps."

Her butler bowed and left the room.

Lord Stafford was here. Why did that make her heart thud harder? *Because last night he kissed and held you, idiot.*

Alice rose and paced the room, shaking her hands. She lectured herself to be exactly who she had always been, strong and independent. When her spine finally stiffened, she left the room. A glance in the hall mirror confirmed she looked as she always did—composed and well put together.

The parlor door was open and Alice entered. He stood at the window, looking down at the street below. He was immaculate as always; his broad shoulders were encased in deep blue today, hair slightly mussed. Large body seeming at ease, unlike Alice. Everything about the Marquess of Stafford was big and intimidating, but she would never let him see that. Alice showed no weakness. She had worked hard to be the cool, emotionless woman society saw. A shield she'd built because no one, apart from Charles, had ever protected her.

Thankfully, her father had not forced her to marry. She kept his affairs running smoothly, and a son-in-law might have complicated that.

"Lord Stafford."

He turned, shoulders first, eyes locking on hers before the rest of him followed. The man moved with surprising grace for his size. In moments, he was before her, bowing deeply. His gaze flicked briefly toward the open door.

"Is your aunt joining us?"

"She is not." Alice's eyes found the darkening bruise on his jaw from the fight last night.

He nodded. "Forgive me for my actions last night, Lady Alice. The only excuse I can offer is that when I fight, it takes me a while to calm down, and sometimes I am not entirely rational."

Alice had seen that smile before, across ballrooms. She'd heard ladies tittering over him, calling him swoon-worthy.

"So, what you're saying is I was the handy vessel to rid yourself of excess—"

"I would not call you a handy vessel, Lady Alice. You are an exceptionally beautiful woman, and let no one tell you otherwise. But what I did was wrong. I behaved like an animal. I hope you can forgive me."

He thought she was beautiful. The words left her momentarily speechless. When had anyone last spoken to her like that? She couldn't remember a single time.

"Of course, and I was not entirely blameless," she conceded. Honesty mattered to her.

His lips twitched at her words.

"Perhaps the moment overcame me as well. Now," Alice

said, eager to move from uncomfortable territory, "is that all that brings you to an unmarried woman's home at such an hour?"

"Your reputation is safe. No one saw me, Lady Alice. And as for why I came, it is to ask again what I asked last night, why were you there?"

"I believe I told you my actions are no business of yours, Lord Stafford."

He studied her, and she had the uneasy sense he saw far more than anyone else ever had. It disturbed her, but she did not look away.

"Were you there because you knew it was possible Kenneth Jackson might attend, my lady?"

Alice was an excellent actress. By sheer willpower, she kept her face composed, or so she hoped.

"Why do you ask?"

"Because a year ago, I received some alarming news about him. I have been hunting him since."

"You've not seen him since Blackwood Hall?" she asked, raising a brow.

"Some men have paid for what they did to us and to others, but not Kenneth Jackson. He disappeared from our world. Once we left, we never saw or heard from him again. That changed a year ago, and I realized I wanted justice. I have been hunting him ever since."

Hunting him?

"What news reached you?"

"News that Kenneth Jackson was still committing unspeakable acts against young children. This time at a charity school here in London."

"Dear Lord," Alice whispered.

"He fled the facility when confronted by one of the benefactors after rumors of his actions reached him," Lord Stafford added.

"And someone told you?"

"I overheard a conversation," he said simply.

They fell silent, eyes locked for long, heated seconds.

"I know your brother was a Blackwood boy, Lady Alice."

She nodded.

"Did he speak of his time there? Is that why you wish to find Jackson?"

Emotion choked her as it always did when she thought about the cruelty Charles had suffered at Blackwood Hall, and how it had broken him beyond repair.

"Why are you asking me this?" The words emerged hoarse, stripped of her usual composure.

"I have no wish to upset you, my lady."

Alice turned from him to the window, staring down at the street below to steady herself. She knew he was still watching her. Breathing deeply, she turned back.

"You suffered terribly, didn't you? Like my brother?" She hadn't meant to ask but the words had escaped before she could stop them. She didn't expect an answer. He gave one, with a single, grave nod.

"I…I'm sorry."

He said nothing, his eyes unreadable.

"Charles was there for two years before he came home ill," she continued. "He never fully recovered. His spirit was broken in Blackwood Hall." She looked down at her clenched fists.

She heard him move, and moments later his boots stopped inches from hers. Polished black leather gleaming. Alice forced herself to meet his gaze.

"I knew he was a Blackwood boy, my lady. We have a list."

"A list?"

"My friends, Lords Hamilton and Corbyn. We entered Blackwood Hall together. When we left, we made a list of everyone who had attended. Everyone who may have suffered."

"Why?"

He looked so calm speaking of something that had to have scarred his soul.

"Because we made a vow when our torment ended—"

"When did it end?" she whispered, regretting the question at once. She didn't want to know how long he had suffered.

"That is not my story alone to tell, my lady."

"Of course." Her voice softened. "What was your vow?"

"No Blackwood boy would walk alone."

He spoke the words quietly, but his eyes had darkened, hardening with something fierce and implacable. Alice shivered. This was not a man one wished to make an enemy of, and she would do well to remember that.

CHAPTER SEVEN

J AMIE HAD DECIDED the minute he opened his eyes that he needed to speak with Lady Alice. First, there was the apology he knew he must deliver. Second, there was his need to get to the bottom of why she was there last night, and what her intentions going forward were with regards to Jackson.

He'd gone through his morning routine of dressing and then eating a large meal while reading the newspaper. When his horse arrived, he'd left the house. He now sat in the Smythe parlor with a woman who he thought wished him anywhere but here.

The Lady Alice he'd known for the last few years should not have been frequenting a bare-knuckle boxing match. She was proper, aloof, and the epitome of a gently bred society lady. It appeared she'd been fooling everyone.

Yes, she was unwed, and old enough now to be classed as on the shelf, but still, he had never once heard a whisper of a scandal surrounding her, or a whisper of impropriety. If news of what she was about reached people, she would be shunned from the world she'd been born into. He needed to move carefully now, to get her to talk to him.

"I'm sorry for your brother's suffering, my lady."

He watched her shoulders straighten under the soft cream of her day dress, and the anguish leave her eyes then. Once again, she was the cool Lady Alice, and had he not seen that look of anguish for himself, he'd never have believed her capable of such devastation.

It was clear her brother's loss had hit her hard, but more than that, the suffering he endured.

"Thank you."

Her eyes were a color he'd not seen often. More amber than brown, and the right had a lighter patch close to the pupil. He'd thought her beautiful and meant it, but Jamie was fast beginning to realize she was much more than that. She was exquisite, but he, and no doubt many men in society, had not taken the time to get past her standoffish façade to notice.

Her hair was in a simple bun today, with a few tendrils loose. She wore a cream dress with rose pink embroidery around the cuffs at her wrists and hem. But on her body the effect was stunning. A body he now knew was curved and lush.

He was not a man who gave into urges, but last night he'd touched and tasted her, and he knew that he would have those urges again, no matter how much he'd told himself otherwise. What had happened between them would be a memory that would stay with him for a long time.

But he would never again act on that need, because there would be no future for him with Lady Alice Smythe, and she was a lady. Don't forget that, Jamie, he reminded himself. Because he had last night and the consequences had been dire.

"Tell me what the name Kenneth Jackson means to you please, my lady?"

"He played a hand in killing my brother," she said.

Jamie knew there was more to that statement, so he stood in silence, watching her and waiting.

This, what they were talking about, was not easy for him, because until now, he'd never discussed what had happened in Blackwood Hall with anyone but Toby and Anthony. There had been others whom they'd helped, who suffered also, but they'd never spoken about what they endured. It was just accepted that they had. Now, however, that was changing, because if he needed Lady Alice to tell him what she knew, he had to acknowledge the suffering of her brother.

"So you believe your brother died as a direct result of what took place in Blackwood Hall?"

"Kenneth Jackson did not hold a gun to my brother's head, but the torture he endured broke his mind," Lady Alice said. "He never recovered and suffered terribly."

Which likely meant she, in her own way, had suffered also, Jamie thought.

A knock on the door was followed by a tea tray, which a butler carried into the room, to place on the small table before the sofa. It was loaded with two plates full of food. Jamie saw three wedges of cake, and another plate filled with scones. His eyes went to Lady Alice. Clearly, she did not nibble her food like many.

"Are we expecting visitors, Phipps?" She raised an eyebrow at her butler.

"No indeed, my lady, but as you have a visitor, I thought to add another plate." He smiled at her.

"Thank you, Phipps. Scones are a particular weakness of mine," Jamie added, smiling.

"That will be all, thank you," Lady Alice said to the butler, moving around him to the table.

Jamie waited for her to pour, and then take the seat on one end of the sofa. He then took the other, and the cup she handed him.

"I have never spoken about how my brother suffered, Lord Stafford. I have two staff members who know some of what happened, and whom I would trust with my life, but no one else. This was his private battle and not one that he would wish to share."

"As I am aware of what took place at Blackwood Hall, I can assure you that anything you say to me today will go no further. But I will add that Lords Hamilton and Corbyn are my friends and endured much there too, and I would trust them with my life."

Her long, slender fingers tightened briefly around the handle of her cup as she took a sip of her tea.

Jamie loathed teacups. They were always too small for his hands, and he far preferred a mug. Alas, that was not what was served in the correct parlors and drawing rooms of society.

He always felt awkward attempting to hold a cup and not spill the contents down his front.

"Is there a problem, Lord Stafford? You are frowning at the tea. Do you take it stronger?"

"No, this is fine, thank you," Jamie said.

She took a sip of her own.

"Just so we are clear, Lady Alice. Are you looking for Kenneth Jackson to seek revenge on your brother's behalf?" Like Jamie, he believed this woman was someone who liked to get straight to the point. No prevarication needed, even on such a delicate topic.

That he was even discussing this was a shock. Jamie never talked of that time, and yet here he was doing just that with Lady Alice.

"I am," she said, her voice strong. "I wish I knew who else was involved, but as my brother only mentioned Jackson, I do not."

"Let me assure you that the other men involved have received punishment for their wrongdoings, through different means. However, as yet, not Jackson."

"I am pleased to hear that, but it is time for Jackson to suffer for his crimes."

He wanted to tell her to stop this revenge now. The gentleman in him needed to protect her and make her understand the animal she hunted. The man who would rip the innocence from boys who had been put into his care. A man so ruthless he would laugh when they begged him to stop. Age hadn't dulled his wickedness from what Jamie learned when he'd gone to the charter school.

The two boys he'd spoken to had recounted their punishment in halting voices, each word dragging up memories Jamie had long tried to bury. What they described was the same torment he and his friends had endured. Cruelty disguised as discipline. Jamie had spent a long time with them afterward, doing what little he could to offer comfort, though he knew words offered nothing when the pain ran deep. He'd told them that Kenneth Jackson would pay for what he'd done, that justice would come. More than that, he'd urged them not to let that monster define who they became.

"Do not give him that power," he'd said quietly, watching their too-young faces shadowed by fear and shame. "You survived him. That is victory enough for now."

But as he looked into their eyes—empty, hollowed, and far too old for their years—Jamie knew healing would not come easily. It would take time, perhaps a lifetime, before they could look at themselves and not see the marks left by Jackson's cruelty. And God help him, he understood that truth better than anyone.

He'd not left his townhouse for two days after he'd spoken with them, as the memories had come back harder and more punishing than before.

Closing his eyes briefly, he forced down the images of the time in his life that had changed him beyond recognition from the one who had arrived at Blackwood Hall, eager and ready to face this next journey life was presenting him.

"Jackson is a dangerous man, Lady Alice. The word evil embodies him. I would not advise you to ever confront him alone."

"I know the man he is, my lord," she said in a cold, hard voice. "My brother told me some of what he suffered, but after he passed, I found a journal of his time at Blackwood Hall. It went into detail of the torture."

Christ. He could only imagine what she read in there, if her brother suffered as he and his friends had. The thought of her learning about what cruelty he'd endured made him feel slightly nauseous. There was also vulnerability. Jamie felt exposed when for so long he'd taken steps to hide his pain and what he'd experienced at Blackwood Hall.

"My brother made me promise something before his death, Lord Stafford. He wanted me to seek retribution on his behalf against Kenneth Jackson."

"No." The word was out of his mouth before he could recall it.

"No?" She raised a brow.

"I'm quite sure your brother would not wish to throw you into the path of a man like him, Lady Alice," Jamie added. "Was he in his right mind when he asked this of you?"

"How dare you speak of my brother in such a way?" She snapped the words at him like the crack of a whip.

"This is no game, my lady—"

"Oh yes, you can imagine how amusing I find the memory of my brother weeping in his sleep as he relived the hell he went through, or lashing out as the anger gripped him. Watching him slide into a madman because he could no longer face the hell of living!"

Her anguish reached out to him then, and the sheen in her eyes told Jamie tears were close.

CHAPTER EIGHT

"LADY ALICE, I did not mean—"

"I lost my brother long before he drew his last breath, my lord." Her words cut him off.

She got out of her seat then and moved back to the window. Jamie stayed where he was, watching her. Her arms folded tight around her waist as if to protect herself from something. Memories, Jamie thought, as he was no threat to her, and vowed right then never to be so again.

This woman had suffered deeply; he could see that clearly now.

"Sorry is a word that should mean something to you in this moment, Lady Alice, but I know it doesn't. However, I am that, and as someone who went through what your brother did, I know how he suffered." Jamie regained his feet, but did not approach her.

It wasn't an easy thing to say, acknowledging the suffering, but right then she needed to hear those words, because only then might she decide to trust him.

"And yet there you stand before me with all the appearance of a gentleman who doesn't suffer."

The anger came then, fast and fierce, even though he knew she was lashing out in retaliation for his previous words. Jamie took a few seconds to calm down before he spoke.

"Because I do not show it does not mean I don't battle my

demons, Lady Alice, as do my friends."

She sighed. "Forgive me if you thought I was in any way suggesting you didn't go through what my brother did, Lord Stafford. That was not my intention. In fact, I don't know what I meant by those words." She didn't look at him, her eyes still on the window. "I had believed Charles strong, but—"

"I survived because I had my friends, Lady Alice." He cut her off. "Without them, I would not have. If your brother was alone, then his struggle would have been greater."

"So yes, I am seeking revenge on behalf of Charles, Lord Stafford, and there is nothing you can do or say to change my mind on this." She returned to her seat then, and Jamie retook his.

He looked at the uneaten plate of cake and realized that, for the first time in a long while, he had lost his appetite. He also knew in that moment there was nothing he could do or say to dissuade her from her revenge, just as no one could sway him.

"Very well, but perhaps we could work together in finding him, and then we will both be safe," Jamie said.

She turned in her seat, studying him. Jamie withstood the look. Anthony's three aunts, after all, who were world class at it, had stared him down many times.

"You are just saying that so you can keep track of my movements, aren't you?" Her amber eyes narrowed. "Let me assure you I do not now, nor ever, need a man to protect me, Lord Stafford, and especially not one who is a stranger."

"Are you always so untrusting, Lady Alice?"

She was right, of course. He was trying to ensure she did not stumble into danger, or get close to the animal that was Kenneth Jackson, but he would not be telling her that.

"Yes," she said, chin lifting. "I have been given many examples in my lifetime of what trusting someone can bring me. I no longer do so without knowing a person well, and even then—"

"I take your meaning," he interrupted, raising a hand.

"Excellent," she added primly, which only annoyed him

more.

This woman was a danger to Jamie simply because she could *get* a reaction out of him, and not many could, save perhaps his oldest friends.

"Why were you fighting in that ring?" she asked, eyes narrowing. "You, a wealthy, powerful peer of the realm, stripped to the waist and behaving like those beneath you."

"Not all beneath us are common, Lady Alice," he said, his voice roughening to a growl.

"I did not say they were. And do not think that I believe money and title maketh a man, Lord Stafford, because I have ample evidence to the contrary."

Jamie's jaw clenched. Why did he enjoy sparring with her when she wrenched so many emotions from him? Why did she intrigue him when so few ever had? Her wits were sharp, her intellect keener still. Anyone who looked at her and saw an empty-headed, gently born woman would be sorely mistaken. Lady Alice was far more dangerous than that, and he was fast coming to understand it.

"I have my reasons for fighting," he said. "Reasons I will not discuss with you, my lady. But you must not go there alone again. It is far too dangerous, as evidenced by those two men mistreating you when I found you."

She studied him, her expression unreadable. Then, to his relief, she nodded once.

"I will make you a deal, Lady Alice." He held her gaze, searching for something, anything he could read. "If you tell me what you know, I will share my information with you."

"I will do that, Lord Stafford, if you promise to take me with you when you get a lead on Kenneth Jackson."

He hesitated. He didn't want to say yes because most of his hunts for Jackson took place in the early hours, and in places no lady should ever be. Yet he knew she would simply take it upon herself to do the same without him.

"Very well," he said at last. "You have a deal. But I insist that if the situation we face is dangerous, you will take instruction from me."

"Absolutely not. I take instruction from nobody. I can shoot better than most men and am handy with a knife."

"That may be, my lady," Jamie said evenly, though his pulse had begun to thrum, "but a man's strength will always be greater than yours."

"I am stronger than I look," she countered, with that infuriating gleam in her eyes. "And I have someone who ensures that is the case."

"Who?"

"That is no concern of yours, Lord Stafford."

"Your aunt—"

"Knows none of what we speak of, and I wish to keep it that way."

He studied her for long seconds. She didn't flinch beneath his gaze, instead, lifting her chin, meeting him head-on. She had courage—too much of it, but that could land her in trouble.

Jamie could think of no way to stop Lady Alice, no way to keep her safe. If he excluded her, she'd continue her inquiries alone, but if he included her, at least he could watch her movements.

"Very well."

She extended her hand, and he stared at it.

"Have you never shaken the hand of a lady, my lord?"

The little witch was mocking him now. He took her fingers. Neither of them wore gloves, and her skin was warm in his. The moment lingered longer than it should have before he released her. Jamie barely resisted the urge to step back. He'd felt that touch all the way to his toes.

"What information do you have?" he asked, voice rougher than he intended.

"I have several informants and have followed multiple leads, but I have yet to run Jackson to ground. He is elusive," she said, blowing out an irritated breath that made her look like a frustrated child.

"He is that," Jamie murmured. "But between us, we may succeed. We must."

The words came out harder than he'd planned. He had no wish to spend his life chasing Kenneth Jackson, but feared now that he'd begun, only success, or Jackson's destruction, would appease him.

"Does your father know what you are doing, Lady Alice?"

"He is in France, and has been for many years."

Her voice cooled, shutters slamming down behind her eyes. Whatever had passed between Lord Smythe and his daughter was not for him to know, so Jamie let it drop.

They talked for another half hour. She was sharp and direct, and he found himself admiring her mind as much as her spirit.

Only later, when he rode away, did Jamie realize the true danger he had invited into his life. Not just Kenneth Jackson.

But her.

Because there was something about Lady Alice that made him forget every vow of caution he had ever sworn. And that, he suspected grimly, might prove his downfall.

The woman had nerve. He would give her that. But courage, no matter how admirable, could get her killed.

Jamie turned his horse down a quieter street away from hawkers and the rumble of carriages, with thoughts churning over and over inside his head.

Alice's information had filled gaps in his own, and she had searched in places he had not, but still, they were no closer to locating Jackson.

Partnership meant trust, and trust was a luxury he rarely afforded himself with anyone but those closest to him.

When he reached his townhouse, he'd collect his sword and leave again immediately for Angelo's. Jamie needed an outlet and exercise would provide that as it always did. Fencing would mean he could quiet the thoughts inside his head briefly.

He thought to protect Lady Alice Smythe from her reckless

actions. Now, he was beginning to wonder who would protect him from her.

<h1 style="text-align:center">CHAPTER NINE</h1>

"**I** AM TO go driving in the park today with Thaddeus and Eloise, Aunt Gwen," Alice said to her aunt across the dining table.

It had been two days since Lord Stafford had called to see her. Two days of mulling over what she'd learned from him, which if she was honest, was not a great deal that she didn't already know.

But one thing had come clear to her. Jackson must be stopped for those who had suffered at his hand in the past, and those like the children at the charity school who still could be harmed.

"Lovely, dear. Make sure you take a scarf. I fear there could be a chill in the air today."

Her aunt was not a morning person. She rarely woke before ten and then stayed in bed drinking tea and reading until she was ready to face the world...namely, Alice, because she was a morning person who woke ready to start the day the minute her eyes opened.

They'd established a routine since Aunt Gwen had moved in after Charles's death that was comfortable to both.

"There is to be a picnic at Lord and Lady Sinclair's soon, dear. We shall go, as there will be plenty to do."

"Lovely," Alice said with the same enthusiasm she would have for eating pilchards—very little. If there was one thing she loathed more than a ball, it was a picnic. People sat about on blankets eating and chatting, while watching each other for the slightest indiscretions. Society fed on gossip, and thus far she'd managed to avoid being fodder for the more voracious members, but Alice was sure that given time, she'd slip up in some way.

"There will be croquet, and cards, I believe."

Alice pulled off the crust of her toast and ate the middle so she didn't growl.

"Crusts are good for you, and make your hair curl, Alice."

"No, they are not," Alice teased her aunt. "They're just bread like the middle parts, and I already have a curl in my hair." She'd never eaten crusts since she was little and choked on one. Charles had whacked her on the back, dislodging it.

"What plans do you have for the remainder of the day, Aunt?" Alice asked.

"I am at a particularly tense part in my latest novel, so I will retire to the parlor and read that, if you do not need me."

"Well then, enjoy your book, and I shall ready myself to depart."

After kissing her aunt's cheek, she headed for the door.

"Alice."

Turning, she found Aunt Gwen's eyes on her.

"Are you happy, my dear?"

"Why are you asking me that?" Alice tried to make light of it, because the deep ache inside her chest told her that was never likely to happen again. Not the kind of happiness that reached every inch of her body. She could laugh and smile, and be content. But happiness? No.

"I worry about you. Charles has been gone a while now, but I fear you still feel his loss keenly."

"He was my brother," Alice said with more force than required.

Her aunt's eyes softened. "I know, my love. Just as I know you loved him very much. Seeing as you had hopeless parents, you and he were very close, and I do not say that lightly, as one was my sister."

"It's all right, Aunt Gwen—"

"It's not, dear. But alas, there was little I could do about it."

"Why are we having this discussion now?"

Her aunt's eyes looked sad. "Because I see the turmoil inside you when you believe no one is looking. I worry for you, Alice. Worry that you will never find happiness, or marry—"

"I have no wish to wed." The words came out flat and cold.

Her aunt sighed.

"There is no need to worry about me, Aunt Gwen." Alice softened her tone. "Really. I am fine, and happy here with you. If you are happy, that is?"

"Of course I'm happy. I live here in this wonderful townhouse with you. I get to visit with my friends. Before I came to live with you, my life was uncertain. I just worry about you, Alice."

She went back to her aunt and hugged her close. "There really is no need. I am fine, and happy with everything, just the way it is. Now I must hurry to change, or the twins will be here, and I will not be ready."

Her aunt rarely asked her questions like that. In fact, for the most part they just rubbed along together, sharing a house, yet doing what they wanted. Why had she asked those questions of Alice now? Had someone been talking to her? Alice hoped not; she didn't need anyone meddling in her affairs now.

After changing, she made her way back down to the front entrance, where her butler now stood.

"A missive has arrived for you, my lady," he said, holding it out to her.

"Thank you, Phipps." Taking it, Alice opened it.

A man meeting the description of Kenneth Jackson entered the Black Dog in Wapping. He's been seen there twice now, and asking plenty of questions. I will meet you there at midnight.

It could be another dead end, Alice thought, tucking the note into her reticule. Or it could lead her closer to Jackson. Either way, she would be attending, even if she must enter the Black Dog in Wapping, a place she'd never been before.

Usually, she met an informant in the small park, a ten-minute walk from here, with Ezra. Alice wondered why now she was being told to go to the alehouse?

It matters not, Alice, only that you have another lead. What she had to do now was notify Lord Stafford, or she could deal with it and speak to him tomorrow?

Then she remembered the solemn nod he'd given her when Alice had asked if he too had suffered at Blackwood Hall. He had a right to know what she'd found, just as she did to avenge her brother. She had to tell him, as he'd promised to tell her if he had a lead, as had she.

A knock sounded on the door, and Phipps opened it, and there stood Thaddeus, looking his usual well put together self.

"Imagine my shock that a Thomas twin is punctual," Alice said.

"Yes, well, we won't be making a habit of it. My reputation will be destroyed." Thaddeus leaned in to kiss her cheek. "You look beautiful as always."

"And you look handsome as always."

He bowed deeply and then held out his hand.

"Where is Maggie?"

She turned at these words to find Ezra standing behind her with Phipps.

"If you will cast your eyes to the phaeton, you will see my dear friend Miss Thomas already seated there, so I do not need Maggie, Ezra. Stop fretting."

Her footman stepped out of the doorway and looked at the phaeton. Eloise waved as he glared at her.

"Take care of her," he then said to Thaddeus. "You'll not turn sharp corners with her on the outside in that thing."

"Enough, Ezra," Alice gritted out while glaring at her footman.

"I will ensure she is returned to you in the condition she left," Thaddeus said solemnly.

They then made their way to the carriage. He helped her up,

and she took the seat on the outside. It wasn't exactly a squeeze, but if she wasn't close with the Thomas twins, it wouldn't be a comfortable ride.

"He's still watching us, isn't he?" Thaddeus whispered.

"Pay him no mind," Alice said, waving to Phipps and Ezra who were both watching as they rolled away.

"I've never known servants who protect their mistress quite like your household staff do, Alice."

Alice hissed out a breath between her teeth. Ezra had declared in curt words his displeasure when they'd arrived home after the night she'd seen Lord Stafford fighting. About impropriety and danger, and any number of other things she could no longer remember.

"I should fire all of them."

"No, you won't," Eloise scoffed. "I think it's rather lovely they care for you so much."

Secretly, she did also, even though sometimes their meddlesome ways annoyed her excessively.

"We play cards some nights. All of us in the household. My aunt is a whizz and beats us constantly."

"I can't imagine playing cards with any of my father's staff. They're all stuffy," Thaddeus said.

Alice looked around her as the twins discussed which of their staff would unbend enough to play cards with them.

The day was a warm one, and it showed London at its best. Sunlight glinted off the windowpanes, and people stood about enjoying its warmth.

She preferred the wide open spaces of the country, but sometimes, like now, she thought London had its benefits. Anything you wanted was right there. Sweets, which she was partial to, and teashops.

But then so were the poverty and squalor. Young children who had hollow cheeks with their eyes too big in their faces were everywhere. Alice and her aunt had joined numerous charities to try and put their efforts into helping some, but sometimes she feared the task was too great. However, her latest acquisition, she hoped, would aid some of those in desperate need of medical attention.

"Eloise, do you and your brother involve yourself in charities?"

"Pardon?" Alice's friend looked at her.

"Father wishes to purchase a property to set up a clinic to offer medical care to those that don't have access to it." Alice always had to use her father's name, even with her friends, as no one could believe that she would actually want to be involved in such things. Business was not something with which a woman should sully her hands.

"Pardon?" Eloise said again, looking shocked.

"You have to know there are people out there who cannot just send word they need a doctor as we do?"

"I—ah—well as to that, Alice. It's not something I've thought about," Eloise said.

She'd been wrong to bring this up. Her friends had been raised in a wealthy family, with parents who loved them, and the darker side of life had yet to touch them. It hadn't exactly touched Alice either until her brother died.

Then she'd felt restless and needed to do more to forget the pain of losing Charles. It had been Maggie who had told her about the plight of her cousin Eunice and those in the tenement where she lived. How there was no hope for her now she'd fallen ill.

"Please forget I brought it up. I'm not sure what I was thinking," Alice said. "'Tis a lovely day for a ride through the park."

"Forget you brought up a subject like people are suffering as they cannot access medical help?" Thaddeus said, looking around his sister to Alice. "I hardly think that is something we can dismiss with ease."

"The problem as I see it, Alice, is that we rarely think about anyone other than ourselves," Eloise said, frowning.

"You're two of the best people I know," Alice said.

"Perhaps, but perhaps not," Eloise added.

Had she just ruined her friendship with the two people she actually liked in society? *Why did you say anything?*

The problem was that, at times, the life she lived felt obscenely privileged. Surrounded by people who were spoiled and indifferent, Alice could not help but feel disgusted knowing that while the wealthy squandered their comforts, most of London went without. She had seen the seedier side of the city on her visits to the orphanages with her aunt, and those images lingered.

"Explain about this clinic," Eloise said, waving her hand in front of Alice.

"It doesn't matter."

"Well, clearly it matters to you," Thaddeus said. "Or you would not have mentioned it."

Alice thought about what she should say, and decided only the truth would do now. If she lost her friendship with the twins after that, then were they ever really her friends?

"My maid Maggie, who is married to Ezra, the footman who glared at you, Thaddeus, approached me one day about her sister who was unwell."

"He does have a formidable glare," Thaddeus added.

"Eunice, her sister, had a fever which was from a sore on her leg. She would have died, had I not had her brought to my father's townhouse and insisted a doctor tend her," Alice said.

"And this started you thinking about a clinic?" Thaddeus asked.

"It did, and so Father and I decided to purchase a building and set it up in an area where those in need could access it."

"That is a wonderful idea, Alice, and one I would never have thought of." Eloise looked curious now. "Mother does some charity work with the orphans, and Father is a patron to a few things."

"And we live an indolent life and do little for anyone other than ourselves," her brother added.

"I did not mean—"

"We will be involved," Eloise cut her words off. "In some capacity, and we will be discussing the matter with Father."

"Will we?" Thaddeus asked as he navigated them around a cart filled with something smelly.

Fish, Alice thought.

"We will," Eloise said. "You have reminded me that we have much, and others don't."

"Many will think it is not right, what I'm doing," Alice cautioned her friends. "I have no wish for you to fall foul of your family for helping me. Perhaps another charity—"

"So it's quite all right for you to fall foul of people, and yet not us?" Thaddeus demanded.

"I don't really have anyone to worry about. I care little what society thinks of me," Alice said.

"But you still have to live within its confines, as do we," Eloise added. "We will help, and you will tell us how when the time comes. My mind is made up."

"Well then, if your mind is made up, far be it from either of us to change it," Thaddeus said.

"You couldn't even if you tried," Eloise scoffed.

And they were off again, and in fact their argument lasted until they drove through the gates, and into the park.

CHAPTER TEN

HE WASN'T SURE why he'd done it, and was now regretting his actions, but Jamie had asked Miss Devlin when he arrived in the park if she wanted to take a walk with him.

It was that bloody list, of course. Miss Devlin's name had been on there, along with Lady Alice, and Miss Timothy. He wanted to rid his mind of Lady Alice, and to do that he thought, foolishly, that walking with Miss Devlin might help. It hadn't.

"I always find a walk in the fresh park air invigorating," she said.

They'd been walking for ten minutes, and to Jamie, it was turning out to be the longest ten minutes of his life.

"Extremely invigorating," he agreed.

"Here you cannot easily smell the more unpleasant scents you could if you were walking a London street."

She then proceeded to wave to everyone she met, in between talking to him about a variety of topics he had no interest in.

"Miss Primrose is quite a gossip, you know, my lord. Why, just last week I had to tell her I had no wish to hear such things about society members."

Miss Devlin then went on to explain the things she hadn't meant to hear, but clearly had, as she was very detailed. And this was why he didn't take young, innocent women walking in the park. Their conversations were mind numbingly boring.

Glancing around them, Jamie saw plenty of colorful parasols

to shade women from the sun, as they wandered closer to the Serpentine. Vendors called out their wares, and a few servants scurried to them to secure refreshments for those in carriages. It was a typical scene, and one he'd taken in many times, yet today it felt different. He felt different, and could not quite put his finger on why.

"Of course, I never gossip, as it really is not done, Lord Stafford."

Jamie let her rattle on with the occasional noise when it was required of him. He knew not all were like Miss Devlin, and in fact it was likely she was nervous walking with him. Maybe he was just too jaded to be in the company of innocent people.

The hand life had dealt him by putting him in Blackwood Hall had darkened his soul. He wasn't sure that would ever change.

He knew for his family's line to continue, he was expected to marry, but never to someone like Miss Devlin. Lady Alice slid into his head. *Absolutely not.* He did not want passion with his future wife. He wanted companionship. She would not be comfortable—far from it in fact.

They would do what they must to seek out the monster that was Kenneth Jackson, and then he would be keeping his distance from that woman.

"Lord Stafford?"

"Sorry, I missed that, Miss Devlin. What was it you said?"

"Are you to attend the Fotheringham house party? I heard it will be quite the occasion, and everyone is going." This was followed by a trill of laughter which confirmed to Jamie, if he'd needed confirmation that was, that no way in hell could he face this woman across his breakfast table.

"I am unsure at this stage."

"Oh, you must."

"And here is your mother." He didn't exactly drag her across the grass to the woman smiling at them with a smug look on her face, but it was a near thing.

"My daughter is so accomplished, Lord Stafford. Why, just this morning I listened to her playing a sonata by Mozart, and her performance was faultless."

Lady Devlin was no different to many who had daughters in society. Their main goal was to secure them good matches, and it was for the young women to present themselves in just the perfect light to achieve that. Jamie knew this was the way things worked, even as he disliked it. Mainly for the young women. He wasn't sure why this was suddenly bothering him when he'd been witnessing it for years…but it did.

"Wonderful. I always think pianoforte playing an excellent skill. I'm quite hopeless at it," Jamie said. He then bowed deeply. "Thank you for the walk, Miss Devlin." Before either lady could speak another word, he'd headed the other way, his eyes searching for someone, anyone, he knew and was comfortable with. They landed on her.

Lady Alice was walking with the Thomas twins.

"Well now, this is fortuitous."

Turning to the right, he saw Anthony, Evie, Toby, and Liberty approaching. Slowly, he unclenched his muscles and made himself focus on them, rather than Lady Alice. Jamie also made sure the bruise on his chin was not facing his friends.

"Is Miss Devlin on the list?" Anthony asked.

"List?" Jamie raised a brow.

"We know you have one, and I'm quite sure we shared ours with you," Toby said.

"Never let it be said that I have a say in who you wed, Jamie," Liberty added. "But not Miss Devlin if you please. She is not suitable at all."

"She chatters incessantly. Even if she is on the list, I agree with Liberty—"

"Of course you do because she's your wife," Jamie said. "You always agree with her."

"As he should. Now, let us stroll," Liberty said.

"Where is Florence?" he asked Toby and Liberty, placing his

hand over the bruise now, casually. Florence had been a little girl when she'd come to live with Toby when her parents, Toby's cousin, Thomas, and his wife, passed away. At the time, it had been terrifying for both of them. His friend had been a bachelor who had no plans to wed, but now, he, Liberty, and Florence were a happy family.

Jamie had come to love the little girl very much, and spoiled her, as did the others.

"She and her nanny, Miss Haigh, are studying nature today in the garden," Toby said. "I wanted to stay, as it sounds rather fun actually, but Liberty told me I had to accompany her."

"It certainly sounds more fun than this," Jamie agreed, looking around him. He found Lady Alice with the Thomas twins.

"I like that woman," Evie said, following his gaze. "Is she on the list, Jamie?"

"This conversation is over because I will not marry," he said, feeling like his neckcloth was tightening on its own around his neck.

"But is she on the list?" Liberty said with a sweet smile.

"That look may have your husband yielding to your every wish; however, it will not move me."

Toby clutched his chest. "Are you actually refusing her? I must try that sometime."

"Very amusing, husband, but still he has not answered."

"What is the bruise on your cheek from?" Evie asked, grabbing Jamie's hand and tugging it from his face. Suddenly, the silence was deafening, and Anthony and Toby's smiles changed to scowls.

"Ah, do you want a lemonade, Evie?" Liberty said, looking at her husband. "We shall procure some and cake—I think they will definitely need cake after the talk that is coming."

"You will not make a scene here," Evie said, patting her husband's cheek. "I'm wondering if we should stay and mediate?"

"They'll tell us later anyway, but we shall pretend they won't," Liberty said.

The women then wandered off, leaving the three men all now standing in a tight circle glaring at each other.

"You told us you were done with fighting," Anthony snapped.

"Promised actually," Toby added, scowling.

Jamie hadn't thought he'd see his friends today, as they were usually in their houses playing happily married couples, and had hoped the bruise would have faded by the time he saw them again.

"I walked into a door," he lied.

"No, you did not," Anthony gritted out.

The sound of someone banging on a drum had them all jumping. Looking left, Jamie found a military band had begun to play nearby. At least they would not be overheard.

"You were fighting again, weren't you?"

The anger in Anthony's voice had Jamie's rising.

"He lies better than anyone I know, so it's hard to say," Toby said, leaning in to look at Jamie's face.

"I'm not answering any of your questions. I have more important things to talk about."

"More important than you being used as a punching bag?" Anthony's words were chilly, as was the look in his eyes.

"Christ, Jamie," Toby said. "You said it had stopped. What happened to make you—"

"Look, just leave it, will you? I need to tell you something else. What I do when you're not with me is my business." Jamie saw the hurt his words put in his friends' eyes, but he didn't care. He wasn't done talking yet. "You both have wives now, and lives to live. Let me live mine."

They stared at him for long seconds and he withstood it, even as he wanted to shuffle his feet.

"You think because we are married and in love with our wives, we are no longer invested in your life? That you don't matter, and the past that we have shared is suddenly no longer important?" Toby said, his tone solemn.

Hell.

"You became our business the first day we walked into Blackwood Hall, and will always be so," Anthony said. "We are brothers, and our wives have no bearing on that."

"Of course they have bearing on that," Jamie snapped, not even realizing until now that he was feeling cast adrift. "They are your sole focus now, as they should be."

"No," Toby said. "Absolutely not."

"Agreed. You," Anthony jabbed him in the chest hard, "are stuck with us, and I want the truth right now. Have you been fighting again?"

He'd never been able to lie to these two.

"Speak," Toby snapped.

"Fine, yes."

"Why?"

"Look—"

"Why?" Anthony said again, but this time in a low growl.

"I enjoy it." It wasn't a lie exactly. He did enjoy the fight, but when his demons were howling at him, he needed to do something to push them back down inside. Fighting did that, more so than just any form of exercise.

"What's going on? Why did you feel the need to fight? Why did you not come to us?" Toby asked. "Was it after the ball, which we both attended, so you could have talked to us there."

"There are just some things I need to do alone," Jamie said. He saw her then. Lady Alice was walking the path nearby, and her eyes were on him. They widened briefly as she passed. *Did that mean she wanted to speak to him?*

"We don't keep secrets from each other," Anthony said.

Jamie snorted. "You don't actually believe that, do you? You had secrets, such as the extent of your gambling."

"If you feel the need to fight again, I want you to tell one of us," Toby said before Anthony could speak again. "We will be there in support."

"I won't need you, because I always win." Jamie said the

words with a cocky smile, hoping to lighten the mood.

"What do you want to tell us?" Anthony muttered, clearly still annoyed.

"Not here. But soon. Right now, I need to speak to Lady Alice."

Both his friends raised their brows at that.

"Not in that way; it's to do with her brother. He was a Blackwood boy. But I need your women to help me get her alone."

"Why?"

He knew he'd have to tell them, and that they would not be pleased, but not here in a park full of society members.

"I promise I will explain everything, just trust me in this. I need to speak to her now."

"Very well, but we will have a full accounting," Anthony said.

Liberty and Evie returned with two lemonades.

"Give those to your men. I need to speak to Lady Alice, and you two are going to help me," Jamie said, taking the cups and handing them to Anthony and Toby.

"Why can't we come?" Anthony demanded. "We could distract Thaddeus Thomas."

"For pity's sake, fine, come then." He then held out his arms for their women.

"You may want to smile before we approach Lady Alice or that look will have her running for the hills," Liberty said out of the side of her mouth.

"I need you to draw her away from the Thomas twins."

"Really?" He could feel Evie's eyes on the side of his face. "That's an exciting development."

"It absolutely is not a development, but I have something I must discuss with her," Jamie said.

"Damn," Evie muttered.

"I feel like a spare carriage wheel wandering along in his wake, while he monopolizes our wives," Anthony said from behind them as he drank the lemonade.

"It is complicated, but I will tell you the reason I need to speak to her later. I promise."

"Oh, well then, if you are promising, Jamie, I guess we must," Liberty said. "I like her by the way."

"As do I," Evie agreed. "Determined, strong willed, and does not suffer fools. Her aunt is lovely too. Not sure about the father as I believe he lives in France, or so Anthony told me when we were discussing the perfect woman for you."

"What?"

"You have excellent hearing, so I know you heard, Jamie."

"Leave him alone, Evie," her husband called from behind them. "He is looking a little panicky."

"I am not panicky, but I will add that just because you are all experiencing wedded bliss, does not mean I must."

His friends all gave him a look that suggested he was protesting too much, so rather than confirming their suspicions, he shut up.

He wouldn't wed until he was ready, and then it would be comfortable. Someone like Lady Alice was likely the least comfortable woman he knew.

CHAPTER ELEVEN

"I SAY, DON'T look now, but we are being approached by several noble people."

"You can't swing your parasol around here without hitting a few, so could you be more specific, brother?" Eloise asked.

But Alice knew who was approaching, because he'd interpreted the signal she'd sent him when passing. Lord Stafford. Before Thaddeus could say their names, she heard someone calling to her. Turning, she watched the group approach.

Lord Stafford walked with the wives of his friends on each arm, while their husbands ambled in their wake. He looked calm, with none of the unleashed power she'd seen in that boxing ring, but Alice knew it was there beneath the surface.

Greetings were exchanged, and then Lady Hamilton said, "How lovely it is to see you out here on such a beautiful day. We are to take a turn along the Serpentine. Would you all care to join us?"

"We would love to," Thaddeus said with his usual enthusiasm, before the two women with him could comment.

Soon they were strolling. Alice watched Lord Stafford release his friends' wives and move to her side. He then held out his hand to her. Eloise shot her a speculative look.

"Thank you." She put her fingers on his arm. They then let the others walk on, and fell in behind.

"What did you want to talk to me about?" he said softly.

"I received a note this morning from one of my informants."

"How many do you have?"

"That has no bearing on the matter at hand, Lord Stafford."

Alice turned as he did and their eyes collided. She felt the punch of heat at his nearness in her stomach and looked away.

"Just curious. Forgive me. Pray continue, my lady."

"Are you mocking me?" Alice hated men doing that to her. She ran her father's estate and finances, and likely better than most men, even if she couldn't inform them of that. She would not tolerate anything but respect from this man.

"No, I was not mocking you, Lady Alice. Are you always this sensitive?"

She blew out a very unladylike breath. "Probably."

He snorted out a laugh.

"What did the note say, my lady?"

"A man meeting the description of Kenneth Jackson entered the Black Dog in Wapping. He's been seen there twice now, and asking plenty of questions. I will meet you there at midnight."

He was silent for a while as they both stared at their friends who wandered before them.

Alice was far too aware of this man. Every time his body brushed hers, she tensed. It had to stop.

"You will not go alone," he said softly.

"As I believe I have already explained, you have no say in what I do—"

"Where is your father?"

The change in conversation threw her for two heartbeats, and then she regained her wits. "That has no bearing on what we've just discussed, my lord."

"I know he's in France, but does he play no part in your life, or watch over you at all?"

A dark scowl marred his handsome features now.

"Look, Lord Stafford, I am not your concern, and never will be, and if you persist with these questions, or demands, I will no longer let you know when I receive word, but do as I wish."

This time it was he who exhaled loudly.

"Fine. I will get a hackney and collect you. Then we will proceed to the Black Dog, which let me assure you is not a place for ladies such as yourself to be seen—"

"Let me be clear on something, Lord Stafford," Alice hissed. "I refuse to listen to your recriminations or lectures any further, so if this is to work, you need to learn to be quiet!"

Lord Hamilton, who was directly in front of Alice, must have heard her words, as he turned with a smirk that he directed at his friend.

"Are we clear?" Alice said in a quieter tone.

"Crystal," he snapped back.

They continued to walk behind the others, but the tension between them was palpable. Alice was pleased when they were finally heading back to the carriages.

"Shall we wander to the band?" Thaddeus asked.

Before Alice could refuse, they were all heading that way.

"Bloody brilliant," she muttered.

"Tut tut, Lady Alice. Such language."

"Go to hell, my lord." Why did this man get a rise out of her? Why did she want to kiss him one minute and slap him the next...*no, not kiss, Alice!*

He gave a loud bark of laughter that had all eyes turning their way. She noted that Lady Devlin was glaring at her, and wanted to tell her not to worry, as she was no threat to her daughter's marriage prospects.

"So, you will need to wear—"

"I have left the house for such reasons before. Please do not lecture me on what I need to do or wear, Lord Stafford."

"I do believe that sentence just took ten years of my life," he whispered. "Tell me you did not go alone?"

"I did not. I have a footman, one of the staff members I told you about, who is...ah, well, let's say zealous in his protection of me, thanks to my brother."

"How so?"

Why did I say that? She never talked of private things with anyone. And yet hadn't she already told this man far more than she should have?

"Just know that I rarely leave the house without a large escort, Lord Stafford."

"I feel like that was a threat."

"Take it as you wish. I will make my own way there," Alice said.

"You bloody will not," he whispered in a furious voice.

"Then I will collect you in my carriage. We will discuss this no further. Be ready, as I shall wait no more than five minutes, my lord."

His hiss of breath had her smiling.

"Is this informant reliable?"

"He is."

"Very well," he said but added nothing further.

After listening to the band for a while, they then wandered some more, and Alice heard the conversation going on around her while wondering how soon she could excuse herself and leave. Not easy considering she'd come with the twins, but perhaps she could plead a headache.

Lord Stafford wasn't an easy man to be in the company of, especially when she was as aware of him as she felt right then.

"We shall take this path down to the water," Lady Corbyn said, further heightening Alice's need to flee. She wasn't fond of water, possibly because she'd not spent any time in it, and also she couldn't swim, so there was no way she was taking a chance of falling in.

"What are you doing?" Lord Stafford asked her as Alice moved to his other side, which placed him closest to the water.

"Moving away from the water."

"Because?"

She shot him a look, and met his eyes.

"Need I have a reason?"

"Absolutely," he replied.

"I don't like water."

"Any and all forms, or just large bodies of it?"

She could see the small tilt to his lips. He was enjoying teasing her.

"Large," she said with a smile on her face that in no way reached her eyes. "We all have phobias, Lord Stafford."

"Oh indeed, Jamie loathes snails," Lord Hamilton said from in front of them, as clearly he had been listening again.

She couldn't be sure, but thought Lord Stafford's teeth just snapped together.

"Indeed, if you want to bring him to heel, wave a snail in front of him. It's the slimy underside that makes him squeal."

"I have never squealed a day in my life, and I'll thank you not to share any more of my secrets or I shall start doing the same." Lords Hamilton and Corbyn said nothing further. Their wives, however, weren't so quiet.

"What secrets do you have on them?" Lady Hamilton demanded.

"Nothing," both Lords Hamilton and Corbyn said at the same time, making Alice laugh.

Lord Stafford smiled at her and this time it was genuine, and the effect had her blinking. The man looked younger suddenly, and approachable. As if he was not plagued by demons as her brother had once been. She found herself returning the gesture.

They continued to move with the others along the Serpentine, as a breeze stirred the water, rippling the surface like someone was stroking it. Her skin prickled suddenly, the fine hairs at her nape rising. Looking around, she tried to discover why. Was someone watching her?

She glanced sideways, careful to keep her expression blank, but her eyes flicked across those nearest. People were strolling, chatting and laughing. Nothing amiss. And yet, beneath the polite bustle of the park, she could feel it. Something wasn't right.

"What is wrong, Lady Alice?" Lord Stafford murmured, his deep voice pitched so only she might hear.

"Nothing."

"Your shoulders are rigid. Like a horse about to bolt." His head bent, his lips dangerously close to her ear. "What do you see?"

"Nothing," she said swiftly. Too swiftly.

His gaze lingered on her profile, but he said nothing more.

Up ahead, Lady Hamilton had slowed her step so the women could examine the feathers on another lady's bonnet. The conversation swirled with chatter about Paris fashions and the impossibility of obtaining the right dye for ribbons this Season. Alice answered when addressed, but her eyes drifted again across the crowd.

There, by the boats. A man in a plain brown coat, his hat pulled low. His stance was too still amid the movement around him. She could not make out his features at this distance, but she had the unsettling impression that he was studying her.

Lord Stafford followed the direction of her glance. His hand closed ever so lightly over hers, where it rested on his sleeve. The brief pressure startled her, and she nearly pulled away.

"Do you know him?" he asked softly.

"No." Alice forced her lips into a polite curve as Lady Devlin studied them, frowning, as they passed the group she and her daughter stood in.

"And yet he has you unsettled?"

She looked up at him.

"Perhaps it is not you he is watching, but me."

"Do you know him?"

"I could not say from this distance, but it's possible, and as I'm sure you don't have enemies and I do, then it's very likely it is me he is observing."

"What enemies do you have?" Alice asked before she could stop herself.

"I may appear a gentleman, my lady, but let me assure you that is not always the case."

"I do believe that sounded sinister, Lord Stafford." Alice

pushed the words past the dryness in her throat.

"One piece of advice I will impart now we are to be working together to find Jackson is, don't be suspicious of everyone, Lady Alice; it will drive you mad. Sometimes a man is just out walking with a woman, or enjoying a solo jaunt around the park."

Her eyes went back to the man, who was now bent at the waist speaking with a young boy. Why had she believed he was looking at her? Why had she felt that prickle of awareness? *Was he right? Was she just being suspicious?*

"Are you all right, Alice?" Thaddeus asked.

"Of course, but if you are ready to leave, then I am."

Thaddeus studied her, but whatever he saw in her face had him not questioning her need to leave.

"Jamie!"

Everyone in their party turned at the shriek, but it was Lord Stafford who started forward. In fact, he was nearly running by the time he reached the two women walking toward him.

"His sisters," Lady Hamilton said. "Lovely ladies. They do not spend a great deal of time in London, but Jamie is always happy when they do.

Alice watched him kiss his sisters' cheeks and give a bark of laughter when they said something.

"Come along. You will love them," Lord Hamilton said to Alice and the twins. "They are not grumpy and aloof like their brother."

Alice thought most peers were aloof but kept that to herself. She could just leave, taking Thaddeus and Eloise with her, but then Lady Hamilton took her arm, urging her in the direction of Lord Stafford and his sisters.

She kept a polite expression on her face as they reached them. However, she did not look at him. Alice was unsettled; there was no getting around that. First, there was the conversation they'd shared today, and then that man, who Alice thought had been watching them.

"This is Lady Alice," Lord Stafford said to his sisters.

She dropped into a curtsy and smiled at the two women. Something in their eyes made the hair on the back of her neck rise. Calculating, she thought. But why? Until today, she'd never met either woman.

"How lovely to meet you, Lady Alice," the sister closest to her said.

She opened her mouth to say something further, but her brother cut her off with a question about his nieces and nephews. After a few more minutes of general chatter, Alice sent Thaddeus a look, which he clearly understood.

"Well," Thaddeus said. "It is time for us to take our leave."

They said their goodbyes, and were soon heading back to her townhouse.

"I found it interesting that Lord Stafford singled you out, Alice."

"Not interesting, Eloise. He also singled out Miss Devlin."

"Yes, but—"

"No buts. There is nothing between Lord Stafford and me, so we will leave it there if you please."

Surprisingly, the twins complied with her request, and the rest of the journey was conducted in comfortable silence, even if inside Alice was feeling far from that.

After arriving home, Alice went straight to her room and opened her journal. She wrote, in careful, deliberate strokes, everything that had happened that day. When she finished, she lay back on the bed and let the room grow quiet around her. The thought of the man who had killed her brother filled her mind as it always did. She had lived with him in her thoughts for so long that she wondered, for a moment, what it would be like to wake and not think of him.

"I'll find you," she whispered into the dark. "And you will pay."

For now, she told herself, nothing else mattered. Her purpose was set, and she would not deviate. Lord Stafford would not hinder but help her to achieve that. From this point on, she would keep her dealings with him strictly professional. Alice was certain he could be dangerous to her in more ways than one otherwise.

Chapter Twelve

THE NOTE ALICE had received that afternoon contained only five words: *I will meet you there.* It had been signed with an *L* and an *S*, written in large, sweeping black loops, bold, confident, and entirely like Lord Stafford.

Relief had followed her initial apprehension. She would not have to endure a nighttime carriage ride alone with him after all. Still, she couldn't help but wonder why he had changed his mind. Had he discovered something? Or perhaps he simply wished to keep control of the meeting on his own terms. With that man, it was difficult to tell.

Alice dressed with care for her trip, in a dark bonnet, cloak, and sturdy boots laced high. Lastly, she buttoned black gloves to her wrists. Ezra's disapproval was clear as he followed her out the door and down to the carriage which awaited them.

"Who is it we are meeting in the Black Dog, my lady?" he asked, opening the door.

"Lord Stafford. I have recently learned he was in the same hall as my brother, and suffered, too. He's also searching for the man responsible for Charles's death."

Ezra's jaw tightened. "It's my hope that every soul who mistreated those boys will answer for it," he said.

"I believe some already have," Alice replied. "At Lord Stafford's hands… and those of his two friends."

Ezra's mouth twitched. "I like him already," he muttered,

closing the door firmly.

Through the small glass pane, Alice watched him climb up beside Bernard, the stable hand he trusted. They would keep close watch during the journey—Ezra always did. Whenever she insisted on venturing out at such ungodly hours, he insisted just as stubbornly on being there to see her safely home again.

The carriage lurched forward as they started moving, and Alice leaned back against the seat, hands clasped in her lap, and let her thoughts drift.

She had made herself brave after her brother's death. Pushed aside the things she feared, to do this for him, and for her. The deep ache of vengeance inside her begged to be appeased. Right or wrong, she feared it would consume her if it was not.

She looked out the window as the carriage rocked gently as it left the wide avenues of Mayfair behind. Through windows, Alice caught the gleam of lamplight on polished brass knockers, the soft glow of drawing rooms where even at such an hour some still lingered over syllabub and gossip. She saw a vendor selling roasted chestnuts, the scent wafting into the carriage briefly.

If the wrong person were to see Alice in the Black Dog, her reputation would be ruined, which didn't worry her overly, but what did worry her was her aunt, who loved being part of society. She had no wish to bring shame down on her, and so must be careful.

The streetlights grew fewer, and the shadows stretched long across the cobbles as Ezra directed the carriage toward Wapping. Fine houses gave way to narrow brick lanes. The buildings had shuttered windows, the plaster cracked. The air thickened with the scent of coal smoke and the tang of refuse tossed into the gutter.

Alice had been out at night a few times before this. She'd come to realize that London at night was two cities. The glittering one of ballrooms and musicales, and the other smelling of desperation and survival. And with every turn of the wheel of the carriage, she was leaving the first behind.

Alice drew her cloak tighter. Under her skirts were a pistol and a knife should she need them.

As the carriage slowed, she inhaled and exhaled slowly, trying to temper her breathing and calm her galloping pulse. She might appear cool and in control, but she was an excellent actress. In fact, the majority of the time she was terrified doing anything dangerous. However, if she acted like she wasn't, she could pull off anything.

When the door opened, Ezra's large form stood there. He wore his permanent scowl. Alice placed her hand in his and climbed out.

"We are close. While we go in, Bernard will walk the horses, as I fear for him and them here, in such a place."

"Thank you, Ezra. I realize you would rather be home with—"

"Your brother asked me to watch over you, so I will see this through. But, when it is done, I'll be pleased. I fear for you, my lady. It would be a lie to say otherwise. You may never find this man, even as I wish for him to be punished for what he has done."

She patted his arm, as this conversation had been carried out many times, and he was never happy with what she said, so she chose to say nothing.

"Be alert now, my lady."

They began walking along the street with the cloak of dark settling around them. Alice stayed pressed to Ezra's large side, as the signs of fear began to slither into her body. The crawl of sweat slipped down her spine despite the chill of the night, and the prickling at the back of her neck indicated that someone was close.

I can do this for Charles.

She'd been a child who had feared much, and Charles had been her savior then, but now it was her turn. She could be brave for him.

"'Tis ahead to the left," Ezra said. "You'll not leave my side,

Lady Alice. I'll have your word on that."

"I have a feeling you've asked this of her many times."

The deep words made Alice give a muffled shriek, and then he came out of the shadows, wearing a long black overcoat, which made him look bigger.

"And you'd be?" Ezra said, stepping in front of Alice.

She pushed at his back, but he didn't move, so she stepped to the right.

"I'm Lord Stafford," he said calmly.

"I'll warn you now, my lord, that if you're a threat to Lady Alice in any way, you'll be going through me to get to her."

"I told you we were meeting Lord Stafford, and why, Ezra," Alice said as the two men stared at each other.

"I'm just checking his intention is all," her footman muttered.

Instead of being angry, Lord Stafford nodded to her footman. "I promise you, Ezra, that my intentions toward your mistress are entirely honorable, and I am seeking out the same enemy."

They stared at each other for long seconds, and then Ezra nodded. Lord Stafford then held out his hand, and her footman shook it.

Men were odd creatures, Alice thought. Women would want to chew over every detail for a while longer before they decided to like each other.

"It's a foolish thing she does, my lord, but I understand loyalty and vengeance as good as the next man," Ezra added.

"Ezra—"

"He's right, it is a foolish thing for a lady to do," Lord Stafford said.

"Then leave, and I shall do this myself, and we can go about the same business separately."

"There is no need to be testy, my lady. Even you can see this is no place for a lady surely," Lord Stafford said in a tone that had her wanting to slap his handsome face.

Alice refrained from hurling an insult at him. They needed to get this done and leave.

"You'll have the devil's time convincing her of that," Ezra said.

"I've already worked that out," came the deep reply.

"If you're done, we will proceed," Alice snapped.

"If you will stay at her back, Ezra, I shall go first, and then Lady Alice," Lord Stafford said.

Lord Stafford shot her a look when she didn't argue, but Alice was quite happy with being placed between the two men. She was nobody's fool, and knew there would not be many women inside the Black Dog, and those that were there would very likely be more than capable of handling the advances of men, drunk or not.

"My informant will be looking for me," Alice said.

"And will see you if he looks hard enough," Lord Stafford added, which had him receiving a grunt of approval from Ezra.

They moved as one toward the building, which had a sign above the door shining on a black iron post. She eyed the large black dog and hoped that he was not awaiting them inside also.

Alice pushed her shoulders back as the door before them swung open and a man staggered out. After shooting them a blurry-eyed look, he headed off down the road.

"Be diligent," Lord Stafford said over his shoulder.

He ducked to enter, and they followed, Ezra doing the same. The Black Dog was likely no different than many alehouses all over England. Flickering tallow candles and firelight barely cut through the gloom.

They were greeted with the sounds of rough laughter and slurred voices. A fiddle was scraping out a tune in one corner, and someone was attempting to sing along. Alice heard the clatter of carriage wheels and the distant church bells before the door closed behind them.

Sawdust, damp from spilled ale, gathered under the hem of her cloak as she walked. Exposed beams above her holding up the low ceiling were blackened with soot. All in all, it wasn't a place she'd ever return to, Alice could say with absolute certainty.

Lord Stafford made his way to the bar, and Alice stayed as close as she could without touching him. *You can do this.* She saw two women, their skirts faded and dirty, laughing with men, and realized again how lucky she was that her life was not this one. That she did not have to earn her money by raising her skirts.

A hand in her back nudged her forward and she carried on walking behind the broad-shouldered marquess.

Reaching the bar, he stopped. Alice moved to stand beside him, and Ezra stayed behind them.

"Who is your informant?" Lord Stafford leaned down to speak to her, and his shoulder pressed to hers.

"I'm not sure which one, but it will be Huckle or Bea," Alice said, looking around them. "It is hard to see with so many people all jammed in here." Looking down, she saw the railing around the bar and climbed onto it, bracing her gloved hands on the sticky surface. She saw Huckle then. Seated in a booth to her right, he was alone and his eyes were on Lord Stafford.

Alice would have some fast talking to explain why the marquess was here and she'd not come alone.

"What'll it be?"

The man now before her was as large as the one at her side, with huge hands braced on the wood. He had the look of someone who had seen everything life had thrown at him and wasn't terribly impressed by it.

"Three ales, please," Lord Stafford said, and Alice wondered if one was for her, but doubted it.

With the drinks, they made their way to the booth, where the tall, thin Huckle sat.

When Alice had first begun investigating Kenneth Jackson, she'd gone directly to Blackwood Hall. No one there had known where to find the housemaster and all were unwilling to speak of the years that had clearly put a dark stain on the Hall's reputation. One week later she'd received a note from Huckle. It had told her to come to the park near her street in London. He'd then explained that he'd worked at Blackwood Hall when Jackson had been a housemaster and had seen much.

Alice had not pushed for more information about if he'd suffered too. She'd also never questioned Huckle as to who had directed him to her. For now, it was enough she had someone who knew Jackson. Since that day, she'd paid him handsomely to dig up any information he could on the man. Thus far, Jackson had remained elusive. She hoped that was about to change.

CHAPTER THIRTEEN

J AMIE HAD ARRIVED at the Black Dog early, after making one more stop on the way to chase a lead on Jackson. Like the others, it had come to nothing.

Every instinct in him rebelled at the sight of Lady Alice in a place like this. It was dirty, loud, and crawling with danger. But experience told him that ordering her to leave would be a waste of breath. Even on short acquaintance, he already knew she was the sort of woman who did exactly as she pleased.

One of his sisters was the same. He'd spent a lot of time with Briar growing up, following her around and then extracting her from the trouble she sometimes fell in.

Jamie felt a small measure of relief that her large, surly footman was at least keeping her company, but if anything went wrong and they got into a fight with a handful of men, then what would happen to her? The thought made him go cold.

One look in her eyes when they'd met outside and Jamie had known she was not as calm as she wanted him to believe. But she held herself still, unlike one of his sisters who waved her hands about when agitated.

He slid into the seat opposite the man Lady Alice had said was awaiting her. She took the space next to him, and Ezra stood, arms folded, and glared from beside her, effectively blocking her from leaving until he was ready for her to do so. *Good man.*

"You sent word you wished to speak to me, Huckle?"

Jamie, who had been looking around them, snapped his gaze back to the man across from them.

"Huckle?" He was almost unrecognizable from the boy who had once collected their laundry daily at Blackwood Hall. He was losing his hair and had lines on his face that had not been there when last they'd seen each other. But it was his height that shocked Jamie the most. He'd been small as a child, but now he was tall, with broad shoulders.

"Aye, 'tis I, Lord Stafford." Huckle bobbed his head.

Jamie looked at Lady Alice and then back to the man who had taken beatings right alongside him, and no doubt they had continued after Jamie, Anthony, and Toby's had ceased. They'd shielded him as best they could, and yet had been unable to save him completely. He'd then been moved to different lodgings and they'd not seen much of him after that.

"I—you're well?" Jamie didn't know what else to say in that moment, because he was suddenly ridiculously pleased to see the man before him. Like him and his friends, Huckle had survived, it seemed. But, he was sure, also like him, Huckle had memories that haunted him too.

"I am, thank you, Lord Stafford, but I'd be better if you found that"—he shot Lady Alice a look—"nasty individual, and rid the world of him."

"Agreed," Lady Alice said. "What news do you have for us, Huckle?"

"You work for Lady Alice?" Jamie asked, ignoring her.

Huckle nodded. "I have been searching for him on her behalf, my lord. In between working with my father, and I think I may have something."

"What business does your father have, Huckle?"

"He is a corn chandler, my lord."

Jamie wasn't entirely certain why a sense of ease settled over him upon learning that Huckle now worked with his father, weighing and measuring dry goods for households. Yet it did. He had thought of the boy often—one among many who had suffered—and wondered what had become of him. Now, at last, he knew.

"Excellent. Where is the business located?"

Lady Alice waited patiently while Huckle gave him the address. Jamie would from now on ensure his and his friends' households got their supplies from there.

"Now, tell us what information you found, Huckle?" Jamie asked.

She didn't flick her fingers or move in her seat, because he would have felt her, as their legs were brushing in the cramped seat. Lady Alice had her hands settled in her lap and watched Huckle as Jamie did.

He smelled her scent above the stale ale and myriad of other unpleasant odors. Soft, and floral.

"I've been hearing some things coming out of somewhere." Huckle's eyes dropped to his hands that were clenched before him on the table.

"If you have something to say, please say it, Huckle. My sensibilities are not delicate. If they were, I would not be even now sitting here in this tavern," Lady Alice said.

"You'll pardon me for saying so, Lady Alice, but some things a lady should just not hear," Huckle said.

"Are you convinced he is still in London, Huckle?" Jamie asked before she could speak again and deny those words.

"I am. And I heard about a place—" his eyes shot to Alice again before he continued, "—it's a place of vices…ah, you can get any needs met there."

And suddenly Jamie knew exactly what the man spoke of. He knew of these places where men could go to act out whatever fantasy they wished. He met Huckle's eyes, and a look of understanding passed between them.

"What are you not telling me?" Lady Alice demanded. "You are sharing a look."

"I will explain later. Now, continue your story, Huckle."

Thankfully, she did as Jamie asked, but he sensed her frustration at being left in the dark and knew she would be questioning him about the matter soon. Lady Alice was not one to let things slide.

"I've managed to make contacts myself around London. Often I do my father's deliveries, and when I do, I talk to people. Two of the places are near this location. Servants gossip, and I heard that there have now been three instances of women being attacked by a man while they… when he was with them."

"But surely Jackson is not the only man who would behave in such a way around women?" Lady Alice said.

Jamie wasn't sure why those words sent a chill down his spine, but they did. Had someone mistreated her? The thought of anyone touching this woman, or any woman for that matter, made him angry. Yet, he knew it happened, just as it had happened to the Blackwood boys when they were young and helpless.

If Huckle was right, and these women were harmed in one of these dens of depravity, then it must be bad indeed, as Jamie knew what went on in those places, and they were not for the faint of heart.

"My reasons for believing it is Jackson are that when I spoke with one of the staff at the den, the description fit him. They did not mention his name, but I'm convinced."

Lady Alice drummed her fingers on the table before speaking. "But surely you have not seen him in many years?"

Huckle met Jamie's gaze. "The women he hurt said his laugh was strange," he added quietly. "That was how they knew it was him."

Jamie felt every muscle tighten. The memory struck hard. He remembered that laugh.

"They described it," Huckle went on, "as something like a foghorn—loud, harsh, and in short, awful bursts."

Jackson had moved on from the charity school pupils to a brothel, it seemed. And just like that, Jamie was back at Blackwood Hall in his mind. The sound of Kenneth Jackson's laughter as he inflicted punishment on the boy on his knees before him. He hadn't realized he'd made a sound until he felt fingers on the hand he had clenched on his thigh. The smaller ones wrapped around the top of his fist and squeezed. It had the effect of jerking Jamie from his nightmare.

"There were other factors, but to me that was the most telling."

"What other factors, Huckle?" Lady Alice asked, her hand still resting on top of Jamie's.

He moved his thumb, placing it on top of hers, and holding it there. He needed that, to be anchored to someone, anyone would have done, but it was her, and he wasn't letting go.

If I'm touching her, I won't go back there.

"He has a slight lisp, and his hair is thinning," Huckle added.

"I'm shocked he still has any." Jamie forced the words out of his mouth. Made himself speak.

That man will not hurt me again. Cannot hurt me, he reminded himself. I'm the strong one, and he's weak.

The words made the side of Huckle's mouth curve up slightly in a smile.

"I'd hoped he got a wasting disease and died a slow and painful death. Alas, that has not happened," Jamie added.

"We'll finish him."

"Aye, Huckle, we will." Jamie raised his tankard. "When was the last report of him in this location you speak of?"

"I'm unsure, but it can't have been long ago, because I was there just last week."

Jamie nodded, and then questioned Huckle until he was sure he had everything he knew. Lady Alice had removed her hand minutes ago, and Jamie had to say he missed the contact, which surprised him.

Yes, he'd kissed the woman, but they'd both explained that away with him feeling an excess of excitement after his fight. Now, he wasn't so sure, and would go so far as saying that he believed Lady Alice was going to become a problem for him.

"It's good to see you again, my lord."

"You also, Huckle." Jamie handed him some money.

"I can pay—"

"And now I have," he cut Lady Alice off. "Good evening, Huckle, and I'm pleased to have met you again."

He watched him leave, slipping through the patrons toward the door.

"You first, Ezra," Jamie said. "We shall follow."

Lady Alice didn't like it when anyone but her gave the orders. But, as he was now involved in this, she would have to get used to that. He placed a hand on her spine and moved her into place between him and Ezra. She shot him a look, but stayed silent.

"What are you about?" The words came from a woman approaching Lady Alice from the right.

"Step back, please. We're leaving," Jamie said evenly. When the woman didn't move, his voice hardened. "Now."

"There's enough women here already. We don't need another!" she snarled, sending the sharp tang of gin fumes their way. Her lips were painted an unnatural pink, and a large black beauty spot marred her cheek. Once, she might have been called pretty, but her face now bore the weary marks of a hard life.

"I am no threat to you," Lady Alice said quickly. "Move, please."

The woman sneered and shoved her. Alice stumbled, colliding with Jamie's chest. Her body was rigid with fear when he steadied her.

"Please don't touch me!" Lady Alice's anguished cry came out high-pitched and panicky as the woman drew back a fist.

At his employer's scream, Ezra turned. The woman lurched into a man, who stumbled into another. Outrage bellowed through the room, and fists began to fly.

"Get her out!" Jamie roared. Too late. The Black Dog had descended into chaos.

A fist whistled past Jamie's ear, and he turned to face the deliverer. A man was grinning at him drunkenly. Jamie punched him, and his eyes rolled back in his head and he toppled, like a felled tree, scattering those behind him.

Another shriek split the air, and Jamie's gaze immediately sought Lady Alice.

The woman who had pushed her earlier was back, her hands locked around Lady Alice's arms. Before Jamie could reach them, Lady Alice twisted sharply, breaking free, and this time it was she who sent the woman stumbling back with another forceful shove.

Ezra was alternately trying to care for his mistress and fight.

"Make for the door, Ezra!" Jamie bellowed. He then spun Lady Alice and dropped his shoulder. When he straightened, she was dangling over it.

"What are you doing?" she cried.

"Run!" Jamie roared.

Ezra did, pushing people out of the way with his large hands and lashing out with his feet. Jamie had one hand free, so he did the best he could. Reaching the door, they ran through and out into the smog and cold air.

"Put me down!"

He didn't until they were a few feet from the Black Dog. Only then did he lower her gently to the ground.

"I'll get the carriage," Ezra said.

Jamie heard the steady thud of his feet as he ran away from them. Clearly Lady Alice's footman felt Jamie could keep her in good health until he returned.

"How dare you!" She pushed Jamie hard in the chest. He didn't move, instead deliberately intimidating her by leaning closer.

"You should not have pushed that woman, Lady Alice. You should have walked away."

"And you should not have thrown me over your shoulder again!"

Her eyes were a little wild and angry, and Jamie had to say it added another level to her beauty. What did it say about him that looking at this woman, with her bonnet sitting crooked and her cheeks flushed, aroused him.

"I needed to get you out of there fast, because what is going on inside the Black Dog is not something a lady of gentle breeding, such as yourself, should be witness to. A stray fist could have flattened you or worse."

"I can take care of myself, my lord, and have been doing so for many years. I need no man to ensure my safety." The words were spat at him like they tasted foul. "Never manhandle me in such a way again."

"And how," Jamie said with deadly calm, "would you have done that in such a place if Ezra and I had not been there? You were bloody terrified. I heard that scream. It was panicked."

"I would have found a way." Her chin lifted. "And I was not panicked."

"Are you always this ignorant to the dangers around you?"

Jamie raked his eyes over her face, taking in every delicate inch. The line of her small nose and the curve of her chin. He then reached up to right the angle of her bonnet. Her hands slapped at his.

"Don't touch me," she hissed.

He grabbed her wrists, holding them to his chest. "Who hurt you?"

Of all the words he could have asked, those were the ones that came out of his mouth?

"Wh-what?" She tried to back away but he held her close.

"Who hurt you, Lady Alice?" Jamie knew when someone was hiding pain, just like he knew the signs of someone who had been harmed by another. When you suffered, you recognized it in others.

CHAPTER FOURTEEN

"No one," Alice lied.

"That's not true, is it? Because when you have suffered as I and many others have, you know when someone else has endured pain. You were terrified in the Black Dog, as you should have been, but your scream was fear, and nothing like the control you usually exhibit when people get close to you. You put distance between yourself and others with an aloof façade."

"Stop—"

"Who hurt you?"

"You don't know me well enough to know those things," Alice said quickly. Her heart was thudding hard inside her chest, and her palms felt clammy beneath her gloves.

Alice wanted to look away from those all-seeing green eyes, but couldn't. What did he see when he looked at her?

"Let me go," she said, and the word came out more of a whimper than with her usual strength.

"It helps to talk to others."

"Did you...do you talk to others about your suffering?" She wasn't sure why she'd asked that, but suddenly Alice needed to know that someone had been there for this man, as she'd been there for Charles.

He nodded.

"Lords Hamilton and Corbyn?" He nodded again.

"I'm so sorry," Alice whispered, remembering her brother's

pain.

"Who hurt you, Lady Alice?"

The world narrowed to the intensity of his gaze and the pulse pounding in her throat. She wanted to deny him and retreat behind the armor she had worn for years.

"I wish to return home," Alice whispered as she battled the need to say the words she had spoken to no one. *I won't betray Charles that way.*

One of his hands moved to cup her cheek, and she dug her toes into the soles of her boots to stop from flinching, but something gave her away.

"Who?"

"Why do you care? This—us—is about finding Jackson and nothing more. Let me go." She held her breath, waiting for the warm gloved hand to release her, but instead he looked into her eyes, moving closer, so they were mere inches apart.

The lane pressed in on her then. The shadows, the stench, and the memory of Charles's hands trembling with rage as he struck her. She had never told anyone what happened, but of course Ezra and Maggie knew some as they'd been close.

Her dear, sweet brother had turned into a deranged man in his last few months, and he'd turned his anger on her.

"It will destroy you if you don't find a way to let it out." The words were a low rasp. "Trust me, I know this."

"I have nothing to let out," Alice said with a great deal more strength than what she was feeling. Looking up at him, she saw understanding in his eyes, and he confirmed why he did what he did.

All the exercise, and the fighting. The horse races she'd heard he participated in. It was his way of coping with the hell he'd endured. Alice's heart broke again for the child who'd had his innocence stripped away.

He cupped her face with two large palms and looked into her eyes like he could read everything she wasn't telling him.

"H-he didn't mean to, but in the end he was not right in the head." The words came out before Alice could stop them.

"Your brother?"

Alice didn't cry. She'd made herself shut everything that hurt her out of her head… especially what her brother had done in his fits of rage, but right then the tears came.

"Alice." Her name came out as a plea. He released her, but only for a second, and then he was pulling her gently into his arms. Strong arms that held her pressed into his hard body.

The faint smoke of the tavern fire clung to his coat, and for a moment, she allowed it. Allowed him to comfort her, because it felt so good.

The damp stones beneath her boots, the cold night air, the mutter of voices nearby, all faded until there was only the steady rhythm of his hand at her back, and the whispered, "I'm sorry," breathed into her hair. "So sorry."

"H-he wasn't right in his head."

"Shh, now." She felt a hand cup her neck as the other ran up and down her back. "I'm sorry."

"My brother was a good man," she said into his necktie. She breathed in fresh linen and the spicy scent of his cologne. "He wasn't in his right mind after he returned to me."

He didn't add anything to that, just held her, and Alice let him. In that moment she wanted his strength.

Since her brother's death, no one had done this. No one had just held her and said it would be all right. Her aunt had of course supported her, but no one had really known the hell she'd endured. He held her as if she was fragile and would break.

It was that thought that had her stiffening and easing back. Alice clenched her eyes shut briefly, and when she opened them, shame flooded her body. She was not weak. She would not break in this filthy alley in the arms of a man she barely knew.

"I'm sorry."

"For what?" He was still close.

"That." Alice waved her hand at him.

She wasn't used to having to explain herself to people, just as she wasn't used to falling apart as she just had before someone, especially not him.

What were you thinking, Alice?

Ezra had seen the bruise on her face toward the end of her brother's life, and it had been then that he'd said she was not to be alone with Charles anymore. She'd argued, of course, as she'd been the mistress and he the footman, and yet he'd stood firm, and somewhere inside her she'd known relief.

Alice had hated herself for the fear she'd felt being close to her brother when she knew it was not his fault he had turned into the man he had become. One minute he was her sweet Charles, and the next a man so angry he wanted to hurt the only person who had loved him unconditionally.

She'd hated him sometimes, and the guilt had sat heavy on her.

"That, my lady?"

Lord Stafford was looking at her with the expectation she would answer his question. What Alice wanted to do was run fast in the direction Ezra had taken.

"Weakness," she said when nothing else came to her.

"You think that weeping and letting another comfort you is weakness, Lady Alice?" The words were spoken gently as one would if soothing a child.

I am not a child.

"Don't you, Lord Stafford?"

Alice knew the words had hit their mark as the gentle look in his eyes changed, and he was once again the cool, expressionless marquess.

"Would you ever let anyone help you through what you've endured? Or is what you do your way of running from your demons?"

"And what exactly is it that I do?" His voice was cool now. All that warmth and comfort she'd felt moments ago was gone as if it had never been. Alice told herself that was for the best.

"Whatever you can," she said quietly, steadying her breath.

"As fast as you can." She didn't look away.

They stared at each other for long heartbeats until he said, "It is late. Come, I will escort you to your carriage."

She'd comforted him tonight when Huckle had told him what he'd heard about the incidents with those women. About the man's laugh. Alice had felt the change in him. Felt him tense, and the hand on his thigh clench. It had been instinctive to reach over and place her fingers on top of his. Now he'd comforted her, and suddenly it was as if those moments had not happened. They were distant strangers once more.

The clip clop of hooves was followed by the approach of Ezra with her carriage. Lord Stafford opened the door, and before she could step inside, large hands lifted her and she was tossed onto a seat. Alice struggled to right herself, but when she did, it was to see him braced in the doorway.

"Do not go anywhere that could be termed dangerous without me."

She wasn't frightened of many people…if any, but right then she knew he would be a formidable foe should she cross him.

"You—" before Alice could finish that sentence, the door was slammed, rocking the carriage on its chassis. Before she reached the window, she could hear the hum of him speaking to Ezra. Looking through the glass, she watched Ezra nod, and then before her eyes, Lord Stafford started running down the street away from the carriage.

Ezra started the horses moving, and they followed. Alice pressed her face to the window but did not catch another glimpse of Lord Jameson Stafford.

She sank back against the squabs as the carriage jolted forward. Her palms were damp, her breath ragged, and still her skin tingled where his hands had held her. It was unbearable, this sense of being seen when for so long no one had.

She pressed her fists into her skirts, willing herself to calm. She must lock it all away again—the tears, the trembling, the dangerous craving for comfort. What was she thinking, collapsing against him like some foolish girl?

They rolled toward her townhouse as Alice closed her eyes and saw Charles's face. Her brother could smile one moment and be filled with rage the next. He had not meant to hurt her, but he had not been himself. Her heart still bore the scars of his cruelty even if no one could see them.

Lord Stafford had seen them. He had glimpsed her vulnerability, and Alice swore he would not do so again. In a weak moment she'd spoken out against the only man who had ever loved her. Shame washed over her.

Alice straightened, forcing her breathing into an even rhythm. She would not think of Lord Stafford's arms around her, nor the gentleness he showed her. Instead, she would remember the slam of the carriage door, and the cold authority in his command. That was who he was.

And yet she knew she would never forget his words. "It will destroy you if you don't find a way to let it out." He had spoken the truth, and Alice often wondered if she would ever be as she was before Charles had shown her the hell he'd endured.

"I'm sorry," Alice whispered into the darkness. "Sorry that I couldn't save you." She wept then. Hot silent tears for her brother. "But you will be avenged."

CHAPTER FIFTEEN

FOUR DAYS AFTER he and Lady Alice had entered the Black Dog tavern, Jamie was preparing to leave the house again. It was late, and while he'd promised to let her know when and if he found or pursued another lead, she would not be accompanying him for this particular trip, and he would make sure she never found out.

She consumed Jamie's thoughts. He constantly wondered what she was doing, and if she was taking risks and not telling him.

Which is exactly what you are doing. Jamie ignored that voice and took some money out of his desk.

Having returned from a musicale that bored him witless, and that Lady Alice had not attended, he'd changed into dark clothing and was ready to leave.

There had been plenty of pointless conversation and gossip, some awful singing, which usually didn't bother him, but tonight had grated on his nerves. He wasn't sure why he felt like he was on the precipice of something. He would fall or stand but something was about to change, and he didn't know exactly what, but he could feel the tension inside him rising.

He'd been evasive with his friends earlier, and that wasn't like him. But this wasn't something he wanted them embroiled in. They had lives now, and people who would suffer deeply should any harm come to them.

Pushing his pistol into his pocket, he slipped a knife into his boot and made his way downstairs to the front door. His household was silent, his servants dismissed and likely now slumbering in their beds.

Opening the front door, Jamie slipped out, closing it softly behind him. He then made his way through the front gate and onto the street. The air was cold again this evening, slapping him in the face as he began to walk. He would find a hackney, as the walk was a long one, and while he didn't mind that, he wanted this done with.

"Take another step and there's going to be trouble."

He yelped, the very unmanly sound coming from Jamie as the deep words reached him. Turning, he found Anthony and Toby. Both dressed as he was, in dark colors.

"What the hell are you two idiots doing outside my house at such an hour?" He resisted pressing a hand to his chest to ease the pounding.

"You're up to something, Jamie, and we want to know what," Toby said.

"You couldn't have asked me tomorrow? Or perhaps earlier this evening a few hours ago at the Thornton musicale?" Jamie demanded. His friends now stood before him, arms folded, which usually meant trouble.

"You've been avoiding us," Anthony said flatly. "We"—he jabbed a finger into his own chest, then at Toby—"suspected you were up to something. And were fairly certain it would happen tonight, given how on edge you were at the musicale."

"Which, I might add, my ears have yet to recover from," Toby said dryly. "But Anthony's right. What are you about, Jamie?"

"Oh, for pity's sake," Jamie muttered. "You mean to tell me you were planning to stand out here all night just to see if I left the house? Would you have done the same tomorrow?"

Both men nodded.

"That's what friends do," Toby said with gravity. "Especially when the person they're worried about refuses to tell them why they should be worried."

"What's going on?" Anthony said, his voice hard.

"Just so I'm clear on your intentions. You took your women home, then after presumably a few hours, where you what?"

"Drank brandy and ate food while our wives fell into bed exhausted due to their delicate conditions," Anthony added.

"Now you're here." He looked around and saw a carriage parked along the street. "In Toby's carriage."

"Excellent deduction."

"Ambushing me?" Jamie added. He had no reason to laugh, but it was there.

These two men knew him better than anyone, and cared what he did, or what happened to him. Sometimes he forgot that.

"Let's get in the carriage, as presumably you are going somewhere you didn't want us to know about," Toby muttered. "Plus, I'm tired."

"It's only just after midnight," Jamie said.

"I go to sleep earlier these days," Toby said, heading back down the street to his carriage.

"You poor old men," Jamie mocked, following with Anthony.

"Give my driver your address," Toby ordered before climbing inside.

When Jamie had done as his friend asked, he joined them, taking the seat opposite, and not missing the fact his friends had chosen the same seat so they could glare at him.

"Now talk, Jamie," Anthony snapped.

He sighed. "I've been hunting Jackson after word reached me that he'd been abusing children in a charity school.

"What?" Toby growled the word.

"I went there and spoke to two boys. They said the man who hurt them was Kenneth Jackson."

Anthony swore loudly.

"We've never gone after him. In fact, we barely mention his name," Toby said.

"He was the most evil," Anthony said softly. "Also, as he doesn't walk in our world, we never came across him, so it seemed easier never to mention his name."

"I want him to pay now because he deserves that for the suffering he put many Blackwood Boys through. But it is not just that. If we don't stop him, he will hurt others again," Jamie said, knowing it was time for the truth only. "I thought I didn't need to see Jackson brought to justice, but in all honesty I'm not sure I will ever be at peace until he has been."

The carriage passed under the glow of an oil lamp, throwing light and shadows on the dark walls. Elegant townhouses rose neatly to his right and left, some in brick, others in pale stone. The occasional glow of candlelight spilled out of windows.

"And you didn't feel you could tell us?" Jamie could hear the hurt in Anthony's words.

"We told you we are always there for you," Toby added.

"I have done nothing to put myself in danger, and if I was to do that, I would have told you. Just as I know when the time comes to finally confront that bastard, I will have both of you with me."

"At least I believe you in that," Anthony said. "Now what of Lady Alice? What is her part in this? You said that day in the park you'd tell us, but as yet have not."

He told them then—everything.

"Her brother was younger, I know that much, but I never met him," Toby said when Jamie had finished.

"After he returned from Blackwood Hall, he never recovered in his mind or body," Jamie said.

It wasn't his right to tell them everything. He'd held Lady Alice when she'd told him it was her brother Charles who hurt her. Jamie had known anger that anyone would touch her, but he'd also known the dark places he'd gone to when his demons had haunted him.

He had to believe he would never hurt anyone, but clearly Lady Alice's brother's mind had become crazed. Jamie had never felt close to a woman like he did to her. They were united in their goal, but it was more. Something about her, who had taken up the fight to seek retribution on behalf of her brother, touched him. Even if he thought her reckless to do such a thing.

"It was she who cared for him, I believe, which is why she was rarely seen in society."

"You and Lady Alice have clearly had more interactions than you are letting on," Toby said.

"If I promise from this day forth to tell you everything, can we move on?" Jamie said.

"You're holding something back from us still, I can tell," Anthony said. "You care for her," his friend said, smiling suddenly. "Lady Alice has stirred your interest."

"You're deluded, Anthony." But Jamie could not deny that his heart was thudding a little faster at the thought of her. Not that he would act on that, or that she would in any way wish him to.

"Huckle is her informant," Jamie said before they asked him yet more questions about Lady Alice.

Toby whistled. "I often wondered what became of him."

Jamie filled them in on the man Huckle had become and what he'd told them in the Black Dog.

"And I suppose you are going to visit this den of depravity he mentioned now?" Anthony asked.

"Yes."

"Then we shall be going with you."

"Anthony, you and Toby are to become fathers. I have no wish—"

"Shut up. We are coming, and that is that. Besides, you are in my carriage, and presumably have just given the address to my driver," Toby said.

The Crimson Serpent was located in St Giles, and by the time they'd arrived, they'd worked out a plan. Jamie would enter the premises through the front door as a client, and his friends would circle around the rear and find an entrance that way.

They walked in because the roads around here were too

narrow for expensive carriages.

"Be alert," Jamie said. "Are you armed?"

"I'm not sure if I'm insulted or pleased he's so worried for us, considering we have been in more dangerous positions than this in our lifetimes," Toby said to Anthony.

"You're both soft now. I have to watch out for you," Jamie replied.

The jab he received in his side from Anthony made him grunt. "You may be more athletic than Toby and me, but in no way are you more intelligent."

They moved as though they had nowhere else to be, and yet all three were aware of everything around them.

The street they turned up was little more than a crooked lane between leaning tenements, their upper stories sagging so close they almost touched. What light the moon offered was swallowed by the overhanging eaves. The air was thick with scents Jamie had no wish to identify.

Laughter spilled from one of the doorways, the high-pitched giggles of a woman mingling with the gruff voice of a man.

"It's at the end there." Jamie pointed. "Huckle told me about the light."

A red lantern burned faintly above the lintel, its glass filthy but the glow easy to see in the dark night. The door itself was scarred, half-hidden in shadow.

"The Crimson Serpent is hardly a name to inspire lust," Anthony mused.

"No, but it does inspire intrigue and danger," Toby added.

"Be careful," Anthony said before he and Toby slid into the shadows and disappeared.

Jamie walked on, senses open, and aware of every move around him. Reaching the building, he looked up as a shrill whistle filled the air.

In the window above him stood two women, their pale rouged faces peering down at him.

"Hello, lovely. You look like a fine gentleman!" one called

down. "What you got a taste for? We can meet all your needs."

"You're too kind," Jamie called up to them. "I shall come inside and see what takes my fancy."

"You're a big boy. I'm sure you could handle the both of us, and we might actually enjoy it."

This produced raucous laughter from both ladies.

"I shall do my best," Jamie said.

He rapped on the door with his gloved knuckles as the ladies continued to hurl bawdy comments down on him.

Jamie could feel a constant undercurrent swirling around them. Desperation, hunger, and menace. This was no Mayfair dalliance, no gilded boudoir with velvet curtains. Here, vices were raw and unchecked, in a place where men disappeared and no one thought to ask why.

The door swung open, and there stood a tall thin man with a moustache that could only be termed sinister. With not a stitch of hair on his head, he was dressed in black like them, but unlike Jamie and his three friends, he was sure this man had not an ounce of civility in his body. Eyes as black as the sky above them, his face was narrow. Jamie knew what evil looked like; he'd seen it in many forms. It came off this man in waves.

"I wish to enter," Jamie said.

"Have you frequented the Crimson Serpent before, sir?"

"I have not."

The man eyed him thoroughly, and then stepped to one side.

"Please come in."

He did, stepping into the entrance. Inside, the light was little better. Jamie took in the heavy crimson drapes and the darkened floor beneath his feet. To his right loomed a huge gilt-framed mirror, its surface dulled by grime, while flickering candles cast weak light over stained plaster and peeling wallpaper that had once been a garish red.

"If you'll come this way," the man said.

Jamie's boots thudded on the hard floor as he followed him, and the sounds of music and the rumble of voices grew louder as he moved deeper into the house. He was ushered into a small parlor that held a chair, a fireplace, and little else.

"Someone will be with you soon." The man left, closing the door behind him. It was not five minutes later when it opened again.

"Good evening, sir."

Easily as tall as him, the woman had a hard look in her eyes that matched the man who had let him in, and if he was to guess, he'd say they were related. She had the same dark coloring and angular features.

"I am Madam Ravelle. May I have your name, sir?"

"I am Lord Stabler," Jamie lied, giving a false name. The man no longer frequented society, so unless this woman knew him, he was safe.

"What desires do you wish us here at the Crimson Serpent to fulfill for you this evening, Lord Stabler?" She held out a tray, and he took a glass.

Unlike the women leaning out of the window, who had looked a little worn and faded, this one wore a gown of peacock blue silk, and the style could be seen at any society event. Her hair was piled high and held in place with sapphire pins that Jamie had a feeling were real jewels.

"What can you offer me?" he said after a sip of surprisingly good whiskey.

Were Anthony and Toby inside?

"Perhaps a tour, my lord?"

Those eyes were cat-like and cunning, he thought. Assessing, working out what was needed to achieve her needs. Whether he was worth her time.

"Thank you."

Jamie followed her out the door.

"We offer viewings, where you will not be seen but can watch," Madam Ravelle said as they climbed to the next floor. "We have prostitution at all levels. From cheap street girls to courtesans dressed in silks."

Jamie listened as she listed all the services her girls offered as if she were reading a list of household supplies.

"Flagellation, bondage, and of course a particular favorite with nobility, role play. We also have restraints should that be your wish," she continued as they walked down a long, dark hallway that had doors leading left and right off it.

"The depravity climbs with the floors," she added calmly.

A loud scream followed by a crash had the woman cursing.

Was that noise due to his friends?

"Take the last door on the right. You can view what is going on in there. I shall return shortly."

Before he could speak, she'd retraced her steps and started climbing to the upper floors.

He needed to find someone to talk. Someone he could pay to give him the information he sought, and he must do that now while Madam Ravelle wasn't with him.

The thud of feet coming down the stairs had him reaching for the closest door. Opening it, he slid inside.

CHAPTER SIXTEEN

A CANDLE LIT the room, and whatever light the open window offered allowed him to see the two women leaning out of it.

A huge bed dominated the space. Its massive frame of oak was scarred with age, and the posts were fitted with iron rings and worn leather cuffs dangling and ready. A set of drawers stood open in the corner, spilling their contents across a stool. Jamie ran his eyes over the whips, paddles, and lengths of knotted rope. On the wall, a chain hung from a bolt, ending in manacles.

The floor was strewn with discarded garments. Silks in bright colors, torn stockings, a gentleman's crumpled cravat. A chair sat nearby, its arms padded but fitted with straps, angled toward the bed as though for an audience.

"Well now, you're the one we saw below."

The ladies he'd seen when he arrived were staring at him. One of them got off the windowsill and sauntered toward Jamie. Shorter than the other who was now doing the same, she wore a dress that did little to hold in her ample breasts.

"We're awaiting a client, but I think, considering what you're offering, we could make him wait a little longer when he arrives. Fancy a tumble with us, love? This is Molly, and I'm Ada," she said.

Jamie was used to women eyeing him as a prospective husband or lover, but these two reminded him of hungry wolves stalking their prey. Eyes, ringed by something dark, ran over his body.

"I don't want your services, but I want information and I'm happy to pay for it." They eyed him as he pulled out the notes he'd put into his pocket.

"We don't want trouble."

He nearly laughed at those words from one of the women. Everything about the Crimson Serpent was trouble.

"I have no wish to bring trouble down upon you, but what I do want is someone to inform me when a certain man comes into this establishment."

They shot each other a look before returning their gazes to Jamie.

"We need our work," one said.

"I have no wish to cause trouble for you, but you will be handsomely rewarded if you help me."

It was a risk—Jamie knew that. They could just as easily tell the madam and the man who had opened the door to him, but it was one he was willing to take. They must find Jackson, and to do that they needed eyes in places he would go. If Huckle was right, this was one of those places.

"Sure you don't want a tumble, lovely? We don't need to use—"

"Ah, no thank you. Perhaps another time," Jamie said, feeling his neckcloth tighten.

"Well then," one of them said, exhaling loudly. "What do we get?"

He named a sum and they didn't look overly impressed.

"Well, what do you want?" Jamie asked.

The coy, playful smiles had left their faces and were replaced with cool, calculating looks.

He was nobody's fool and knew that life for these women, and what they were forced to do and endure, was not good…and never would be. He also knew that their future was uncertain, because when their looks and bodies grew too old to do what they were now doing, they'd likely just be tossed out on the streets and replaced by younger ladies.

"More money, and when the time comes, we want enough to leave London. Me and Molly."

Jamie studied the women and noted the similarities. *Were they mother and daughter?*

"I will give you enough money to leave London if you help me find a man. Tell me who runs this place first?"

"Madam Louisa Ravelle and her brother Mr. Gideon Ravelle," the one called Molly said.

"Both mean, tight fisted, and wouldn't part with a farthing if their lives depended upon it," the one called Ada said. "We do all the work and they get all the money."

"I'm after information about a man called Kenneth Jackson. My informant thinks he frequents the Crimson Serpent, and he has a reputation for hurting women."

"Why do you want him?" Molly asked.

"He has hurt others, badly, and needs to pay for those crimes." Jamie withstood their looks.

He loathed talking about Jackson, but it seemed lately he was being forced to do just that. Jackson was the only person who could truly unsettle Jamie—or had been. Now Lady Alice could be added to that very short list.

"What does he look like?" Ada asked him.

Jamie gave them the description Huckle had given him. "He also has an odd laugh."

"He's been here," the taller one said after a minute. "Calls himself Master Jackson, and laughs like a foghorn. Has dark hair, and a voice like yours, and his eyes are too small and close together. He's used to being obeyed." She tilted her head and studied him.

"He's a man who enjoys inflicting suffering on others," Jamie said. He forced the words out of his tight throat as he felt the room close in around him.

"That's him," Molly said. "He wasn't one of the regulars. He liked the private rooms for when he took his pleasure in the girls." Her fingers twisted a length of silk absentmindedly. "If he came now, we'd make sure no one new took his notice. Us older ones can handle him, but two of the newer girls were hurt by him. He's an animal, like many, and Madam Ravelle should have known better than letting him get his hands on Jenny and Mary."

"They don't care what happens to us as long as he pays," Ada added, her lips twisting into an angry snarl. "He's come with others too."

"Names?"

They exchanged another look at Jamie's load of notes. Ada stepped forward and lowered her voice.

"There's a ledger. Not kept by the madam herself, because her brother likes to keep his own accounts. A little book, names and initials, the rooms they favored, some notes. We—the girls— think he keeps it so he can blackmail people. If you could get to that, you'd find entries, but not sure they would help in any way, or give over addresses. But it's all we've got for you."

"Where would I find this book?" Jamie asked.

"He keeps it in a room off the parlor where everyone goes before and after... well, those that know about it do. There's a bar, and plenty of women to serve you," Molly said. "Gambling and any other vice that isn't found up here, you'll find there."

Jamie wanted that ledger, because at this stage he'd take anything that would give him a lead in finding Jackson.

"How do we find the parlor?" he asked.

They spoke in whispers now, giving him the layout. "There is a narrow staircase behind the last door on the right. Once there, you'll see the bar, and behind that to the left, there is a thick, green velvet curtain. Gideon's room is behind that."

"There's a back entrance too, but that is usually guarded because they were robbed once when he got too drunk to stop the man entering. He cleaned him out," Ada added.

"Where the bloody hell is he?" The whispered words came from outside the door and were loud enough for anyone close to hear.

Taking two strides, Jamie opened the door to find Toby and Anthony outside.

"Get in here," he whispered. They did as he asked, and he shut the door.

"Well now, you three are more handsome than many we're forced to see," Molly said.

Toby bowed and smiled, and Anthony followed suit.

"These ladies are Molly and Ada. They are going to keep an eye on things, and we are going to pay them handsomely for any and all information they give us," Jamie said. "Now, we need to get back downstairs, and you two need to cause a distraction so I can slip into a room and steal a ledger."

"What ledger?" Anthony demanded, looking around the room.

"One that may have Jackson's name in it, or the names of those that come with him." Jamie looked at the women again. "Can you give me an exact date that Jackson may have been here?"

Surprisingly, Molly did, because Ada said she was the sister that remembered things.

"Toby!"

His friend raised his head from inspecting the array of devices on a stool.

"Need me to give you a lesson in what they're used for, love?" Ada asked with a saucy wink.

"Alas, I am wed to the woman I love," his friend said.

Both women sighed. "Not common in your world," Ada said.

"No, indeed."

Before Toby could settle in for a chat, Jamie handed over more money than he'd originally thought he'd be parting with, and his card.

"Send anyone to this address if you have more information, and I will come."

"Have a care how you go below stairs," Molly added. "Madam Ravelle is not fond of strangers asking too many questions, and Gideon likes to watch people like a hawk. If he hears the wrong thing, he'll have more than words for you."

"Don't betray us," Jamie said, throwing the woman a last look. "I promise that if need be, I will get both of you out of London safely, if for any reason it comes to that."

The women nodded, and then Ada said, "And if you three change your mind…" she gave him another wink.

Jamie, Toby, and Anthony left the room.

"Are you sure you can trust them?" Anthony asked after they'd moved away from the door.

"I don't think there is much choice. We need someone in here who can notify us when and if Jackson comes back. I have hopefully secured their trust with the money I handed them."

Anthony nodded, but didn't look convinced. "We found nothing upstairs other than debauchery. None of the men we encountered were Jackson."

"I'm not sure I'll ever recover from seeing so many naked men and women." Toby shuddered.

"Did you recognize any?" Jamie asked.

"The Earl of Pankhurst, and that surprised me," Anthony said. "I will never be able to look at him again without seeing his spotty bottom."

"Come. Madam Ravelle—who brought me up here for a tour, before leaving to tend to something upstairs—will return to look for me soon, if she hasn't already. We will head downstairs."

"And what is the plan?" Toby asked.

"If Gideon Ravelle is downstairs in the parlor, we're going to enter. And then you'll need to distract him so I can get behind the bar and into his room. I want that book because it may lead us to Jackson."

"Or it may not, Jamie," Toby cautioned.

"I have to try."

"Very well."

Jamie walked to the staircase leading down to the parlor. He opened it and started down the stairs, his friends close on his heels. The sounds below grew louder with each step. When he reached the bottom, he pushed open the door and strode in as though they had every right to be there.

Men sat around the room in various states depending on how far down their tankards they were. Tables were set up in one corner where men gambled. Women dressed similarly to Molly and Ada served drinks and sat on knees. One man had his face in a pair of naked breasts.

"Gideon Ravelle is at the bar, on the right. Two left from the man serving," Jamie whispered to his friends.

Anthony moved around him in that direction, and Toby went the opposite way. He would create some kind of distraction.

So far Ravelle had not noticed Jamie. Skirting the room, Jamie moved to the bar to stand in the shadows to one side of the entrance and wait.

Pipe smoke made his eyes itch and hit the back of his throat as he inhaled. It was warm in here, heat from the fireplaces thickening the air even more.

"Well now, you're a fine one."

The woman who now stood before Jamie was young, and the smile on her lips didn't reach her eyes.

"Can I get you a drink, sir?"

"Whiskey, please," he said to get her away. She nodded and left.

His eyes found Toby, who was standing at a card table watching the play. He stepped back as a woman walked by carrying a tray full of tankards. It was done so fast and looked like he'd genuinely tripped, but seconds later the tray and its entire contents were heading to those seated nearest.

The roars of displeasure drew the room's focus, and Jamie used the noise to ease behind the bar, to the curtain just two steps away. Slipping behind it, he found a door and opened it.

The space beyond was small, and a very male domain. A narrow shelf held books. The desk wasn't big, but had ink, paper, and other things a man would need to run a business. Moving behind it, Jamie searched for what Molly and Ada had told him would hold the names of those who visited the Crimson Serpent. He took precious seconds to go through the drawers and found nothing that looked like what he was after.

Had the women been lying to him?

"Where could you be hiding?" Jamie muttered as the noise beyond the curtain started to ease. His eyes fell on a jacket hanging on a hook beside the entrance. Unsure why he thought the book could be there, he found himself heading that way. Seconds later, he was going through the pockets and found a small black book. Opening it, he read the first page, and then stuffed it into his jacket pocket.

Heading back out of the room, Jamie ran into the barman.

"What are you doing back here?" he demanded.

Just then a loud roar filled the air, and they both turned. Jamie watched someone hurl a tankard at another patron. He hurried to his friends as the barman ran to intervene. Reaching Anthony, who was wrestling with someone, he dragged him free.

"Run for the door now!" Jamie said.

Toby went first, and Anthony and Jamie followed. Shutting the door behind them, they took the stairs up.

"Get them!" The door opened and soon footsteps were following.

"Up," Anthony said. "We'll leave the way we got in."

They ran to the next floor and through another door to an external staircase, which was narrow and attached to the rear of the property. They made it down without falling and were soon running back to the carriage.

"I'm too old for this," Toby wheezed as they rolled away from the Crimson Serpent.

Jamie didn't answer. Instead, he turned up the lamps. Pulling the book from his inside jacket pocket, he studied the pages, running his eyes down the columns.

"Well?" Anthony demanded.

"Initials, money amounts, but not much else," Jamie said as

he slumped back into the seat.

"Well, now we are on board, things will improve," Toby said, "as we are far superior at investigative work than you."

He hoped his friends were right, because the rising tension inside Jamie told him they needed to find Jackson, and soon, before he disappeared completely.

CHAPTER SEVENTEEN

L ADY ALICE PAUSED outside the door, taking in the faint creak of boards above her head and the old musty smells that clung stubbornly to the walls. The house still bore the scars of neglect, with cracks running down the plaster, and a faint draft sneaking in through ill-fitted windows, but it was hers. Or, at least, her father's, even if he didn't know about it. Here the poor and forgotten of London could seek medical help.

The need was great, and Alice knew it would not be long before they were overrun. She pulled her gloves tighter, reminding herself she shouldn't be anxious because this was the path she had chosen.

Opening the door, she stepped into the first treatment room, and the only one so far properly arranged to take patients. Whitewash had brightened the walls. Buckets and basins stood in a clean line beneath the window, and the little iron stove threw out heat. On the tray sat a neat array of instruments that she now knew the names of, as Doctor Hammond had explained them and their purposes. Alice refused to look too closely at the bone saw.

"We have had our first patients, my lady."

"So I understand, Doctor Hammond. The waiting room is currently filling up."

Tall and most often grave, the doctor's dark coat was immaculate despite the dust that settled over everything in the East End, and he was busy washing his hands. His spectacles glinted in the dim light, and his voice carried the tones of a man raised in better surroundings than these. Yet, like her, he was compelled to do better for those who had no one.

"Excellent," Alice said, forcing her shoulders down from her ears. "If we are missing any supplies, please let me know at once. I want nothing to delay your work."

He nodded. "I am attempting to secure the services of another physician, one I think will suit the nature of this place. I shall inform you when he has agreed."

Alice studied him a moment. Dr. Hammond was the picture of composure. Yet his eyes betrayed something deeper, a steady determination that no polish of manners could hide. Alice knew he treated both Mayfair's wealthy and the East End's destitute. Most men of his profession would never dream of dirtying their hands in such a place as the one Alice had set up, but he had said it was his calling to do so.

"Excellent," she repeated again as he dried his hands. "Send word when you know the time for a meeting, and I shall endeavor to find you more staff also." She then excused herself, leaving the man to get on with what needed to be done.

The house had once belonged to a merchant who'd lost everything to debt. Large and old, it had been left to rot until she'd secured the lease. The first time she walked through with Ezra and Maggie, dust lay like a thick carpet on the floors, and damp darkened the walls. It was still far from finished, but the clinic was at least ready to take patients now. The second floor, scrubbed and whitewashed, held the waiting room and two treatment rooms. One day soon, the third floor would be a ward with beds for patients too ill to return to slums and alleys. But for that, she would need more staff. Always more, Alice thought. More bandages, more laudanum, more coal, more food. If she could convince others like Eloise and Thaddeus to help her cause, then perhaps this would not be the only clinic for those in need.

She descended the staircase, trailing her fingers along a once grand banister, now worn smooth with age. From below drifted coughs, the shuffle of boots, the murmur of voices, and a baby's thin, fretful cry from the waiting room. Alice entered.

The space was already crowded. Patients seated along the far wall, each looking as though life had taken more than it returned. A woman with a hacking cough bent over a child whose flushed face spoke of fever. An old man leaned heavily on a stick, eyes glazed with pain and the kind of weariness that lived in the bones. A boy, no more than ten, cradled a swollen hand against his chest, the knuckles puffy.

Alice's heart squeezed. So many, and this was only the first morning. "The doctor will see you soon," she told the old man. "We've a chair by the stove if you're cold," she then told the little boy and the woman, guiding her a step closer to the heat.

She crouched before the boy with the swollen hand. "How did this happen?"

"Barrow wheel," he muttered. "I'm fine."

"You are very brave," Alice said. "But I think you shall be braver still if you let Dr. Hammond bind it, and I will ensure you have a slice of bread after, as a reward."

At the promise, his gaze flicked to her face, suspicious. She stood, remembering her own breakfast of toast and preserves. Alice had eaten until her belly was full. Had this boy ever done that? It was then she heard the voices, low whispers from behind her.

"Madam said one of them gave a fake name," a woman said. "They've made her and Gideon uneasy. Even two weeks on, they're still nervous. Especially since one of them stole his ledger. We must make certain no one knows they spoke to us, Molly. But this could be our chance to put a bit aside. For when we need it."

Alice's head turned fractionally, her ears straining. Two women sat near the door, close together in dresses patched with bright ribbons meant to distract from their worn hems. The taller wore a smudge of rouge on her cheeks. The other, round-faced with yellow ribbons, twisted her shawl between nervous fingers until the wool squeaked.

"I asked Mary about the man who attacked her," the first woman continued. "She didn't name Kenneth Jackson, but it's him, I swear. Matches the description the gent gave us when he came to our rooms two weeks ago and offered to give us money for information."

Alice's pulse kicked. *Kenneth Jackson.*

"He was a right handsome one," the second said. "All three of them were, but that one had the look of trouble in his eyes if you ask me."

"All hell broke loose downstairs when they walked in, so Neil told me," the first said. "They tried to hide it, but they were definitely noblemen to my mind. Madam and Gideon are fuming, and want answers, so we need to be careful."

Noblemen. Alice's breath caught. Could it be Lords Stafford, Hamilton, and Corbyn they spoke of? Were these women from the Crimson Serpent that Huckle had talked about? The thought struck like cold water. Betrayal stung.

The agreement she and Lord Stafford had, had been clear. They would tell each other everything concerning Jackson. No secrets. No private investigations. The danger was too great otherwise. Yet surely here was proof he had gone behind her back, if she could confirm it. Two weeks ago, the woman had said, they'd entered that brothel, and Lord Stafford had neither approached Alice nor sent word, if indeed it was him.

She crossed to the women, with a polite smile even though her heart thundered. She needed more proof. "Good morning, ladies."

Both startled, their eyes widening before they scrambled to their feet, dropping untidy curtsies. Their perfume was so strong it stung her nose.

"Are you here to see the doctor?" Alice asked.

"We are, my lady," the taller one said. "Molly's got an awful earache."

Alice's gaze softened despite herself. "Then he shall see you soon. In the meantime…" She let the pause hang, then lowered her voice. "I overheard you mention Kenneth Jackson. And a gentleman who wished you to send word if you came by any information."

They froze, and fear flickered across their faces. Their eyes darted to one another, then back to her.

"Do not be afraid," Alice said, gentling her tone. "One of the noblemen you spoke of, I'm quite sure, is my friend. We are investigating the man, Jackson, together."

Molly licked her lips. "Your friend?"

"You can trust me. Can you tell me what he asked of you?"

The round-faced girl twisted her shawl again. "He wanted to know if any of our girls ever saw a man named Kenneth Jackson. Said to send word if we did. That's all. Honest, my lady. He paid us a sovereign and said to be careful."

"Did he describe Jackson to you?" Alice pressed.

"Aye," Molly said with a little shiver. "Mary swore that was the man who hurt her. Wouldn't give a name, but… it was him. He hurt another, too. A new girl, but we were told to keep our mouths shut, or we'd be sent packing."

Alice knew what Kenneth Jackson was capable of. The ledger… a record of clients? Debts? Blackmail? If Stafford had stolen it, the danger to anyone named within those pages would be a fuse already lit.

"And do you ladies work in the Crimson Serpent?"

They both nodded.

She drew a coin from her reticule and pressed it into Molly's hand. "Thank you for telling me. And I promise my friend will not mind."

"Is he your beau?" Molly asked, clutching the money. "He's a handsome one, if he is."

"No," Alice said too quickly. "We are only friends."

Someone let out a hacking cough, and a child whimpered. Dr. Hammond then appeared in the doorway, spectacles askew, and beckoned the two women she'd been speaking with forward.

"Next, if you please."

Alice stepped back to let them pass, and then turned away, the stiff smile on her face falling the moment they were out of sight. Walking out into the hallway, she sank onto a bench.

Her fingers curled into fists. Stafford had lied to her. Not in words, perhaps, but in silence. Their pact had been to share everything, and he'd broken it. If he could not trust her with his actions, how could she trust him at all?

A shadow fell across her. Ezra stood there looking down at her, frowning. "Is all well, my lady?"

"As well as it can be," she said. "We shall need more liniment, more vinegar, more everything. And a better lock on the rear door."

"I'll see to it." He hesitated. "You look pale. Sit a moment longer."

"I cannot," she said, standing despite the tremor in her knees. "If I stop, I shall not start again."

They found Maggie in the kitchens, sleeves rolled up, head bent over a list while the cook they'd employed scowled at a sack of potatoes as if it had personally insulted him.

Alice had made the decision that meals would be served to those who were hungry here. She had hired Tom Bibbs to cook for them, because he'd been recommended to her. The man was crotchety on his good days, but the meal he'd cooked for her tasted better than anything her own cook prepared—not that she'd be mentioning that to anyone—so she'd hired him.

Between them they then discussed deliveries, the price of coal, the astonishing greed of the coal merchant, and whether they could stretch the bread by mixing in boiled oats. The practicalities steadied Alice. She was good at this. Organizing was her strength.

After saying goodbye to Doctor Hammond an hour later, she collected her maid and cloak, then stepped outside. A fine mist of rain had settled over London. Climbing into the carriage, Alice fell on the seat, suddenly weary.

"Well, the clinic is coming along, my lady," Maggie said once they were rolling, her tone brisk. "Better every day."

"Indeed. I am pleased with the progress," Alice murmured, watching narrow lanes change into wider streets as they moved west. She had trusted Lord Stafford because, like her brother, he had suffered. She had believed that together they would track down Jackson. It seemed she was wrong. He had been hiding things from her. The visit to the Crimson Serpent, the questions, the ledger. It had to be him who had taken it, and he'd told her nothing now two weeks on.

Heat prickled behind her eyes, but Alice blinked the tears away. She'd wanted to trust him because she had needed that. Needed to believe she was not alone.

You can trust no one but yourself, Alice. No one but those who have already tied their fate to yours. Ezra, Maggie, Dr. Hammond. Lord Stafford was like every other nobleman in the end, no matter how good his mouth felt pressed to hers, which she should absolutely not be remembering when she was furious with him. Like the other men in her life, he believed she was beneath him, and of no consequence. Alice had been wrong in thinking he was different.

She pressed her back into the carriage seat and folded her hands in her lap so tightly her knuckles ached. If Stafford thought to keep her in ignorance, he was mistaken. She had survived worse than his betrayal. She would learn what she needed to alone, and then use it to find Kenneth Jackson.

Outside, the rain ran in rivulets now across the glass. Her reflection looked back at her, pale and resolute, a woman Lord Stafford would underestimate at his peril.

CHAPTER EIGHTEEN

ALICE'S CARRIAGE MADE the last turn and slowed before her father's townhouse. She was more than ready to close herself in her room with a pot of tea and think.

Stepping down, Alice lifted her face, letting the cool rain settle on her skin briefly. All she wanted was to find Jackson, and she'd complicated that by including Lord Stafford in her hunt— but no more.

"Hello, Phipps," Alice said to her butler.

"Lord Smythe arrived an hour ago, my lady."

Alice stared at the butler, stunned at what he'd said.

"He has been asking for you since," Phipps added, his expression giving away nothing of what he felt.

The staff were not fond of Alice's father, which was fine because she was not very fond of him either. She just hoped he had not brought his mistress.

"Thank you, Phipps. Where is he?"

"The blue parlor, my lady."

"Excellent. If you will have a fresh tea tray prepared. I shall tidy myself and then see him," Alice said. "Where is my aunt?"

"She is out visiting with Lady Hetherington."

"Let's hope she stays there," Alice muttered. Aunt Gwen loathed her father too.

The butler left, and Maggie, who took her coat, looked Alice up and down.

"Will I pass, or do I need to change, Maggie? Because my father is not a patient man, so I would like to see him as soon as I can."

Maggie brushed at Alice's skirts, and then fixed some pins in her hair. "You'll do," her maid then said.

Alice climbed the stairs to the second floor and headed for the blue parlor, nerves fluttering in her belly. Why was her father here? He never came to London unannounced.

She inhaled the scent of beeswax and orange oil, her housekeeper's concoction, and looked up at portraits of her ancestors gazing down at her in judgment as she attempted to regain control of herself. Her steps made no sound on the carpet as she reached the parlor door and paused with her hand on the latch.

He will leave again soon, she reminded herself. Just get through this.

She entered.

Her father stood at the hearth with a glass of claret, spectacles low on his nose, and he read from the book her aunt had left in here this morning. His hair had gone grayer this past year since she'd seen him. Tall, elegant as always, he was a man who had aged well. A selfish, spoiled man who cared only for himself.

"Hello, Father. To what do we owe this honor?" Alice tried to say the words without giving away any of the emotion she felt. She'd fought long and hard against her resentment toward this man, who had simply abandoned her and Charles for a woman he was not even married to.

"Ah, Alice." He surveyed her, but made no move to kiss her cheek or hug the daughter he'd not seen in many months. The monster that was resentment roared louder inside her. "You are late."

"I did not receive word you were arriving, so I fail to see how I could be late, Father."

"Where have you been?"

"Out visiting friends," she said.

Alice knew how this worked. He liked to be right all the time and hated anyone challenging him. Loathed the fact that Alice didn't just bow to his every whim and flatter his ego.

She had long ago realized she would always love her father, but she in no way liked or respected him.

"In the rain?"

"She lives in a house, not on the streets, Father."

His lips tightened, and then formed a sneer. "Lord Braxton called to see you. I told him you would be home tomorrow to receive him."

"Why are you here, Father?"

"It is my townhouse, daughter; do not forget that," he snapped at her.

"How could I? It is I who runs your affairs and deals with everything. It is I who sends you and your mistress money." The words slipped out before she could swallow them down. No good ever came from speaking to her father like this, but perhaps because she was already unsettled, she'd done just that.

"How dare you speak to me like that!" he thundered.

"How dare I?" Alice snorted. "I think you have that wrong, my lord. How dare you walk away from all your responsibilities. How dare you put your mistress before your duty." Her words were coated in ice.

"Enough!" He raised a hand. "I have decided you will wed, Alice, and soon, because I wish to return to London, and have no wish for you to still be living in my homes."

Shock had her taking a step backward.

"Clearly, Lord Braxton has an interest in you. He is a sensible young man," her father said. "Attentive, but not—"

"You know nothing about him," Alice said through her teeth. "You have no right to do this. Come in here and demand I wed, when I have kept everything running while you frolic with your mistress."

"I am an earl, and as such can do as I wish," he declared. "We will return for next year's season, and you and your aunt will not be living here."

It hit her then, hard. "You would bring your mistress back here for everyone to see, and to mock?"

"How dare you speak of the woman I love in such a way. We are going to marry."

The word was like a gunshot to Alice. It silenced her and had her reeling.

"You can't mean that?" she whispered.

"Of course I mean it. I am traveling to the country now briefly and will return in a few days to discuss this matter further. I expect by then you will have something to report to me."

"So you came here for a single day, to see me, your only surviving child, who you've barely spoken a word to in years, and tell me you are throwing us out of our house, so you and that…that woman can live here?"

"It is time," he said with deadly finality. "I will discuss this no more. See you find a suitable husband, daughter. I shall return soon."

She moved to the door and opened it, but before she left, Alice had a last thing to say. She'd never taken her father to task, but it was clearly past time.

"You are a selfish, horrible man. You have neglected your children for many years and now want to throw one of them out of the only home she's ever known. This speaks to your weak, mean spirited, and shallow character, my lord. I will be more than happy to never see you again. I will also ensure to never look at another of the household accounts or the investments I have undertaken on your behalf. Your estates and finances are flourishing because of me, but that will no longer be the case."

Her father's mouth dropped open at Alice's speech.

"Rot in hell, Father. It's what you deserve, and know that for your many sins there is a single one I will never ever forgive you for: Turning your back on your son when he most needed you."

She walked out the door to her father roaring her name. In the hall, Phipps, the butler, waited with his impenetrable calm. "A card came for you, my lady. Delivered not ten minutes past."

Her stomach tightened. "For me?"

"Yes, my lady." He extended the silver salver.

Alice did not look. She knew the quality of the card before she turned it, felt it in the crispness of the edge beneath her gloved fingers. Lord Stafford's crest. The ink black as a bruise.

A single line, written in a strong, slanted hand.

We must speak. Tonight.—S.

Heat flared up her spine, as she looked at that bold stroke of a letter. She slipped the card back onto the tray.

"Please send word to Lord Stafford's townhouse," she said, keeping her tone even, "that I will be unable to see him this evening."

Phipps hesitated, perhaps surprised by the steel in her voice. "Very good, my lady."

"And, Phipps?"

"My lady?"

"If any other notes arrive from Lord Stafford, they are to be placed on my writing desk unopened. I will attend to them myself."

"Of course."

She climbed the stairs, rage, hurt, and pain roiling inside her, and made for her room.

Once there, she resisted the urge to hurl herself onto her bed, and instead sat in the chair before the fire. Maggie followed with a tea tray and a small plate of sugared biscuits.

"Eat please, my lady," her maid said, setting the tray by the writing desk, "before you faint on me and give the housemaids stories to tell their grandchildren."

"Why would I faint?" Alice said, picking up a biscuit and nibbling. It tasted like dust.

"I have eyes," Maggie said, and then, softer, "and I can see you are pale and upset."

"'Tis nothing," Alice added. "My father is a fool, but that's nothing I did not already know."

Maggie's brows climbed, but she only bobbed a curtsy and

left, closing the door with the quiet efficiency of a woman who had learned how to vanish when her mistress needed to think.

Alice rose with her tea and went to the desk she'd had placed before the windows. Opening a drawer, she slid out the little inlaid box. Pulling out paper and pen, she began to write.

Ledger stolen. Three nobles in disguise. Questioned girls about K. Jackson, and the men who questioned them, Lord Stafford being one of them.

Look into securing more staff for clinic. Supplies: carbolic, laudanum, liniment—more. Ward: at least six beds to begin; two nurses.

She paused, and ink blotted the paper, before writing *Stafford did not tell me what he was doing, or had uncovered.* She set the nib down hard enough to nick the paper.

Wind rattled the window behind her. Alice looked up as rain rolled steadily down the pane. She heard a carriage roll past. The city went on beyond these walls regardless of whether a gentleman kept his word, or a father abandoned his daughter yet again.

Picking up the pen, she then began to make notes about what she needed to do to secure the future for herself, her staff, and her aunt before her father returned to town with his mistress, who was to become her stepmother. The thought made her shudder.

Alice would not be in society if her father and that woman were there. In fact, she would be long gone. A little house in the country should do.

She had many things to sort out. One of them was how to keep supplying money to the clinic and other causes when her father returned. She would have to cover her tracks well, and ensure she had enough money left to do what she needed to.

Alice closed the box and set it back in the drawer, then took the card once more, looking at the black slanted writing.

"Not tonight," she said aloud to the empty room. "Not on your terms. In fact, never again, Lord Stafford." *You are not to be trusted.*

A knock on her door was followed by her aunt.

"Don't forget that this evening we are to go to the dinner party, dear."

Damn, she'd forgotten about that. Lord Anthony's aunts were hosting it and had called on her to invite Alice and her aunt, who was a personal friend.

"I know your father is here, and I'm afraid he is not invited. Would you like me to see if I can change that, Alice?"

"No, Aunt Gwen. He is leaving London again this evening," Alice said, and noted the relief on her aunt's face at her words.

"Well then, you rest now, dear, as it should be a late night."

The door shut, and Alice rose from her seat. This time she did head for the bed, and fell face first onto the cover. Lord Stafford would be there, she was sure of it. Firstly, because of that conversation she'd had with Lord Hamilton's aunts, and secondly, because he was a close friend of their nephew.

And that mattered not, because she didn't have to speak to him. Closing her eyes, she let exhaustion take its toll. She'd need all her wits about her this evening. Alice just hoped her father did leave before she came downstairs as she had no wish to see him again.

The first tears fell, and they would be the only ones. Alice had plans to make, and she could not afford the weakness of self-pity. Her aunt depended on her, and she would not let her down.

CHAPTER NINETEEN

"ONE WONDERS WHAT favor Lord Redfern owes your aunts, seeing as the man is a powerful peer," Jamie mused to his friends, who were seated across from him in the carriage.

In the two weeks since they'd visited the Crimson Serpent, he'd been investigating the initials on the list. So far, he'd found no trace of Jackson.

Either Toby or Anthony had shown up at his door each day demanding to know what they were doing that day in regards to locating Jackson. It was both humbling and vexing that they didn't let him do the investigating himself, as he'd been doing.

Even now, they'd sent their wives on ahead to the dinner party and had collected him.

"You do know I could have driven myself here?" Jamie drawled.

They waved his words away.

"We don't trust you, so we are watching you," Anthony said.

"I'm the most trustworthy of all of us."

They laughed at that.

"Back to your aunts. How is it that tonight Lord Redfern is hosting a dinner party on their behalf?" Jamie asked.

"I tried to get that out of them, actually—"

"Perhaps I could try; they do love me the most," Jamie added, needling his friends.

"Evie and I have a theory on that," Anthony said.

As he was looking at his friends, he could read the smirks on their faces now.

"What theory?" Jamie demanded.

"Why, it's for you, my friend. After all, you are not showing progress with the names on that list, so they feel it is time to move things along by holding a dinner party," Anthony said.

"You cannot be serious? They would go to all this trouble just to ensure I spend time with the three women on that list?" Jamie felt a sinking feeling at the prospect that this evening was all about him.

"You do know my aunts, don't you?" Anthony asked. "They didn't want to put me to the trouble of hosting a dinner party because of Evie's delicate condition, so they asked their dear friend Lord Redfern is my understanding."

"What names were on that list anyway?" Toby added.

Jamie thought seriously about leaving, but as the carriage was stopping outside Lord Redfern's house, he didn't think he'd get the chance. Mind you, he could outrun his friends.

"I'm not telling you the names," Jamie said.

If his friends were right, then Lady Alice would be inside. He'd only seen her once in the past few weeks, from a distance at a ball. When he'd finally worked up the nerve to approach, she'd turned and walked away. Jamie didn't know why he'd taken that as deliberate—but he had.

He'd even sent her a note the next day, asking to speak with her. Her reply had been polite, stating she was unavailable. Something about it didn't sit right. There was more to her refusal than courtesy; he could feel it.

He pushed aside the flicker of guilt that he hadn't told her what he'd discovered. It was for the best. A woman like Lady Alice had no place in a brothel. He'd tell her about the ledger when the time was right.

You're doing this to keep her safe, he reminded himself. What she didn't know couldn't hurt her.

They stepped from the carriage and then took the stairs up

and into Lord Redfern's townhouse.

Lady Petunia appeared to be waiting for them in the front entrance, elegant in lavender. "I could not hold them off much longer. Where have you been?" she demanded.

"Surely we are not that late, Aunt," Anthony said, kissing her cheek. "And where is Lord Redfern as we are in his townhouse?"

She made a tsking sound. "We are hosting, and he merely offered a larger dining room. In fact, he was excited, as since his wife passed, he's not hosted a ball or dinner."

"Well then, how kind of you to help him with that," Anthony said solemnly.

"Yes, well, your aunts and I thought it time to revive his flagging spirits."

"A whopping untruth," Toby whispered to Jamie. "Now I need to find my wife."

"You're pathetic," Jamie muttered as his friend smiled at the thought of seeing Liberty.

Anthony clapped his hands together. "This is going to be an excellent evening. I can feel it."

He could simply turn and walk out the door; no one would be able to stop him.

"Jamie, you will stop dragging your feet!"

Except maybe her. "Coming, Lady Petunia."

Was Lady Alice here? The thought made his pulse pick up speed. What was it about that woman other than she had lush, soft, and kissable lips?

The townhouse was hushed save for the muted clink of crystal and the faint murmur of voices carrying from somewhere ahead. A footman, immaculate in black, led the way. Candles flickered in polished brackets, their light showing Jamie portraits and cabinets filled with expensive porcelain and crystal.

"Do you know, I don't think I've ever been here," Toby said.

Jamie couldn't remember a time he had either. His father perhaps, but not him.

As they slowed, he put his social smile in place as the glow of the parlor spilled into the hall, accompanied by a swell of laughter and the rustle of silk. The doors were open and he stepped through. The guests all turned their heads as the new arrivals were announced. Jamie wasn't sure why he tensed suddenly, as this was something he'd done more times than he could remember, but he did. When he studied the guests, he instantly realized why.

Lady Alice was here and standing against the far wall from where he'd entered. The look on her face told Jamie she was no happier to be in this place than he was. Yet, despite himself, a surge of something dangerously close to happiness stirred in him at the sight of her. He'd think about that later.

As if sensing his presence, she turned, and the look she gave him was through narrowed eyes. Her mouth tightened, and then she looked away.

Why was she angry? Had someone said something to upset her? Looking at the person she was with, he noted it was the youngest of Anthony's aunts. Perhaps they were pressing her about her marriage prospects?

"And now if you'll all come through, dinner will be served," Lady Petunia announced in tones as commanding as a field marshal. Her voice carried easily to every corner of the town-house, and Jamie suspected even the neighbors two doors down had heard the summons.

Much to his relief, he found himself paired with Anthony's other aunt, Lady Agatha, on his arm. Relief, however, proved fleeting.

"Now, Jamie," Lady Agatha began in her brisk, determined way, "tonight will give you ample opportunity, without hordes of people interrupting you, to chat with the three women on the list."

Jamie stiffened. "I do not wish to marry, Lady Agatha." He kept his voice low and direct, hoping honesty would stall their matchmaking attempts. "I understand you and your lovely sisters want my happiness—as Toby and Anthony have found it—but I can be content without a wife for now, thank you."

"Oh, pooh to that." She waved off his declaration. "You need a wife to help you heal and move on, dear."

The word heal slid under his ribs like a blade. Jamie's fingers twitched where her gloved hand rested lightly on his arm. He had no wish to revisit those wounds, not here, not under the blaze of candlelight and the watchful eyes of Anthony's aunts. He owed this lady and her sisters a great deal, but his marriage was not part of that.

"It is time, Jamie," Lady Agatha added softly, as they entered the dining room. "You're seated here."

Now wasn't the time to continue this discussion, so he inclined his head, and took up his place behind the designated chair. As custom dictated, he waited until all the ladies had claimed their seats before lowering himself.

Directly opposite, Lady Alice Smythe sat in her own chair with her usual composure. Her ivory silk gown caught the glow from the candelabra above, the delicate sheen making her appear almost luminous. Pearls rested against the graceful column of her throat, modest enough in appearance, but the gentle curves above the bodice had his blood heating.

He'd kissed this woman, and held her. Jamie had felt every lush curve of her body pressed to his. *Not now, Jamie.* Having lustful thoughts for a dinner guest was not exactly the done thing in such a setting.

He noted, with a sinking heart, that clearly the aunts had placed the other two ladies on his list beside him to his left and right. Lady Alice, the third, was opposite. He was hemmed in on all sides. To his right, Miss Devlin offered a greeting.

"Good evening, Lord Stafford."

"How wonderful," cooed Miss Timothy on his left, as if being seated beside him were akin to discovering a treasure.

Jamie sent Anthony's aunts a look sharp enough to draw blood. All three, grouped together like conspirators at the far end of the room, returned his glare with indulgent smiles. He was a reluctant pawn on their matrimonial chessboard.

Forcing a polite expression onto his face, he acknowledged both women at his sides before lifting his gaze across the gleaming white linen and colorful blooms on the table to Lady Alice.

She was poised, and distant. There was no trace of the woman who had wept in his arms outside the Black Dog in sight. Tonight she was all elegance and haughtiness, her expression polite as she spoke with the gentleman to her right, Lord Braxton.

Jamie's jaw tightened. Braxton was a second son miraculously turned heir after an uncle's death abroad and a brother's fatal fall from a horse. Elevation had not improved his character, only his debts. And the way he leaned too near Alice, smiling with practiced charm, spoke volumes about his intentions.

Jamie wanted to tell him to sit back, to warn him off. But he had no rights where Lady Alice was concerned. No claim. No promise. Nothing but the uneasy feeling that she was angry with him, though he did not yet know why.

Her eyes turned suddenly and locked on his. The candles flickered, casting her face in a golden hue, but those eyes were once again narrowed. She was definitely angry with him. *Why?*

He'd tried to speak to her, but hadn't in two weeks, so to his knowledge nothing had passed between them to warrant her anger. She looked away first.

Jamie had admired many women in his time, even desired some, but none intrigued him as Alice did. He knew he needed to get her alone. He had to tell her what he'd discovered. It was only fair.

Braxton bent nearer still, murmuring something that drew a polite nod. Jamie caught her slight retreat as she leaned back. The man mistook her distance for coyness, idiot that he was.

Jamie clenched his hands beneath the table. He wanted, badly, to break Braxton's nose.

Which should tell you, he reminded himself grimly, *that distance from that woman is the best course forward.*

Conversation around the table ebbed and flowed. Servants glided in with the first course, tureens of fragrant broth. Jamie nodded for the footman to ladle some into his bowl.

"Shocking business in Covent Garden, shocking," boomed Mr. Rushbridge from Jamie's left, his voice carrying above the general din. "A gentleman stopped in his carriage, bold as brass. Robbed him right there on the street."

Gasps circled the table and then the questions started. Jamie's attention wavered between the conversation and the woman across from him, who still did not glance in his direction again.

"Are you enjoying the soup, Lady Alice?" Jamie said, reduced to seeking her attention. *Fool that I am.*

"Yes, thank you, my lord." Her eyes went to his left ear.

"Are you to attend the theater tomorrow evening? I believe it is Shakespeare's—"

"I am not to attend, Lord Stafford," she said, cutting him off. Her eyes then returned to Lord Braxton. The man smiled across the table, looking smug over the fact Lady Alice appeared to have no wish to speak to him.

Was her anger because she'd found out he'd been to the Crimson Serpent? But who would have told her?

He had promised her honesty. Promised to keep her abreast of his search for Kenneth Jackson. And he had broken that promise, but she couldn't know that.

Jamie emptied his expression, lifting his spoon, though he could not have said what he tasted.

From his left, Miss Timothy asked a question about hunting lodges. From his right, Miss Devlin pressed him about his family estate. He answered automatically, with the ease of long practice. But inwardly, his focus never shifted.

Every movement of Alice's hands, the tilt of her head, the light catching in her hair—these occupied him more than any conversation at his own side.

She was furious with him. He knew it now, as surely as he knew his own name. Just not why.

CHAPTER TWENTY

ALICE SMILED AT something Lord Braxton said, and secretly thought him a fool, as was her father if he thought she'd ever marry the man.

Aunt Gwen had fallen ill late this afternoon with a terrible headache and had been unable to attend. Alice had told her she would send word with their excuses, but her aunt had insisted she attend without her, and seemed agitated when Alice had refused, so she'd given in.

Arriving at the dinner party early, she'd felt a rush of relief when the guests appeared without Lord Stafford among them. But that relief didn't last because he turned up soon after with his friends.

Alice had calmed down enough to understand why he'd not wanted her to enter the Crimson Serpent, but he should have told her what he found, and had not. She didn't trust easily, and this was why. People always broke that trust.

Thankfully, her father had kept his word and left the town-house before Alice had headed to the dinner party. Of course, she had not known that as he'd not made the effort to speak to her again. *Loathsome man.* Phipps had informed her.

"The color of your eyes brings forth the most beauteous sunsets, Lady Alice."

"It's going to be an excessively long meal if you keep posturing, Braxton."

Alice looked across the table and into the eyes of Lord Hamilton after he spoke. He offered her a smile, which she was forced to return. Had Lord Stafford told his friends about what had taken place in the Black Dog? Did they also know she was hunting Jackson to avenge her brother? The two women at the clinic had said three gentlemen visited the Crimson Serpent. Were the other two Lords Corbyn and Hamilton? If so, then they were cads also as far as she was concerned.

Alice had the unfortunate personality trait that if someone wronged her, then she never forgave them. Charles had often said that if grudge holding was a sport, she would be its highest-ranking player.

Lord Stafford had wronged her, and she would not forget that. His friends, however, Alice would wait to see if they needed to be put on that list as well.

Beside her, Lord Braxton brayed with laughter, taking the insult from Lord Hamilton as humor. *Idiot.*

"I'm sure your father told you I called to see you today, Lady Alice," he said.

"He did."

"I want to take you driving."

She would rather have insects crawling over her entire body than go anywhere with this man.

"I am uncertain of my plans for the next week, my lord," Alice lied.

Of course, many had seen Alice as a future wife who came with a large dowry and her father's title at her back. She'd managed to dissuade all of them in different ways, and the ones she hadn't, had been unable to speak to her father about their wishes. That was about to change when he returned to London, however. He also now wanted her wed.

Bastard.

"I am a patient man," Lord Braxton said.

She knew the signs when a man was showing interest in her, and Lord Braxton was making his intentions known. She was just unsure why, as before today he'd not shown any partiality toward her.

Alice thought it was likely that he'd come into his title recently and needed her funds to replenish the family coffers. She might not spend a lot of time in society, but Eloise and Thaddeus kept her abreast of all goings-on.

A deep laugh had her tensing. She wasn't looking across the table but she was aware that Lord Stafford was now in conversation with Miss Devlin. The young woman hung on the marquess's every word. Alice didn't acknowledge the small sting of jealousy as the woman touched the sleeve of his dark jacket.

Jealousy had no place in her life, especially when she was furious at him. Her purpose was set; she would find Jackson alone now, and after that she would think about the future, but not before. Lord Stafford was a means to help her find and destroy the man who had taken her brother from her and nothing more than that. She had to stay focused for Charles.

"And what of you, Lady Alice? Are you like many who fawn over the flowery prose of Byron?"

Alice took a bite of her salmon before answering Lord Hamilton, while beside her Braxton slurped down a mouthful of shrimp sauce loudly. It always amazed her how society valued propriety and manners, yet so few had them.

"I do not spend a lot of time reading poetry, my lord," she said as Miss Timothy giggled across the table at something Lord Stafford said to her. "But Wordsworth is my favorite."

Braxton laughed, showy and loud. "You are clearly a woman of sense who has many passionate pursuits, Lady Alice."

Gnashing one's teeth in such a setting was not the done thing, but the urge was there.

She looked across the table and instantly wished she hadn't. Her gaze collided with Stafford's. He raised a dark brow, as his deep green eyes questioned her. For a breath, neither looked away. It was he who broke the contact as Miss Devlin touched his sleeve.

Alice exhaled slowly. Her chest felt tight, and suddenly she wanted to run from the room. Of course, she would not, as there would be questions, and while she may flout society's rules in her own way, she'd made a decision long ago that she would appear to be everything that was expected of her. Then, in private, do as she wished.

A servant appeared at her side with another tray laden with food. Alice fought back the need to send him away, and nodded. The roast course was rich with gravy and herbs. She ate little, pushing the delicacies around her plate, which was not usually her way. Alice loved food. Around her, people chattered and laughed, Lady Petunia's voice booming, Rushbridge holding forth on some scandal in Covent Garden. She answered when spoken to, but her mind was elsewhere.

Every nerve was aware of the devil seated across from her. The way his hands curled around his wineglass, and the faint line between his brows when one of the two young ladies on either side of him leaned near.

She loathed how aware she was of him when he'd betrayed her, and longed to demand the truth from him, but that would not happen here tonight, surrounded by people. Alice made herself focus, putting on the façade expected of her.

By the arrival of dessert she was weary, her nerves stretched to breaking point. She had never been so ready to leave a table.

Finally, Lady Petunia rose and signaled that the ladies would leave. Alice saw this as her chance. When they were out in the hallway, she moved to where Lady Agatha stood.

"Forgive me, my lady, but I must get back to my aunt. She was most unwell, and I am worried. I must return in case a doctor is needed."

"Yes, poor Gwen. I hope she improves quickly. But I'm sure she would want you to stay a while longer, dear, as the music is due to start soon. Surely a few more minutes?"

"Of course she can spare us a few more minutes, Agatha," Lady Petunia said, taking Alice's arm. "Come, dear."

She was towed along with remarkable force considering the age of the lady at her side. Seconds later, Alice was in a large parlor. A huge grand piano stood at the end of the room. Sofas and chairs formed a half circle around it. If she was to be here for this, Alice did not want the chance that Lord Stafford would be the one to take the seat beside her on a sofa, which, given their recent conversations, could easily be engineered.

"Oh, but I thought the sofa would be more comfortable for you," Lady Agatha said when Alice dropped into a chair inelegantly.

"This will do, thank you. Besides, I will stay for only a few songs and can leave without annoying anyone if I am here, closest to the door," Alice said with a fake smile that did not reach her eyes.

"Tea, I think," Lady Agatha said when she realized she was not about to move Alice.

"They are harmless for the most part, but can be extremely meddlesome," Lady Hamilton said, taking the seat to Alice's right. She was beautiful in a dress of apricot satin. "The problem is, they want everyone they love happy and won't stop until that is done."

"I'm not quite sure I understand what you are saying, Lady Hamilton," Alice lied. Please, God, let her not understand.

"Matchmaking, Lady Alice. They are well known for it, and it seems to me that you are on the list."

"List?" Alice wanted to clutch her chest in horror, but as to this point in her life, she'd never done that and wasn't about to start now.

"Apparently they have made lists for the three friends, my husband and Lords Stafford and Corbyn, that have prospective brides on them."

Alice stared at her, unsure what next to say.

"I'm unsure who is on Lord Stafford's list, but my guess would be the three women seated closest to him this evening."

"Ah...I'm quite sure I don't know what to add to that," Alice said honestly.

"They think of Lord Stafford as they do my husband, and therefore, as he is unwed, they are putting a great deal of effort into changing that. It's really rather sweet, but of course excessively annoying to the three men."

"Were you and Lady Corbyn on the lists?" Alice asked, and then added, "Sorry, I should not have asked such a personal question."

Lady Hamilton laughed. "I'm happy to answer it, and the answer is yes."

"I'm not going to marry," Alice said firmly, and then, "for a while." She said the last because it was not normal for a woman not to want to wed, especially one who walked in society.

"Well then, you have nothing to fear," Lady Hamilton said.

Alice regained her feet suddenly. "I need to leave as my aunt is unwell. Good evening, my lady," she said. Turning, she did the same to Lady Petunia, who was behind her.

"I thought you were going to stay for a while," the older woman said. "I know that Lord Stafford is most desirous to spend more time in your company." The look in Lady Petunia's eyes confirmed what she and Lady Hamilton had just discussed. Alice was on the list.

"Such a sweet boy he was, and now a handsome, intelligent man."

Alice was rarely without words, but right then her mouth was open but no sound came out.

"So perhaps a drive in the park with Jamie, Lord Stafford, would be the next thing for you both. Just so you can spend time together, and see—"

"I really must leave. Thank you for a wonderful evening." Alice patted the woman's hand and fled. Hurrying down the hall with far more haste than grace, she reached the entrance.

"My things, please," Alice said to the startled footman, who had watched her approach at pace.

"At once, my lady."

In the precious moments it took to retrieve her cloak, Alice planned how she could convince her aunt to leave London tomorrow. Of course, that also meant she wouldn't be able to continue with her investigation, but she could send someone to do it on her behalf. There was also the clinic, but again, she could get someone to take care of that too.

Breathe, she reminded herself as the panic rose inside her.

Control, Alice thought. It was important to remain in control, and right then it felt as if it was being wrestled away from her, and that would never do.

"Thank you." She took the midnight-blue cloak—what felt like ten minutes later—and swung it around her shoulders. Raising the hood, she hurried to the door.

The footman ran by her and opened it.

"Thank you, and good evening," Alice said, sounding breath-less.

She needed to get home so she could shut the door and calm down. This entire evening had been a disaster. Alice had known Lord Stafford would likely be here, but what she hadn't realized was how she'd react to him. How hurt she'd feel that he'd done what he had to her—what she believed he'd done to her.

Then there was this list business Lady Hamilton had men-tioned, and Lord Stafford as a prospective husband, or so Lord Hamilton's aunts clearly believed. It was enough to unsettle anyone.

"I shall collect your carriage for you, Lady Alice," the foot-man said, having followed her outside.

Chafing at the delay for no other reason than she felt a des-perate need to flee, she watched the man run down the road. Alice was rewarded precious minutes later with the sight of Ezra's large form on the driver's seat of the carriage now approaching.

"My lady, is all well?" he said when he pulled to a halt beside her.

"Yes, thank you, Ezra. I just wish to return home and check on my aunt." Alice climbed inside after these words and exhaled slowly.

CHAPTER TWENTY-ONE

J AMIE DOWNED THE last of his port and rose abruptly. "Excuse me." Bowing, he left the men, ignoring their raised brows. He needed to find Alice.

When he entered the parlor, where the women were gathered for tea before the music began, he found her missing. Crossing to where Evie and Liberty sat, he bent low between them.

"Where is Lady Alice?" he murmured.

Evie's expression turned guilty. "She left. I may be somewhat to blame."

"What did you say to her?"

"The aunts were being rather obvious with their matchmaking," Evie admitted. "I might have mentioned the lists and—"

"Hell," Jamie muttered. "If anyone asks, make my excuses."

"I'll tell them you've a weak stomach and the soup didn't agree with you," Liberty offered.

He didn't bother to reply, just turned and strode out before anyone could stop him. Had Alice truly gone already?

Snatching his overcoat and hat from the stand, he pushed out into the night. A quick glance right revealed Ezra on the box seat of a carriage, with reins in hand and ready to depart. Shrugging into his coat, Jamie broke into a run.

"Good evening, Ezra."

"Lord Stafford." The man nodded his head.

"I need to speak with Lady Alice. Drive the long way to her townhouse."

Opening the door, he found her preparing to rise, and climbed inside, shutting it behind him.

"Get out of my carriage at once!"

"Hello, Lady Alice. Thank you for offering me a lift home," Jamie said, ignoring her words and settling himself on the seat opposite hers.

"I didn't. Now leave at once," she said as the carriage started moving. "I have no wish to be seen alone in here with you!"

Jamie reached forward and shut both curtains. He then turned up the lamp. Suddenly, they were secluded inside the small space.

"How dare you!"

"Why are you angry with me?" Jamie sat back and looked at her.

She was quivering with rage. Her gloved hands clenched on her thighs, and those beautiful eyes were shooting daggers his way.

"I don't want you in my carriage," she gritted the words out. "Leave at once, Lord Stafford, or I shall scream."

"Please do. I doubt anyone would hear you except maybe Ezra. Do you want him and me to come to blows, my lady?"

Color flushed her cheeks, and if anything, the anger made her more beautiful. Spirited, unlike those vapid women who had fawned all over him this evening. Perhaps an unfair judgment, as it was not their fault they'd been raised with a single thought. Marry, and marry well when the time comes for you to do so.

"Why are you angry with me, my lady?" Jamie said again. "Every time our eyes caught, I could see you wanted to lob something at me. Of course, you were too polite to do so, but the sentiment was there."

She looked down at her hands.

"Alice—"

"Lady Alice," she snapped, looking at him once more. "And I

know about the Crimson Serpent. I know it was likely you that stole the ledger, and that you are paying two women of the night to be your informants! I also know you didn't tell me, and it's clear were unlikely to."

Surprise held him silent for several seconds. How the hell did she get that information?

"So, from that, I gathered you wish to proceed in your investigation into Kenneth Jackson's whereabouts solo, which is fine with me, as I shall do the same." She spat the last words at him in an angry hiss.

"I have so many questions," Jamie said. "The first is, who told you about the Crimson Serpent?"

"Two women at my clinic," she snapped.

"Clinic?"

She waved his words away, but Jamie persisted. "What clinic?"

"That is none of your business," she hissed.

He saw by the jut of her chin she was not about to tell him, so he stored that piece of information away for later.

"Yes, you are correct I did those things, and I do have the journal. And," he held up a hand as she opened her mouth again, "I was going to tell you, but have not had the chance."

"I am nobody's fool, Lord Stafford. Had you wished to tell me, you would have called or sent word immediately. You didn't, and nor did you tell me of your intention to visit the Crimson Serpent—"

"I would not have taken you to the Crimson Serpent, Lady Alice. Never," Jamie added so she understood. "It is not a place for you. For that, I will not apologize, but I will do so for not alerting you to what I learned when we went there."

"We?"

"Lords Hamilton and Corbyn accompanied me."

"It matters not." She turned to look out the window, which allowed her to see nothing as the curtains were drawn. "I will not work with someone whom I do not trust, and I no longer trust you, Lord Stafford."

"I did what I felt needed to be done, and will not apologize for that," Jamie said. "Perhaps I was wrong in not contacting you immediately, but I would have told you what I learned when the opportunity presented itself."

"I don't believe you." The words were cold and hard and spoken to the curtains.

Jamie held himself still, though every muscle in his body screamed to move.

If another man had questioned his word, he would have demanded satisfaction on a field at dawn. That Lady Alice did so with such certainty cut far deeper than a blade could.

"I gave my word, and I keep it. Always, my lady. It is an insult to suggest otherwise. Besides, I sent word—"

"Today, which is two weeks after your visit to the Crimson Serpent." She didn't move, just kept her eyes trained away from him.

Jamie let his gaze drift over the soft curve of her cheek and the arch of her proud neck. Her gloved hands were clenched in her lap. She was furious with him, ready to flay him alive with her tongue, and God help him, she had never looked more alive, more beautiful.

"If a man questioned my word," he said, leaning forward, "I would be extremely displeased."

One delicate shoulder lifted and fell, dismissing him. The gesture was meant to provoke, and it succeeded. Heat licked through him, mingled with anger and something darker, more dangerous.

"Damn it," he muttered, running a hand through his hair. "I have dealt with this alone for so long, but I did not deliberately keep the information from you."

"That's a lie." Her head whipped around, eyes flashing.

"It's not. Yes, I wanted to keep you safe, and yes, I am worried about your involvement in this—"

"It is not your right to worry about me. You promised to

keep me abreast of everything regarding Jackson and didn't. Clearly, this is not working, so we shall pursue him alone from now on," she said.

He surged forward before he could stop himself, his fingers clamping around her wrists.

"You will not pursue this alone," Jamie said. "I promise to tell you everything from this moment on."

Her breath hitched as her gaze locked with his, wide eyed, furious, and yet there was something more there in the beautiful amber depths.

The savage need to taste this woman again drove him to pull her into his arms.

"No." The word held no force.

"Yes," he rasped as his mouth found hers.

The kiss was rough and born of frustration and fury. She gasped, tried to speak, but he swallowed the sound, angling his head to take more of her.

Jamie knew he should stop but his hand was at the back of her head, holding her to him, his other arm banded around her waist as though he could keep her there forever.

She clutched his shoulders, her fingers biting through the wool of his coat. He felt the tremor run through her body, telling him she wanted this as much as he did.

The carriage jolted over a rut, throwing her hard against him. He caught her, pulling her onto his lap. Her skirts tangled around them both, the faint scent of roses rising as pins scattered from her hair as Jamie slipped his fingers into the thick black mass.

"Tell me to stop," he rasped against her lips. His chest heaved, his control a thin thread ready to snap. "Say the word, Alice, and I'll end this."

Her eyes blazed, cheeks flushed. "It's wrong to want this."

"I know." He kissed her again, slower now, deliberate, savoring her as though he might never have the chance again. "And yet, like me, you do."

She made a sound, half anger and half need, and pressed

closer. His hand slid over the curve of her back, feeling the shiver that coursed through her.

More, the word surged through Jamie. He wanted the warm swell of her breasts in his hands, and to taste every inch of her. *I want all of her.*

For a moment, he forgot everything—the danger and Kenneth Jackson. There was only her, alive and furious and kissing him as though she, too, had been waiting forever for this.

He parted her cloak and slid his hand inside to touch the silk of her dress. Trace the curve of her spine. One of her hands was touching his neck now. Even gloved, it made Jamie shudder.

This woman was dangerous to him, and right then he didn't care. Nothing mattered but Alice.

The carriage veered left suddenly, and they parted. Jamie gripped Alice as she fell hard into the carriage door.

"Are you all right?" The words came out a hoarse rasp as his eyes ran over her.

Her lips were swollen, curls tumbling free. The rise and fall of her chest and the quick shallow breaths she was taking showed him she was as affected as Jamie. She had never looked more undone. Never more tempting. He reached out a hand, but she backed away.

"I can't b-believe we did that, again," she said. "What is wrong with us?"

"It's called passion, I believe."

"Well, I want no more of it," she said, folding her arms over her chest. He had nothing to smile about, but it was there as he studied her angry expression.

"Unfortunately, there is little to be done about it, when—"

"Well, I will do something about it. In fact, we shall never be in a situation for this to happen again. From this day forth, Lord Stafford, we will have no need to speak to each other any further."

"Don't be ridiculous, Alice." The lust rampaging through him was rapidly cooling now. "I will call to speak with you tomorrow and explain everything—"

"No. I don't want to hear. I will deal with this alone!"

Jamie winced at her shrill tone, and then the carriage slowed to a halt.

"Goodbye, Lord Stafford," she said, her tone icy.

He beat her to the door and opened it. Stepping down, Jamie held out his hand. Alice looked at it as if it were a seven-headed serpent. He waited, and finally she placed her fingers on his, and he helped her from the carriage.

"Good evening, Alice. I will call upon you tomorrow, and we will discuss my findings."

"Lady Alice, and I will not allow you entry." She then raised her chin and walked away from him, and he let her, watching the rigid line of her back until she reached the front door of her townhouse. It opened, and then she was gone from his sight.

Jamie should have told her about the Crimson Serpent. Every instinct said she deserved the truth, yet he'd convinced himself that a few weeks of silence would make no difference. He'd needed time to dig deeper, to be certain. At least, that's what he told himself.

He'd spent years putting his own safety above all else. After Blackwood Hall, he'd learned to protect what was left of him, never letting anyone close enough to wound him again. His friends were the exception, and even they only glimpsed pieces of him.

But as he stood in the chill night air, staring at the place where she'd vanished, a truth settled heavy in his chest. Lady Alice could reach him in ways no one else ever had. And if he wasn't careful, she'd be the one to undo him entirely.

"Do you wish for me to drive you home, my lord?"

"No, thank you, Ezra, I shall walk."

The man nodded, and the carriage rolled away.

After a last look at the Smythe townhouse, he headed toward his own. He had to find a way to get her to understand before she did something reckless. It was just pure luck she hadn't so far.

But there was so much more to his need to keep Lady Alice safe, even if Jamie refused yet to acknowledge it.

CHAPTER TWENTY-TWO

ALICE SAT AT her desk working through the accounts and ledgers that kept her father's estate and townhouse running, while she tried to push aside that moment in her carriage four days ago with Lord Stafford.

"For pity's sake, Alice, move on. I'm sure he has," she muttered. "Focus on the bookkeeping."

Shutting her eyes tight, she reopened them and studied the ledger before her.

Alice kept two sets of records, which was possibly wrong, but she had to be prepared for the day that she'd thought would never come. The day when her father wanted to be involved in running his life. That day appeared to be here.

She had a knack for making money. Her investments had returned excellent yields, and she'd managed to increase her family's coffers substantially. Alice had also taken the meagre amount of pin money he'd given her and grown that with calculated investments until she had a tidy sum of her own and did not have to rely on her father for financial support.

She had more than enough money to set up a household for herself and Aunt Gwen.

Her father's words when he'd appeared unexpectedly to inform her she needed to wed told Alice that securing somewhere for them to live was best done sooner rather than later.

There was also the matter of the clinic, which she'd set aside money for in the second set of books. After two hours, she'd worked through and checked everything. She and Aunt Gwen would be all right, as would be the clinic in the near future. But now, her need for others to help fund her dream was vital, so she had to talk to some of her peers and get them on board.

Alice listed a few she thought would be interested before closing the ledger.

A knock on the door had her putting the ledgers in the desk drawer and locking it, before saying, "Come in."

Phipps stood in the doorway.

"What is it, Phipps?"

"A Mr. Nevis, from Newbury, Fletcher, and Nevis has called and wishes to speak with you, my lady. Here is his card."

She took the white square card from Phipps and read the words, *Newbury, Fletcher, & Nevis Solicitors*. It seemed her father had wasted little time after she'd told him she would no longer take care of his business affairs. How lucky that she had prepared herself for this.

"A young boy has arrived at the back door also, my lady, and wishes to speak with you. He will not be deterred, even though Ezra tried to send him away."

"Thank you, Phipps. I shall come at once." *Was it the boy she'd met the night she'd watched Lord Stafford fight?*

She took some money from her desk and left her rooms. Hurrying down the rear stairs and into the kitchens, Alice saw Ezra's stance as threatening. Legs braced, arms folded, taking up every inch of the doorway.

"Thank you, Ezra, you can move now," Alice said, tapping his shoulder. It was harder than rock.

"He could be—"

"Move now, Ezra."

Reluctantly, he took a single step back, and Alice was able to slip around him and face the boy she had met that night, and who did not appear in any way intimidated by the large footman. She was sure in his brief life he'd seen his fair share of threatening behavior.

"Hello, do you have something you want to tell me?"

He nodded.

"What is your name?"

His eyes went over her shoulder, and she knew Ezra would be there looking menacing.

"For pity's sake, Ezra, he's a boy, and clearly no threat. Stand down at once."

Her footman grumbled like a disgruntled dog.

"I'm Bobby Mott," the boy said, face expressionless.

"And I am Lady Alice. Now what is it you wished to tell me, Bobby? Pay the large, glowering man at my back no mind; he always looks like that."

A small twitch on the left side of the boy's mouth was the only indication he was amused.

"A woman I know told me about a man who was a right mean one. Roughs up people for fun, especially if he's had too much to drink. Near enough killed a man for challenging him."

Alice felt her pulse kick up a beat.

"There's plenty like that around, but when she gave me his description, I thought he sounded like the man you asked me to find."

She nodded, hope battling with anger inside her. Jackson needed to be stopped from his continued assaults on people.

"I asked her to tell me where I could find him, and she said he moves around a lot, but lately is drinking at the Rusty Hook."

"Where is that?" Ezra demanded.

"Near the docks," Bobby said calmly. "I slipped inside four nights in a row, and the last one I heard someone call out the name Jackson. He matched your description, my lady, so I followed him when he left. He's staying at No. 22, Well Yard, off Marylebone Lane, St Marylebone."

"Thank you, Bobby, that is excellent information. Now tell me, are you hungry?"

The boy looked from her to Ezra, and then back to her. He

nodded.

"Well, you come inside then, and we'll see about changing that."

Alice then turned and waved Ezra back.

"He's a child, Ezra, have mercy," Alice said.

"Who's a child?" Maggie said, entering the kitchen.

"This boy is Bobby. He came with information for me and now needs some food. Ezra is deliberately intimidating him," Alice added.

Maggie was really the only person who could cow Ezra. He would die for her, and when she spoke, he usually listened.

"Move yourself, husband." Maggie pushed him in the belly. "Come inside, Bobby."

"I don't trust him," Ezra muttered.

"He's a boy, and he's hungry. It's not a matter of trust. It's a matter of giving to those that don't have enough food to fill their bellies, unlike you."

Ezra grunted again.

"Sit. You'll intimidate the poor lad." Maggie waved her husband to the chairs around a table where the staff took their meals. "I'll give him a wedge of cake. It may sweeten his sour demeanor." She leveled him with a hard look until he sat.

"Bobby, thank you for your information, and please stay and eat a meal with my staff," Alice said, waving the boy to the seat across from Ezra. "I have someone upstairs who needs to speak with me."

Alice hurried back up the stairs to her rooms and quickly jotted down the address Bobby had given her. Once that was done, she checked her appearance. Happy with what she saw, she headed for the parlor to where Mr. Nevis awaited her.

A short, bald man rose to greet her.

"How can I help you, Mr. Nevis?" Alice said after she'd taken a chair across from where he'd been sitting.

"Lord Smythe has sent a request that the firm of Newbury, Fletcher, & Nevis Solicitors take over the running of his affairs. I am here to take possession of any paperwork that may be here, my lady."

"Did my father tell you that in fact I have been running his affairs while he is living in France?"

The man gave her a tight smile that suggested he didn't believe that for one minute.

"If you will collect the necessary papers, I shall be on my way."

"If not me, then who do you believe has been taking care of things on Lord Smythe's behalf?" It was more curiosity than anything to see what would come out of the man's mouth next as to why she'd asked that question.

"Well, as to that, I couldn't say," Mr. Nevis said.

"And yet you are quite sure all the accounts and papers are in this house?"

He didn't look quite so smug now. In fact, he looked downright uncomfortable. Alice took pity on him. After all, this was not his fault, but her father's.

"I will return with what you require," she said, and left the room.

Alice removed the first set of books from her desk drawer and took them back to the parlor.

"Here you are, Mr. Nevis. Should you require any clarification, then—unfortunately for you—it is me you will have to come to." He said nothing further, just bowed and left.

Alice thought after this development it was time to have a conversation with her aunt about where she would like to live when her father returned to London with his new wife. She also had to decide what to do with the address and information regarding Jackson's location.

Alice paced her room after Mr. Nevis's departure. Returning to her desk, she picked up the slip of paper with the address Bobby had handed her, staring at it as if doing so would give her some clarity of what to do next. She and Ezra would need to go there and see for themselves if in fact it was Kenneth Jackson's location.

Alice sat, elbows on her desk, and allowed herself one long, shuddering exhale. "What am I to do with you, Jackson, when I find you?"

Something had to be done, and the hell of it was, it had been a relief to know Lord Stafford would help her in making that decision. But not now. Now she had to do that herself.

Alice had wondered if she was capable of violence and thought perhaps she would be when she came face to face with the man who had destroyed her brother. But the truth was she doubted she could do more than punch him, so her vengeance had to take another form.

A long voyage was the idea that had been growing inside her. Approach a ship's captain, or someone, perhaps that would fall to Ezra, who would take Jackson on a long voyage to the colonies and dump him there.

A knock interrupted her thoughts. "Come in."

Maggie entered with a tray of tea and a plate of scones. On her face was a smile.

"What has you smiling?" Alice said, pouncing on a scone as the plate was lowered to her desk.

"Ezra and Bobby are now deep in discussion about what it's like being a mudlark. It seems that's how the lad makes his living. 'Tis a right shame, my lady. Those who do that can die from horrid infections."

"It is indeed horrid, Maggie. I'm glad all is well between him and Ezra now. I'm sure Bobby could do with a large, intimidating friend."

Her maid went quiet as Alice looked at her. "Do I have jam on my nose?"

"No. You've got that look, my lady. The one where you're planning to do something that'll either get you hurt or have Ezra shouting until the windows shake."

Alice tried for innocence. "I was merely thinking."

"I know that boy gave you some information about that

Jackson, because Ezra told me."

Alice hesitated. Maggie had the tenacity of a terrier, like her husband. There was no evading. "Bobby gave me Jackson's address—or I hope it is."

Maggie's mouth pinched. "Sweet mercy. And what exactly do you plan to do with that, pray?"

"That is precisely what I am deciding," Alice admitted. "I cannot simply ignore it because, as you know, I've been searching for him for some time."

Maggie gave her a hard look. "You could hand it to Ezra and let him deal with it, instead of going after the man yourself. After all, my lady, what is it you think you can do when faced with him?"

Alice snorted. "Ezra would flatten every man he came in contact with to find Jackson, and then you would scold him for blood on his boots."

The door creaked again. Ezra himself filled the frame, glowering. "I heard that."

"Good." Maggie speared him with a look. "Now you can tell her she's not to go gallivanting after Kenneth Jackson."

Ezra crossed his arms. "You're not to go gallivanting after Kenneth Jackson without me or Lord Stafford at your side."

"Of course." Alice was fairly sure that could turn out to be a lie, but right then it wasn't.

Her staff then left her alone with tea and scones, which she steadily worked her way through as she thought up and discarded plans. Spreading a map of London across her desk, she traced the streets until she reached Marylebone Lane.

Alice would have to be careful. If Jackson spotted her, he might flee, because she knew he'd seen her that day Charles had come home, as she'd seen him.

Taking Ezra would draw attention as he was so large. She just needed proof that this was he, and then she could decide her next move. Perhaps she could stand outside the address and watch it for a while? No one need know, and then she'd come back to the townhouse.

The sound of a carriage stopping made her look out the window. The door opened, and Lord Stafford stepped down and then walked up the path to her door. She didn't want to speak to him. Not after what they'd shared in that carriage, and him betraying her.

A knock had Alice moving to the door and opening it.

"Lord Stafford is here to see you, my lady," Phipps said.

"Tell him I am not taking callers, please, Phipps."

He bowed and left. Alice moved back to the window and watched Lord Stafford leave. Reaching his carriage, he stopped and looked up to where she stood. She knew there was no way he could see her, but she drew back, heart thudding. Only when she heard the clop of hooves seconds later did Alice draw in a deep, shaky breath.

CHAPTER TWENTY-THREE

I N THE DAYS since Jamie had kissed Alice again, he'd called at her house twice. Both times her butler had said she was from home, and he couldn't tell if that was the truth or not, as the man's expression gave nothing away.

He'd then sent three notes stating he needed to speak with her. She'd ignored them. She'd also not attended any society events.

Two things gnawed at Jamie. The first was fear that Alice was out there somewhere in the dark, searching through the most dangerous corners of London in her relentless search for clues about Jackson. The second was harder to name, a dull ache lodged beneath his ribs. He told himself it was simply because he hadn't seen her lately, which was absurd. They'd never spent enough time together for her absence to hurt this much. Yet it did. The truth was simple: Lady Alice Smythe had come to matter to him more than he cared to admit. And for now, that was enough. Whatever the future brought, he'd face it after Jackson was found. Right now, he had to ensure Alice was safe.

Jamie then did something he had absolutely no right to do. He'd paid a man to watch her movements. She'd maim him if she found out, but it was the only way he could be sure she wasn't doing anything rash.

God's blood, what has become of me?

"I fear you're not concentrating, my lord."

"I fear you are correct and at this rate, you will be trouncing me soundly, Fletcher."

Jamie had found out from his butler, Radley, who knew through one of the maids, Ginny, that Fletcher, his footman, was in fact an excellent chess player. As Jamie loved chess, he'd instantly challenged the man to a game. That was two years ago, and they'd been playing often since.

"Well then, if I may say, checkmate, my lord."

"If it wouldn't be very wrong of me, Radley, I'd terminate your employment effective immediately." Jamie sighed. "Forgive me. It seems I was preoccupied this evening. I promise to be more alert next time."

"I shall look forward to it, my lord." His footman rose and put the pieces back in their box before leaving.

It wasn't late, but late enough that he should be heading out the door to a social engagement, but Jamie found little excitement in the prospect. He wanted Alice, and he wanted to find Jackson. Both were consuming him.

When Radley reappeared, he was still exactly where he'd been, staring at the chessboard.

"A Mr. Jonas has arrived, my lord, and wishes to speak with you, Lord Stafford."

Jamie was out of his chair so fast he tripped, but managed to right himself. He was then running out the door, past his butler. Taking the stairs two at a time, he arrived at the front door in seconds.

Mr. Jonas had once been a Bow Street Runner and now worked privately for anyone who needed him. He wore beige and gray, and to Jamie's mind was in perfect employment, as everything about the man except for a spectacular moustache was bland. He stood just inside the door, hat in hand, looking around the walls to where Jamie's austere ancestors hung, casting disapproving glances down on Jamie.

"Good evening, my lord," Mr. Jonas said, bowing.

"Good evening. What news do you have for me, Mr. Jonas?"

"I was watching Lady Alice Smythe's house as you directed, and thirty minutes ago she left it alone. If I may be bold, she appeared secretive. I followed, and she climbed into a hackney. I was able to hear the address she told the driver."

"How did she appear secretive?" Jamie asked instead of giving voice to the anger Mr. Jonas's words created.

"Dark cloak pulled over her head almost covering half her face. Constantly looking about her to see if anyone was watching. Also, she didn't call for her carriage but slipped out alone and then walked until she could hail a hackney. A lady of her rank—if you'll forgive me for saying—shouldn't be out alone and definitely not in a hackney."

I'm going to roar at her for an hour until she has a good grasp on not walking into a dangerous situation.

"I thought about following her, my lord, out of concern, but thought you would want to know with some expediency what she was about," the man said in a calm manner that Jamie was sure settled his clients. It did not settle him one bit.

"What address did she give the driver?" The words came out cold and hard.

"Well Yard, off Marylebone Lane, St Marylebone," Mr. Jonas said.

Not the worst street in London, Jamie thought, but still, she should not be out alone. *Where was her hulking footman?*

"Many thanks for this information, Mr. Jonas." Pulling some notes out of his inside pocket, he handed them to the man.

"Do you wish me to call your carriage, my lord?"

"No thank you, Radley, I shall take a hackney," Jamie said, already heading up the stairs.

Once he was dressed and armed with weapons and more money, Jamie headed out the door and hoped he reached Alice before more trouble befell her.

He ran to the end of the street and then down the next to a busier road and hailed a hackney. After giving the driver the address, he climbed inside.

Hands fisted on his knees with his jaw clenched tight enough to crack teeth, he ran through several different scenarios that could be happening to Alice. None of them made him any calmer. He had always prided himself on being a man of order and restraint, but Alice had reduced him to a raging fool who had hired a man to spy on her. Now he was rolling through London to chase after her.

Opening the hatch above his head, Jamie said, "I will pay you double if you pick up your pace, sir. It is of the utmost importance I reach my destination with expediency."

"Right you are!" the man replied.

Seconds later, Jamie felt the vehicle increase its speed.

"You'd better be safe when I reach you, Alice," he muttered.

The hackney jolted to a halt long minutes later. Jamie stepped down and paid the driver. He then took a deep breath of damp air. Marylebone was not the rookeries, but neither was it Mayfair. Shadows pooled in the narrow lanes, and the smell of coal smoke was thick.

Jamie reassured himself of the weight of his pistol before moving silently down Well Yard. A little cul-de-sac, hemmed in by crooked brick houses that leaned toward one another, it had no light except what the moon offered, or lights from the small windows of the buildings flanking it.

A burst of noise came from an open door as Jamie passed it. *Where are you, Alice, and why are you here?*

Well Yard, off Marylebone Lane, was a narrow, ill-lit close. A thin ribbon of fog crawling low on the ground curled around Jamie's boots as he walked.

Three tall buildings, with little ones wedged between, lay ahead of him. Number 22 stood at the far end, the last on the right, its brickwork dark with soot. A narrow iron external staircase ran up one side. Jamie slowed as he approached and turned up the collar of his coat against the wind.

He then made himself walk the length of the lane once more, boots silent on the stone, to see if he could locate Alice. He turned into the shadows behind the buildings, checking the narrow passage that ran between Number 22 and its neighbor. His eyes strained against the gloom as he searched for movement, or the familiar outline of a woman he could not forget. Alice.

There was no sign of her.

Returning to the front, he took the staircase up.

At the first landing, Jamie paused. The numbers on the doors lining the corridor were faintly visible where the moonlight pooled. Seventeen. The next, nineteen. Too low. He'd have to go higher.

He stepped back toward the railing and tilted his head. The upper floors loomed above, the staircase zigzagging into darkness. A flicker of movement caught his eye at the next level. Someone was looking down at him.

For one suspended moment, he could make out the faintest silhouette. A woman, maybe? Before he could call out, they vanished, the figure swallowed by shadow. Then came the sound of running feet. Light, and quick.

"Alice?" His voice came rougher than he intended.

No answer.

Jamie took the stairs up two at a time. The iron rattled beneath him and the cold air burned his lungs. At the second floor, the first door bore the number 20. He strode along the corridor—21, 22—and kept going to the end where another set of stairs descended at the back.

"Damn it," he muttered.

He could hear her now, or whoever it was, the fading echo of footsteps below. She'd taken the back way. Without thinking, Jamie jumped the last few steps and landed hard, his boots splashing through a shallow puddle.

The passage opened into the cul-de-sac at the far side of the yard. Moonlight silvered the rooftops, but the street itself lay in shadow. Stopping at the mouth of the alley, he searched left and right, heart pounding. Nothing moved except a scrap of newspaper caught in the wind.

Then, voices.

Male and growing louder. Three of them, maybe more, coming from the left. Jamie pressed himself into the shadows. If Alice were still here, she'd have done the same. He prayed she had.

The men turned the corner. One carried a lantern that threw a greasy circle of light across the walls. Jamie caught their faces as they passed, and his breath froze.

Kenneth Jackson.

The shock of recognition punched through him like a fist. Before reason could stop him, Jamie stepped out into the light.

CHAPTER TWENTY-FOUR

JACKSON'S FACE WAS unmistakable even in the patchy moonlight and as smug as the last time he had seen him. The bastard had changed little over the years. Two big men flanked him. Brutes with enormous fists and mean looks in their eyes.

"Well, well," Jackson drawled, his voice slick with mockery. "If it isn't Lord High-and-Mighty Stafford sniffing around where he don't belong. I've been informed that someone has been asking questions about me. Was that you?"

"Don't belong?" Jamie raised a brow and told himself to stay calm. He was outnumbered, and not thinking clearly would not help that. "Come now, one would think, considering you were employed as a housemaster in a prestigious school, you could articulate a sentence correctly, Jackson. It's where he doesn't belong. And, of course, I belong anywhere I choose, because I am a marquess, and you—well, you're a nobody."

Jamie's body thrummed with rage, but he forced his voice steady. "And I'm sure I'm not the only one hunting you, like the animal you are. There are the many boys you tortured for fun at Blackwood Hall before you were dismissed for stealing."

Jackson inhaled, the smug look fleeing.

"I know everything there is to know about you, Jackson. The charity school, the girls in the Crimson Serpent, the list goes on," Jamie said.

"I've been watching you and yours too. I know what you've

been doing," Jackson snarled. "You don't scare me, Stafford. You're a weak-kneed noble, just like you were as a boy at my mercy." He turned to look at the men with him. "He used to cry like a baby all the time. Pathetic, he was."

Jamie had known that when the day came that he confronted Jackson, he'd be bombarded by memories, but right then, he couldn't afford to let them consume him. He had to stay clear headed and focused.

He wants you to get angry.

"Come now, not just any baby, but one of noble birth, unlike you. I walk in society, and sit in the House of Lords, Jackson." The rage on the man's face made him smile.

There was no doubt Jackson enjoyed the treatment he'd meted out at Blackwood Hall, but Jamie and his friends believed some of his anger had stemmed from his birth. He'd been jealous of the titles the boys under his care held, and he'd extracted retribution and money from them for his lack of one.

"I don't need blue blood to be important, Stafford."

Jamie looked at the buildings around him and then back at Jackson. "Yes, I can see how important you are by your current lodgings." The words came out heavily laced with sarcasm. "Come now, Jackson. We both know it bothers you very much that you're not one of the elite in London society, and never will be."

Jamie assessed the situation as Jackson hissed out an angry breath. If he reached for his gun, they'd be on him in seconds, but he had no other options, other than his fists, and those he would be using after he fired the first shot.

"Were you behind the good men who worked with me in Blackwood Hall ending their days in prison?" Jackson snarled out the words. "My friends," he added.

"Good men?" Jamie forced out a bark of laughter. "Do you mean the low-life scum like you who preyed on boys for fun? Men who inflicted pain for some kind of sick and twisted thrill?" The words came out like a low growl of thunder. "Yes, I harmed your friends and made them pay, and now it's your turn."

"You were a sniveling boy," Jackson snarled, "and cowed like a baby when I beat you and your friends. You—"

Jamie moved so fast the two men with Jackson didn't see it. He then punched the man as hard as he could in the face. The satisfying crack of his nose was his last thought as the two brutes were on him seconds later, while Jackson howled in pain and dropped to his knees.

Jamie reached for his gun, but he had no time, as one man lashed out with a fist. This would be a fight for his life.

He swung, punching the man hard in the jaw, but he didn't go down, just grunted. The second charged, slamming Jamie into the nearest wall. Pain shot through his shoulder, but he shoved him back and drove a punch into his gut.

Then Jackson, who had staggered to his feet, blood pouring from his nose, lunged. Jamie ducked the first blow, landed one to Jackson's ribs, but he didn't go down. Short but solid, the man could clearly take a punch.

"I will end you, Stafford, never doubt that now," Jackson hissed. "Your death will come at my hands—if not now, then soon!"

Two against one became three against one, and Jamie's body began to take the punishment. Fists to his gut, knees to his ribs, a brutal swing that split his lip. He gave as good as he got, but the numbers weren't in his favor. He managed to punch Jackson again, and this time he stayed down. At least he would meet his maker, if that happened, knowing he'd inflicted pain on the man who had given him the same and worse.

Jamie spat blood onto the cobbles as a fist smashed into his stomach, folding him in two. Another cuff caught him behind the ear, sending stars spinning across his vision. He staggered, nearly dropped to his knees.

And then—

"Stop!"

A voice cut through the night like a whipcrack.

All four men turned. Jamie managed to straighten.

Alice stood a few feet from them, cloak thrown back, pistol raised with both hands. Moonlight gleamed off the steel barrel, and her eyes blazed with fury. At her side was a boy.

"Step away from him," she said, voice ice cold.

For a moment, none of them moved. Then one of the men laughed. "Well, ain't this a pretty picture? Little lady come to rescue her lord with a mongrel. Put that pistol away, sweetheart, before you hurt yourself."

"I ain't no mongrel like you," the boy said in a hard voice. "You're scum."

Alice cocked the pistol with a snap that echoed off the walls and fired as one of the men lunged for the boy. He staggered back, clutching his shoulder, howling in pain.

Jamie pulled his pistol from his pocket. He could barely see as his vision was blurred and his body one big ache.

"Give me that." Alice took his pistol and handed hers to the boy. She aimed it at the only man still standing. "Now we are leaving, and if you try and follow, I will shoot you as I have your friend."

Jamie was looking at Alice, but when he turned back, it was in time to see Jackson fleeing, throwing over his shoulder the words, "You'll die at my hand soon, Stafford!"

"Damn," he muttered, knowing there was no chance he could follow in his current condition.

"We will get him, but now we are leaving," Alice said in a cool, clear voice. "Can you walk, my lord?"

"Aye," was all Jamie could manage. "You go first, Alice."

If the man decided to come at them for retribution, it would be through Jamie, even if his body was one large ache, and he wasn't sure how much longer he'd be standing. He'd been in pain before, and this was no different.

"Foolish men," she muttered as one of the thugs hoisted his friend over his shoulder and disappeared into the darkness behind Jackson.

"Alice," he rasped. "You shouldn't be here."

"You're welcome," she said tartly, though he noted her hands trembled as she lowered the pistol. "Now, can you walk or not?"

"Of course, I can walk," Jamie said, straightening, only to wince as pain lanced through his ribs. "Mostly."

"Mostly will not do." She slipped an arm around his waist, ignoring his protests. "Take his other side, Bobby."

The boy moved and slid an arm around Jamie's back.

"Come on. Hackney's waiting."

"I don't need—"

"Do not finish that sentence," she snapped, hauling his weight with surprising strength. "You'll only embarrass yourself."

Jamie gave a hoarse laugh, then groaned. Together they stumbled down the lane. Alice helped support him, pistol still clutched in her free hand. Jamie cursed under his breath with every jolt, but he let her guide him.

The hackney driver's eyes went wide as they approached. "Good Lord!"

Between her and the boy, they got Jamie inside. He slumped against the seat, breath ragged, face bruised, blood trickling from a cut above his eye. Alice climbed in beside him.

"You too, Bobby."

"I'll make me own way."

"No, you won't. Get in this carriage at once."

The boy looked from her to Jamie. "I'll sit with him." He pointed upward, which Jamie thought meant the driver.

"Give the driver my address," Alice said.

The hackney lurched forward seconds later, and they were rolling away from Well Yard.

Inside, silence stretched, broken only by Jamie's uneven breathing. Finally, he turned his head, swollen lip quirking in a faint smile. "Alice Smythe, my savior. You'll never let me live this down, will you?"

She glared at him, though her eyes shone suspiciously. "Not in a thousand years."

"Good." He let his eyes close, exhaustion dragging him under. "Then perhaps you'll finally stop ignoring my notes. But just so you know, I will be yelling at you for the reckless risk you took tonight when I can…yell, that is." Jamie hurt everywhere.

"I believe I have told you already, you have no say in what I do, Lord Stafford." She took a handkerchief out of her pocket and pressed it to his lip.

"If I apologize again for my high-handed behavior, will you this time forgive me?" Jamie's words were muffled by the cotton.

"We shall see," was all she said, and for now it was enough. Jamie sat back and closed his eyes and tried not to think about the fact Jackson had escaped him, but he wasn't as angry as he should be, because Alice was here with him.

❦ ⬦ ❦

CHAPTER TWENTY-FIVE

THE FIRST THING Alice noticed was the blood.

It dripped from the gash on his cheek and trickled onto his split lip. The handkerchief she pressed to it was soon stained. Her hand shook so badly she nearly dropped the linen. Alice felt her stomach twist with ice-cold fear.

Dear God, he looked terrible. What if there was something more sinister than what she could see going on inside him? Something that would snuff out the life of this man.

No, don't think like that. He would be all right—he had to be.

Bruises already mottled his face, and one eye was swollen. He had to have damaged ribs, because those men had battered them with their fists. Alice had seen it all from the shadows, where she and Bobby were hidden.

"Wh-where are you hurt, my lord?"

His eyes remained closed, lashes dark against his pale skin.

"Jamie," he breathed. "My name is Jamie. And you are Alice. I think after what we've shared, we are beyond titles."

Alice's heart clenched. He was speaking. He was alive. That had to be good—didn't it?

She moved the handkerchief higher, pressing it firmly against his cheek. His jaw tightened, but he didn't flinch.

"And I hurt everywhere. But I have felt this way before, so this too shall pass."

She wanted to shake him. Foolish man. He was bleeding,

broken, yet still determined to sound as though this were nothing more than a trifling inconvenience. *Is this how the beast that was Kenneth Jackson in Blackwood Hall had left him feeling?*

Alice could not think of that now, because that would mean she would think of Charles and his suffering.

"Where did you find Bobby?" he rasped.

"'Tis a long story."

"As you see, I am not going anywhere until we stop." His lips twitched faintly.

She'd seen so much violence tonight. Her entire body had trembled witnessing it. But Alice was strong, and she wouldn't let it show. She'd learned to hide just as this man had.

"When I saw you fighting that night in that warehouse," she said, "I came across him. I asked whether he had heard the name Kenneth Jackson before. Bobby said he had not. I offered him money if he would come to me with any information about him. Children are often seen and not heard.

Jamie's head moved, the smallest of nods, slow and stiff as if the motion cost him dearly.

"He came to my father's townhouse with information that Jackson lived at Well Yard off Marylebone Lane."

Jamie's lashes lifted. His eyes, dulled with pain but still sharp, locked on hers.

"You should not have gone there alone, Alice."

Her chin tilted, anger and fear roiling inside her. "Neither should you, considering it is you before me bruised and battered, and I was not alone. I had Bobby. I found him watching the property." She pressed the cloth harder. He hissed between his teeth.

"Had those men set upon you," he said tightly, "the outcome might have been more than a few broken ribs and bruises. The boy could not have saved you." The words were muffled behind the cloth.

"I had planned only to observe," she shot back. Alice then asked the question that had been bothering her since she'd seen him fighting with those men. "How is it you were there tonight, my lord?"

The carriage lurched over a rut, and his whole body stiffened. The hiss of pain was loud in the small space. Alice winced.

"My lord—"

"Jamie," he interrupted, breath rough. "Say my name, and I might tell you the truth. Not that it will please you. But in the interests of honesty… and the belief that you won't harm me in this condition, I will." His cracked lips curved slightly in a smile again.

"Jamie." The name felt foreign on her tongue, and forbidden.

She eased the cloth away, noting the bleeding had slowed, and then took the seat across from him.

"There now, that wasn't so hard," he murmured, opening his eyes. Pain glimmered in their green depths.

She folded her arms, fighting to keep her face composed. Alice would hear the sound of those men punching him forever, she was sure of it.

"I had you watched."

Alice froze. Her mouth opened. Closed. Opened again. Finally, she found her words. "I beg your pardon?"

"When you refused to speak with me," he said without the slightest trace of guilt, "I paid someone to watch you. In case you threw yourself headlong into trouble again, which you did tonight."

The sheer audacity robbed her breath. He sat there, bloody, bruised, impossibly handsome despite it all, and confessed to such high-handed behavior as if it were no more than commenting on the weather.

Alice squeezed her eyes shut, attempting to regain her wits. When she opened them, her gaze was narrowed. He was big, broad, steady, and a man built to be leaned upon. A man people like his friends and family trusted. But not her. Never her. She had loved and trusted once, and when Charles died, it had nearly destroyed her.

"Speak, Alice, before you explode," he said mildly. "My sisters hold their thoughts when I annoy them, and the suspense of their retribution is terrifying." His words came out slurred, his lip swollen, but the arrogant grin remained.

"Your sisters have my sympathies if they must endure you as their brother." She surged forward, trembling with fury. "How dare you! And how bloody dare you laugh at me!" Her hand itched to slap that look from his face.

"I am not laughing, I was merely—"

"You had no right!" the words exploded out of Alice, "to behave in such a—such a—high-handed manner!" She jabbed a finger in his direction. "I—I—"

"For pity's sake, take a breath. Your face is going red."

Alice inhaled sharply, because he was right, and she loathed him for it. She then exhaled with enough force to extinguish a hearth fire.

"In my defense, it was concern that had me doing what I did. Worry over what Jackson is capable of." He lifted his battered hand, knuckles raw and bleeding. "I know first-hand how evil he is, and I wanted to ensure you remained unhurt if you took it into your head to find him again."

Those words did not mollify her one bit. "I am a woman who can look after herself, damn you!"

"When the man I stationed outside your townhouse came to report to me you'd left the house alone," Jamie continued calmly, "he said your actions appeared secretive."

Alice's cheeks burned hot. Her earlier terror and worry for him were abating. Now she just wanted to yell at him. In fact, she enjoyed the rush of heat anger gave her, because it pushed aside the fear.

"I," she jabbed a finger into her chest, "have looked after myself since my father left to be with his mistress, and my brother returned from Blackwood Hall broken." Her voice shook. "I run my father's estates. I make him money, and do not need any man," she jabbed the finger in his direction now, "interfering.

How dare you have me watched!"

Her shriek rang off the carriage walls, making him wince.

The roof hatch above banged open. Bobby's wide eyes appeared. "Is everything all right, Lady Alice?"

"Yes," she gritted, teeth clenched. "Thank you, Bobby."

The boy hesitated, then vanished. The hatch snapped shut.

Jamie's smile fell from his lips. "Your father left you to go to France to be with his mistress?"

Alice drew in a steadying breath. "My point is—"

"He left you to care for your brother?" His eyes burned with fury now, but it wasn't aimed at her. It was for her. Alice refused to acknowledge how good that felt, because it was rare someone worried about her other than her aunt. *Don't soften. Stay angry.*

"I'm sorry, Alice."

She stiffened as he leaned forward, his long legs bracketing hers, trapping her in the narrow space. Even bruised and bleeding, his nearness unsettled her.

"I don't want your pity," she hissed. "I want you to understand that, unlike others in society, I need no man to assist me with anything."

He studied her in silence, gaze steady, penetrating, even considering the pain he must be suffering.

Then the carriage jolted again, and a ragged groan tore from his throat.

"For pity's sake, sit back, you fool," she snapped.

He obeyed, settling gingerly against the seat. A long breath rattled from his chest. His head tipped back, eyes closing once more.

Alice was still angry, but beneath it lay something far more dangerous, she realized. Relief that he still breathed. She would think later about how much she needed this man to live.

She glared at him, hands clenched tight in her lap, and yet her heart thudded unevenly as she understood just what she'd learned this night. Lord Stafford was coming to mean something to her.

A heavy silence settled inside the hackney as they headed toward the Smythe townhouse. Alice turned to look out the window, thoughts swirling around inside her head. If she had not arrived when she had, there was no doubt those men would have killed Jamie.

"Unclench your fists, Alice. Everything will be all right." There was no humor or mockery in his words now. She turned from the window to look at him then.

"You can't know that."

"You're right, I can't, and between us we know the darker side of life, but I will promise you this."

"What?" Alice asked as his eyes held hers.

"I promise I will get Kenneth Jackson and make him pay for what he did to me, Charles, and others. I also promise from this day onward, I will not keep secrets from you."

Emotion threatened to choke her then. Why was he the man to make her feel things she'd never felt before? It was messy and uncomfortable, and she wanted none of it.

"Thank you for saving me," he whispered, and then he closed his eyes again, as if just speaking those few words had sapped his remaining strength. "And just so you understand. I did not have you protected because I didn't think you strong enough to look after yourself. It was because I watch over the people in my life who I care for."

CHAPTER TWENTY-SIX

N O, HE HADN'T meant it like that, at least, she told herself he hadn't. She wasn't *important* to him, not in the way his words had suggested. He'd only been worried she'd gone after Jackson, and that she'd left the house chasing a lead. That was all.

But still… he'd said *care*.

The word echoed in her head as warmth unfurled through her, no matter how she tried to smother it. Jamie was in pain, and he hadn't meant to say what he had. He'd never bring it up again, and she'd pretend she didn't remember. People said things they didn't mean when emotions ran high.

But that single word lingered, refusing to fade, no matter how hard she tried to let it go.

The carriage swayed as thoughts tumbled around inside Alice's head, and then slowed as the familiar façade of her father's townhouse appeared. She pushed the turmoil aside, relieved that they would soon be out of here and someone could help Jamie.

The door swung wide before the carriage had fully stopped, and Bobby stood there.

"I need you to go inside and rouse Ezra, Bobby." The boy took off up the steps and soon disappeared inside the house.

"Come along, we shall get you inside, Jamie."

"Alice, I should go to my townhouse." The words had no strength and were more a painful wheeze now.

"I have a maid who tends to anyone who is sick in my household. She will tend you, and then we will send you home."

"Where have you been, Lady Alice?" Ezra's bellow was loud enough to reach all residents on the street.

"Someone is unhappy," Jamie whispered.

Ezra stomped down the steps behind Bobby. Her footman nudged the boy to one side as they reached the hackney, and looked in.

"No time for censuring now, Ezra. We need to help Lord Stafford."

"You're not very good at watching her, Ezra," Jamie said, the words sounding slurred as he battled the pain.

"I didn't know she was sneaking out of the house," Ezra snarled.

"I'm sure it's not the first time," Jamie added.

"Yes, thank you, that will do," Alice told both men. "We need to get him inside for Maggie to see to his injuries, and then get him home."

"I could have called a doctor."

Ezra snorted at Jamie's words. "A doctor has little skill. My wife, however, does. Now come along with you." He reached in to help her from the carriage. "You and I will be having words soon."

"As you can imagine, it's a moment I'm looking forward to," Alice muttered.

"I can get myself out," she heard Jamie protest.

"I can see the state you're in, my lord. It's best you let me aid you."

Jamie appeared with Ezra helping him. Then Ezra and Bobby took a side, and they walked slowly up toward the front door of the townhouse.

They made a strange procession up the steps. A bruised lord, a stubborn lady, a barefoot boy, and her angry footman. In the entry hall, the lamps had been turned up and Alice noted Maggie and Phipps were standing inside.

"Take him to the first room upstairs," Alice said. "Maggie,

bring your things. Phipps, get a basin of water and some cloths.

"And shall I call a doctor, my lady?"

"No, thank you, Phipps, we shall see what Maggie says first."

Orders steadied her and always had. When Charles came home a different person and after her father left, it had been her that people turned to for instruction.

They got Jamie upstairs, and he'd stopped protesting in favor of panting from the exertion as they finally lowered him onto the bed.

"Did his body take a beating also?" Ezra asked her as he stood glowering down at the marquess, who was now leaning on the pillows.

"It did, yes," Alice said.

"Well then, let's have your jacket off, my lord."

Ezra began removing Jamie's clothing. He hissed in pain several times, but finally the jacket was off. Next came his necktie.

"Right, then, let's see what we have," Maggie said, bustling in as Ezra was removing Jamie's shirt. "You'll step back, or better yet, leave the room, Lady Alice, but knowing your stubborn streak, I'm doubting you'll do that."

She should leave the room. Alice knew that. It wasn't right for her to be here with him while he wore no shirt. But then, it wasn't right for him to be here in her father's townhouse either, she reminded herself.

The linen peeled away. Alice swallowed. The sight should not have winded her, yet it did. The breadth of him, the pale stretch of torso now marred with bruises forming over his ribs. A long mark scored his side. Had someone's ring done that? Dark hair dusted his chest, trailing lower to the line of his trousers where her eyes had no business dwelling. Her gaze moved back up his body and collided with his.

His mouth wore a small smile, and Alice couldn't believe he had the nerve to be amused.

"I'd like a few words with those who did this," Ezra growled.

"Aye, well, you're not," Maggie said, dropping a cloth in the basin. She then touched Jamie's body with fingers that had soothed fevers and aided any number of household ailments, including Alice's, over the years. Jamie's jaw clenched under each probe. When Maggie touched the worst of the bruising along his ribs, a moan escaped him.

Alice stood still and wanted savagely—not for the first time tonight—to destroy the men who had done this. Jackson needed to pay for those he'd hurt and tormented.

"Bruised ribs," Maggie diagnosed, her tone grim. "Not broken through, praise be. Your cuts will need cleaning. You'll curse my name for the next quarter hour, and after that you'll rest easier. Laudanum?"

"No," Jamie said.

"Yes," Alice added.

His eyes met hers again. "I will not lose my wits by drinking that stuff."

"You'll be in agony if you do not," she returned. "A small dose, Maggie. Enough to take the edge and no more," Alice insisted.

She ignored his protests and took the liquid Maggie poured onto a spoon. He refused to open his mouth, looking like a small child.

"I will hold your nose, while Ezra is holding down your hands if you don't take this, my lord," Alice said, leaning over him.

"I don't want to dream."

The words were whispered, but she heard them. There was pain behind them. Had he been forced to take laudanum when he was hurt at Blackwood Hall?

"I promise to be there if you dream," Alice whispered so only he could hear.

For long moments she held his eyes, and then his mouth opened and she poured the liquid down his throat. He grimaced at the bitter taste.

"Right," Maggie said, "we need to bind those ribs now. Help

him rise, Ezra."

"I can do that without help."

"I'm sure you can, but as my wife gave an order, you'll forgive me but it must be obeyed," Ezra said.

He then levered Jamie forward by sliding an arm around his back. Alice moved to the other side of the bed to help keep him there. His skin felt hot, and his body hard beneath her hand. She focused on her maid's actions and not the fact that Lord Stafford was half naked in her house.

Maggie wound the bandage tight around Jamie's ribs. With each pass, he went rigid, then forced himself to relax. Alice could feel every tremor that didn't show on his face. On the third pull of the bandage, his hand shot out and caught the fingers of her other hand.

"Nearly done," Alice soothed.

Maggie tied the last knotting of the bandage. "Lie back, my lord."

Alice and Ezra eased him down and he released her fingers. Sweat beaded at his temple, and she hoped the laudanum would ease some of his pain soon.

"Now we need to clean the cuts," Maggie said. "And you get him something to put on that is not torn and bloody."

"Pass a cloth," Alice added.

Maggie held one out to her, and she took it. She dabbed the cut high on Jamie's cheek, and then moved to the split in his lip. He watched her face, the intent look in his green eyes unsettling.

"You have a determined expression," he murmured.

"I am determined not to let you bleed on my sheets, my lord."

"Jamie."

She finished with the lip and then smoothed some salve Maggie held out to her over the cuts.

"I have brought tea and brandy," Phipps announced from the doorway.

"He can't have brandy surely if he's just had laudanum?"

Alice asked.

"I am sure my constitution requires it," Jamie said gravely.

"Your constitution requires sense." Maggie nodded to the glass Phipps carried on the tray. "A small sip only if you please, my lord, and then you'll rest."

This time he braced himself, easing upright to settle on the pillows. He then took the brandy and a small sip.

"You have my thanks for taking care of me, Maggie," Jamie said. "I feel a great deal better already."

Ezra returned with some clothes and placed them at the foot of the bed.

"I'll be back soon to check on you," Maggie said, collecting her supplies.

Alice's staff then all left, with Ezra the last. He left the door open wide after giving her a look she had no idea how to interpret.

She should leave. Move away from the bed that held the large disturbing male and go to hers. She needed to wash, and then sleep, but Alice knew she would not get much of that knowing that Jamie was close.

"Thank you, Alice." The words were whispered and a little slurred, which told her the laudanum was now working.

"You've already thanked me, so you need not do so again. Now I think you need to lie down again and sleep, Jamie. It is the best thing for you. When you wake, we shall get you home."

He did as she said and eased back down the bed, resting his head on a pillow. She watched his dark lashes lower on to pale cheeks, and only a few minutes went by before he slept.

Standing there looking at this strong, powerful man brought low enough to fall asleep in her company made something stir inside her. Alice had to fist her hands to stop them from stroking his hair or cheek.

She dragged her eyes from Jamie when Ezra returned. He stepped to her side.

"Bobby said he went outside to check the street in front of

your townhouse, Lady Alice," Ezra whispered, mouth grim. "Says he saw a man in a dark coat loitering across the way. When I went out to take a look, he'd gone."

"Lord Stafford had a man watching the townhouse," she said, not meeting his gaze. "It could be him. But in case it is not, then Bobby should not go outside again, Ezra," she whispered.

"I know that, but he's used to doing as he wishes, my lady. He is now safe and will be going nowhere again. Phipps is making him stay here."

"Good." Alice didn't know what she would do for the boy, but she knew she wanted to do something.

"While it relieves me Lord Stafford set a man to watching your townhouse, I'll still have your word you'll not go back there, to where Lord Stafford was harmed, my lady."

"Ezra—"

"It's not right for you to do so, and you know it. He's hurting because of the people he met there, the same people who could have hurt you."

She sighed. "I know, and I'm sorry I didn't tell you."

That mollified him slightly because his scowl eased. He looked at Jamie.

"I'll not wake him now to change him, as it's my belief he'll sleep right through until morning after the beating he's taken," Ezra said. "But I'll check on him again soon, before I find my bed."

"Thank you, and yes, rest is the best thing for him." Alice looked back down at Jamie. He hadn't moved, but she knew that in the morning, to do so would cause him a lot of pain.

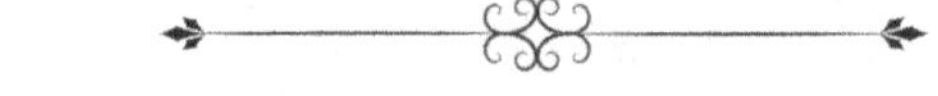

CHAPTER TWENTY-SEVEN

JAMIE WOKE SUDDENLY when he felt the lash on his back.

"A dream," he reminded himself. Heart pounding, he forced himself upright until he was seated on the side of the bed. His body ached as he moved, but he wouldn't lie there and fall back into another nightmare.

Inhaling deeply, he exhaled slowly. When he was calmer, he pushed himself up and off the bed. His ribs tugged viciously, but if he moved, it would help rid his head of the lingering dark, the feel of that whip and the other things he'd been tortured with alongside his friends.

It was seeing Jackson again that had stirred everything up inside him.

It had been years ago, and yet still the remnants of that hell lingered. Rearing their heads to remind him of what he and so many others had endured.

Running a hand through his sweat-drenched hair, Jamie paced slowly to the window, moving his abused body to loosen it up.

He loathed any form of weakness inside him. Loathed being vulnerable, and kept himself in peak condition so no one would ever control or hurt him again. But he'd not been able to stop those men, and that chafed at him, because he'd not been able to stop those who had abused him as a boy either.

Pushing the curtain aside, he noted it was still the early hours of the morning. He had not been sleeping long. That bloody laudanum. They'd held him down at Blackwood Hall and forced it down his throat. He'd loathed it ever since.

The sound of the door opening had him turning, body tensing. He watched her walk in and look to the bed. Finding it empty, she searched the room and located Jamie.

"Is everything all right, Jamie?"

Alice moved closer slowly, and the weak light coming in the window allowed him to see she was wearing a white nightdress and a thick woollen shawl. The soft material floated around her ankles as she moved. Jamie felt his pulse quicken.

He knew he couldn't let himself get closer to Alice, because he had nothing to offer a woman more than his title and perhaps a child, that was. Alice deserved more from her future husband. She deserved to be loved.

"All is well, Alice. Go back to your bed."

Jamie knew she wasn't one to follow orders, but he had to try. She kept walking until she was inches from where he stood. Her eyes studied him, running over his face.

"What has happened?"

"Nothing. How could it here in your townhouse?" But he heard the rasp of uncertainty in his voice, just as she did.

"Did the laudanum give you bad dreams?"

Her hair was in a long braid and hung over her left shoulder. Jamie clenched his hands into fists so he wouldn't reach for it. He wanted to test the texture and bring it to his lips.

"You need to go back to your room, my lady." He'd used her title deliberately to put distance between them. She didn't speak, just stood there watching him.

"Why are you here in this room, Alice?

"I woke and thought to check on you, to ensure you needed nothing," she said. "Would you like help to get back into the bed?"

"I managed to get here. I'm sure I can make it back." He sounded petulant, and didn't seem able to stop himself.

They stared at each other then, and Jamie knew his eyes would be filled with hunger. Leaning closer, he saw something in hers. Wariness perhaps? She had every right to feel that way, because right then, he wanted to touch Alice. Wanted to lose himself in her to chase away the pain and lingering traces of what had woken him. If he was in his townhouse, he'd go to his room and punch his bag.

"I will leave," Jamie said, not moving. "No one can know I am here."

"No one knows," she said, her tone soothing. "I'm sure we can get you home without detection, Jamie."

"It is not me I am worried for," he snapped back.

"I care nothing for that. In fact, I am making plans to leave London and likely never return."

"Why?" That he may never see this woman again disturbed him a great deal.

"Some things have changed, but that is nothing that concerns you. Now come, you need your sleep." Her hand touched his arm. It was only brief, but he felt it.

Jamie looked down at her fingers and could do nothing to stop from settling his over them. Hers turned and slid through his.

"Alice." Her name came out strangled. "Leave here now."

"You will not hurt me, nor could you in your current condition," she said with a small smile, as if teasing him.

She should be bloody terrified. He wanted to pull her close and feel all her heat and lush curves pressed to his body. Wanted to lose himself in this woman he'd come to need.

He should step away. Instead, he lifted their joined hands and placed them against his bare chest. Her gaze flicked up as she no doubt felt the thud of his heart.

"What really woke you, Jamie?"

"I was dreaming," he admitted.

"And I promised to be here, so here I am," she whispered. "Do you dream of Blackwood Hall often?"

Her lovely eyes were steady on his and Jamie saw the compassion and felt the last of his restraint start to slip. He didn't bother to deny her words, so he nodded.

"I want that bastard to hurt as he hurt you and my brother."

Her words surprised a huff of laughter out of him because he'd not expected them.

"He will pay, Alice. Have no fear of that."

"We will make him pay," she added.

She stood on her toes and then, with a boldness that stole his breath, brushed her lips to his cheek. The simplest of touches, and yet heat rolled through him at the feel of those warm lips.

Move away from her, Jamie. She is not like other women. She's not someone you can touch and walk away from.

"What are you doing, Alice?" His words sounded raw and hungry.

"Let me light the lamp," she said instead of answering him. "You look pale." She backed away, but only one step.

"No."

"Will you sit then?"

"I am strong enough to take a beating, Alice. Have no fear I am about to faint." He'd been telling himself he was strong for many years. In fact, since he'd left Blackwood Hall, it was a constant refrain running through his head.

"I know you are strong, Jamie, but anyone who took the beating you did still needs to take care of themselves until they are healed."

"Will you tell me about this clinic of yours, Alice?"

"You have an excellent memory."

He didn't answer, just studied her.

"I run a medical clinic where those who can't afford it get help. I have a wonderful doctor, who actually treats nobility, who was willing to work with these patients three times a week.

"You are an amazing woman, Lady Alice," he said quietly. "And I want to know more about that, soon. But not now. Right now, I have another question." Their eyes met. "Why will you leave London, Alice?"

If he kept talking, perhaps he could stop his mind from fixating on the way that thin cotton nightdress clung to her body, and how much he wanted to strip it away.

"It need not concern you," she said, voice cool and steady.

"So I am to bare all," he countered, "and you will tell me nothing in return?"

"You are as secretive as I, Jamie, and you will not convince me otherwise."

She wasn't wrong. Few were ever granted access to his innermost thoughts. Sometimes his two closest friends caught a glimpse, but never anyone else. Not even his sisters knew the dark things he carried inside his head.

"You know something about me only two others and those responsible do," Jamie replied.

"Yes, I know what you suffered at Blackwood Hall, and am sorry for it."

He moved closer, taking one of her hands in his. He squeezed gently, but did not speak.

"My father came to visit me yesterday."

"And that was a bad thing?" Jamie took the other hand she now had clenched into a fist.

"I shouldn't be telling you this," she whispered, looking down at her hands in his.

"Your secrets are safe with me, as mine are with you, Alice."

"He wants to bring his mistress back to London to marry, and then live in society."

He knew there was more, so Jamie kept quiet, watching the emotions in her pretty eyes.

"But he has no wish for his daughter to be here when he does. So I am to find a husband and be gone from here and his estate. Apparently, Lord Braxton would be the perfect candidate." The words came out cold.

"No," Jamie said instantly. "He will not be."

Her eyes lifted to his. "I would rather marry a rodent."

The lingering fear from his dream was gone, and in its place was anger. No parent should force a child from their home, and especially not the daughter who had kept everything running while her father gallivanted with his mistress in France!

"I do not know your father—"

"You are lucky in that. He's a weak-kneed imbecile," Alice snapped, cutting him off.

"Unlike his daughter, who is beautiful, intelligent, and perhaps a little rash," Jamie added.

Her eyes settled on his then, and he had no idea what she was seeking, but knew it was something.

"I will not marry," she whispered, her soft breath brushing his lips. "I have plans that do not include being under a man's control."

"What plans?"

"It matters not—"

"It matters to me."

"Why?" The question was a whisper.

Jamie wasn't sure who closed the distance but soon they were kissing. Just a brush of their lips but it was enough to ignite him. Her scent, so familiar now, wrapped around him.

"Alice," he rasped as he eased back. "We shouldn't do that."

"I know." She tugged her hands from his and framed his face. "But I fear I can't help myself."

The honesty of her words undid him more than any seduction. He turned his head and pressed a kiss to the inside of her wrist.

"You need to return to your room, Alice. Go now before I can't let you." The words were harsh, his intent to get her away from him before he gave in to the need pounding through his body.

"Of course, you're hurting. I should not have come in here." She turned from him.

"That is not the reason, Alice." He touched her shoulder. "I want you very much, but you're a lady, and I won't hurt you."

She faced him again. "And what if it is my choice? What if I wish to know what can be between a man and a woman just once?"

"You will wed, because no man can resist you." His words came out a rasp as the hand on her shoulder slid to cup her cheek. So warm beneath his palm.

Her laugh held no humor. "I'm quite sure you're the only man who believes that."

"Then they are all fools." The leash on his control snapped and Jamie slid his other hand around her waist, pulling her into his body. "Damn me to hell, because nothing but that would stop me from doing this now, and even then I would bargain with the devil for you."

He took her mouth again, this time deeper, letting her know his words were the truth. Jamie let his hands travel along the line of her back to the tie of her braid. He tugged it loose with fingers not quite steady, and then eased it free. Her hair spilled warm and heavy into his palms. Jamie drew it forward over a shoulder, letting his fingers test the texture.

He knew this was wrong and that tomorrow there would be regrets, but for once his control had slipped.

She kissed the corner of his mouth, his jaw, the place below his ear that made heat shoot through him. He answered with his own explorations, tracing the clean line of her throat with his lips, then lower, where the nightgown's ribbon tied. He caught the end of it between his teeth and tugged until it loosened. She made a sound that tightened every muscle he owned, but when he looked up, her eyes were steady.

"May I?" he asked, and the asking cost him more than any fight.

"Yes," she whispered.

He drew the linen aside only enough to reveal the slope of her collarbone, and the delicate hollow between. He ran a finger down and over the curve of her breast, and her breath caught in her throat.

"I am not afraid of you," she said.

"You should be," he said, dragging his eyes from the swell of her breasts. "Not because I would harm you. Because I am not fit to keep. I have demons, Alice, and that is why I will never let another close."

Her eyes held his for long heartbeats before she said, "One night, Jamie. That is all we will have, and it will be enough. Teach me what can be between a man and a woman."

He could grant that and still be the man he must be tomorrow, but he knew that he would remember this night always, and with that memory would come a pain in the region of his heart.

CHAPTER TWENTY-EIGHT

JAMIE SLID AN arm around Alice and took her with him back to the bed. His ribs would protest, and his body would ache like the devil tomorrow, but right now he didn't care. He turned her when they reached it and kissed her softly, swallowing the quiet sigh.

"Can we—will this hurt you, Jamie? Perhaps—"

"You will be gentle with me, I'm sure," he replied, knowing she spoke from her own fear and worry for him. "If at any time you wish to stop, I will do so, Alice.

"I know you are a good man."

This time it was he who snorted softly. "Not many would agree with you."

"They are fools," she whispered.

"I want to see you, Alice."

She nodded, and his hands went to the hem of her nightdress. Alice raised her arms, allowing him to pull the garment up and off her body. Jamie then felt the breath leave his lungs as he stepped back to look at her. She didn't shy away or hide herself, instead keeping her eyes on him.

She was a goddess. Silken pale skin, perfect breasts his fingers ached to cup, and nipples that he would taste. Jamie wanted to devour her. Run his hands and mouth down the planes of her stomach to the curls below, and further. Nothing would stop him now.

"Can I see you also?" The words weren't weak; she spoke with strength and a need that matched his own.

Jamie bent to push off his breeches, the action making his ribs tug viciously, but he didn't care. He wanted this as much as she did.

Alice's eyes followed the movement of his hands, her breath catching when she took in his erection. Jamie straightened and kept his eyes on her as she had him.

"Jamie, I worry about your pain. You have suffered terribly already. Surely you—"

"I feel nothing when you are close." It was a lie, but it would have taken five men to drag him from this room.

Her fingers moved beneath his, so he released them, and then inhaled as Alice traced the lines of his chest with whisper-soft strokes. When she leaned forward to press her lips to his heart, his control splintered.

"Alice." His moan was deep and guttural.

"Lie down. You are pale," she whispered. "I won't allow you to hurt yourself more."

"Parts of me hurt," he muttered, but sat. His hands then reached for her hips to pull her down to the bed with him. Jamie rolled, placing her beneath him and then rose to brace himself above her. He kissed her again, their bodies touching, and the contact was heaven and worth any pain he was suffering. Her gentle sigh told him she felt it too. The connection Jamie had felt with no other.

"More," Alice whispered. She was innocent, and yet showed no fear of what would happen. The world narrowed to the heat between them, and the soft slide of skin, the ragged catch of breath. Every touch was a promise, and every kiss an offering. He would be gentle, because his body and her innocence demanded that of him, but he could not stop now.

Jamie kissed down her neck to her breasts, licking long strokes over the curves until she was arching beneath him, her breath coming in pants. He then took the taut peak of her nipple into his mouth and sucked.

"Oh, my Lord," Alice whispered.

Jamie continued to torment first one and then the other breast, driving her moans on until her fingers dug into his arms. Only then did he move a hand down her stomach.

"Open your legs, Alice."

She did, and he ran his hands through the curls and lower. His first touch had her shuddering. He ran a finger over the damp folds. Back and forth, until the tension climbed inside her, only then did he ease a finger into her wet heat.

"Jamie." His name came out in a rush.

He slid another finger inside, stretching the delicate muscles, never once stopping his ministrations to her breasts. Alice gasped out a breath then and experienced her first orgasm.

Lifting his head, he watched her eyes close and her mouth fall open as she rode the wave of pleasure. It was a sight he wanted to see again, and the thought that he may not, and another may, infuriated him. But that was a thought for another day. Right now, he wanted this woman to be his.

"Be sure, Alice," he whispered as her eyes opened, their depths dazed with passion.

"I'm sure."

Jamie lowered himself between her legs.

"I can stop if—"

"Jamie, I want this," Alice said.

Christ, he was the one who felt like it was his first time. Jamie had never slept with an innocent before, but Alice was that.

He eased inside her. Gritting his teeth, and with every muscle clenched in his body, he slowly inched forward, the tight muscles yielding as he breached her sheath. Watching, waiting for her to wince, to cry out, but it never came. Instead, her arms slid to his shoulders, holding him close.

Jamie moved slowly, as her silken muscles stretched to accommodate him, and then he breached her innocence and was sheathed deep inside. He stopped and looked down at her.

"Alice?" His voice was a dry rasp. It took every ounce of his control not to pull out and thrust back into her. "Are you all right?"

She nodded, her eyes steady on his. "It eases."

Thank God. Jamie pulled out, watching her for a reaction, and then thrust back into Alice's body. She arched up and into him, so he did it again and again. The only sound in the room was the harsh rasp of their breathing. The world outside the four walls vanished. There was only the two of them.

He felt her tension climb, and knew his climax was also close.

"Again, Alice," he ordered. She cried out his name as she shuddered beneath him once more. Jamie thrust twice and then followed her as wave after wave of pleasure shot through him. He then slumped down beside her on the bed. For a long while, neither of them moved, the only sound the rasp of their breathing.

"Are you all right?" he murmured at last, his voice low and rough.

She nodded, lifting her head just enough for him to see her eyes. They were soft and sated. "I didn't think it would feel like that," she whispered. "Thank you, Jamie, for showing me how it could be. I will treasure the memory always."

Jamie felt a spike of irrational anger at her words. "I don't want your thanks."

"Why are you angry?" She moved, climbing off the bed to look down at him. "Are you in a lot of pain? I could rouse Maggie."

"No, and I'm not angry, just tired," Jamie lied. In fact, he was bloody terrified suddenly at the emotion swirling around inside him. Emotion she clearly did not feel if she was thanking him.

Had he been wrong to believe she'd felt more? You're irrational if you want that from her, when you can promise her nothing but what you've just shared.

"I understand," Alice said with a calm he was far from feeling. "You should rest. I'm sure that..." Her eyes moved from him to the bed, and she waved a hand about. Jamie saw her nerves for the first time then, and fickle bastard he was, it made him feel better.

He raised a brow. "That?"

"What we just did is not helping your injuries." The words came out fast.

"I wanted to do what we just did, and I have been in a worse condition than I currently am, Alice."

She'd been pulling on her nightdress, covering all that lovely flesh he'd just run his hands and mouth over, but stopped. Her eyes went to him again, and she looked sad at his words, but only said, "Sleep now." He then watched her continue dressing. When she'd wrapped the shawl around her shoulders, she hesitated.

Jamie knew he should say something—anything to tell her what they'd just shared meant to him. Fear kept him silent.

"Good night," Alice then whispered, and he watched her walk across the room and open the door. After a last look at him, she walked out, closing it softly behind her.

Jamie lay there in the silence as the sun began to filter silver light across London, wondering what he should do now.

He'd chosen a life of solitude, with the prospect of one day marrying to have an heir, but little else. He wasn't a complete bastard and knew that he had to offer his future wife comfort and politeness, but he'd never thought there would be more. Never wanted more, and then Alice had stepped into his life.

"Damn you," Jamie whispered. She muddled with the order he craved. Alice had turned his life on its head, and he didn't know how to change that. Perhaps distance would mean he'd forget her.

Her father wanted her married and out of his house, but Alice told him she had other plans. What plans? Was she about to take more risks and hurtle herself into danger? What of her aunt? Surely if she was under Alice's care, then danger would not be involved.

The two men in her life who should have loved her had failed

Alice. Her brother, for one, and yet he could not blame the man for sliding into madness. He'd been close a time or two after what he'd endured in Blackwood Hall. But to hurt her was unacceptable, and Jamie had no doubt after what Alice had told him that Charles had done that.

Her father had failed her terribly, as well, and when he saw the man, he'd make sure to tell him exactly what he thought of him.

She was a brave woman, and he knew that hadn't always been easy. But Alice had persevered and survived. Jamie had no doubt she'd kept Lord Smythe's business and estates running, and running well.

He lay there for a while, letting thoughts tumble over and over inside his head, and finding no way to clear them. Finally, he felt the need to move and put some distance between him and Alice. It was for the best, anyway. If anyone saw him leaving here in daylight hours, it would cause trouble for her.

He rose from the bed, feeling every ache and pain in his body. Searching the room, he found a shirt and his jacket on a chair. His boots were harder to get on, but Jamie managed with a lot of grunting.

Walking through the silent house, wincing as he took the stairs down, Jamie thought about the woman he was walking away from. A woman who had done something no one before her ever had. She'd made him feel, and Jamie feared that feeling was something a great deal stronger than he'd ever be brave enough to acknowledge, because no good could come of that, for either of them.

He stepped outside the front door as the rain started and began walking, head still full of a woman he could never have. No one should be married to a man with the demons he had in his head.

London was waking, and the sky was gray and dark as the rain increased in intensity. Jamie huddled in his coat and increased his pace. His body hurt too much to run. He'd be having a bath when he reached his townhouse.

He was turning onto his street when he felt a shiver of unease run down his spine. Turning, he was too late to stop the hand from covering his mouth. He inhaled instinctively and a vile smell filled his nostrils. He tried to fight, but soon his limbs began to feel heavy, and he felt himself slide toward darkness. His last rational thought was for Alice and the fact that he would never see her again.

CHAPTER TWENTY-NINE

ALICE HAD TOSSED and turned during the few hours of sleep she'd managed to snatch. Finally, the rain forced her out of bed. She had woken with a stuffy head, aches in places that had never ached before, and a crotchety temperament that boded well for no one.

She'd given her innocence to Jamie and asked for nothing in return, not that he'd offered anything. Which was what they both wanted. The problem was that when his hands had held her, and his kisses had caressed her body, she had hoped for a brief moment that they could have more, and that had been a dangerous thing for two people who had vowed never to love.

"What a mess," Alice muttered as she sat on the side of her bed. But she'd never regret what happened last night. She'd asked him to show her what could be between a man and a woman, and he'd done that with tenderness and passion. But she was not foolish enough to think what they experienced had been commonplace.

Alice had once read a book that had the words, *their souls had touched, and laughed.* She was not laughing now. In fact, she felt desperate and off-balance. Jamie had taken her to a place she'd never thought to go before. He'd made love to her as if she was important to him—well, she thought he had—but perhaps he did that with all the women he'd slept with. The thought annoyed her enough to pick up one of her pillows and hurl it across the room.

What has become of me?

She prided herself on being strong, and yet right then she was not. He'd done this to her. Jamie had made her feel and made her think about a future he didn't want. *You don't want it either!*

God's blood, Alice, get yourself together!

When Maggie arrived, she called for a tub and bathed, forcing herself to smile when a staff member came close.

"That look would scare rodents," Maggie said, holding out a drying cloth. "What has you out of sorts this morning?"

"Nothing, I'm just weary, and I loathe the rain, as you know. How is Lord Stafford this morning?"

"No one has gone to him yet, because his lordship needs sleep to heal. Perhaps you could check on him after you're dressed, my lady, and call me to come and look over his injuries?"

She nodded, but said nothing further. Jamie's skin would be warm when he woke, she was sure of it. Last night it had felt—

No, don't go there, Alice. You wanted a single experience with a man, and you got it. Now focus on being who you've always been. She could do that, had been doing that for years. Hide what was really going on inside her head behind a cool, emotionless façade.

She dressed in soft lilac, one of her favorite colors. A light-gray shawl rested over her shoulders, and after Maggie had threaded a lilac ribbon through her simple bun, Alice finally felt ready to face Jamie.

As she walked down the hall, she focused on her breathing, slow and steady. At his door, she paused and tapped softly before pushing it open.

The bed was empty.

Her gaze swept the room, searching, hoping, but he was gone. Sometime during the few hours she'd slept, he had left.

Alice sank onto the edge of the bed, the truth hitting harder than she expected. She hadn't realized how much she'd wanted to see him this morning until now. Foolish woman. Because in that instant, she understood that she'd never felt like this before.

"Dear God," Alice whispered, voice trembling. "Is it possible that what I'm feeling is love?"

With a shaky sigh, she let herself fall back onto the bed and stared up at the ceiling. *Surely not.*

She spent a few minutes composing herself before leaving the room. Alice then made her way downstairs to the front door. Opening it, she looked up and down the street as sheets of rain fell. If Jamie had walked, he would be soaked in minutes. Surely he must have taken a hackney considering the condition he was in.

When had he left?

Alice was about to shut the door when she saw someone running down the street toward the townhouse. As they drew closer, she noted it was Bobby. *Did that boy never sleep?*

When he noticed her, his pace increased, and seconds later he was beside her on the doorstep, dripping wet. A single look at his face told her something was very wrong.

"What has happened, Bobby?"

"Lord St-Stafford," he wheezed. "I saw him leave and followed. Th-they got him before I could reach them."

Icy cold fear slithered its tendrils through Alice.

"Who got him, Bobby?"

"Men. They snuck up behind him and placed a cloth over his mouth. He fought, and then stopped, and they threw him into a carriage. I recognized one of them. He was the same man who helped hurt Lord Stafford last night."

"No!"

"Yes. I tried to follow, but they were moving too quick," Bobby said, his face pale. "I ran down lanes, but they were always out of my reach, and then they were gone."

"What's amiss?" Ezra said the words from behind Alice. "Why are you wet, boy?"

"I ran in the rain," Bobby said.

"Well, get to the kitchens and dry yourself. I'm sure there will be something warm for your belly too."

"Ain't no time," Bobby said, not moving. But he was shivering now from the cold.

"Do you need my assistance, my lady?" Phipps asked, appearing next.

Numbing fear was crippling her. *Not Jamie. Please don't hurt him anymore.*

"Lady Alice, what is wrong!" The boom of her footman's voice snapped her out of it.

Her butler gasped, horrified.

"C-carriage, we need it at once, Ezra."

"Why?"

"Go with Ezra to get the carriage, please, Bobby," Alice said, taking off her shawl and wrapping it around the boy. "Tell him what is going on. I need to collect some things, but be as quick as you can. There is no time to lose, as Lord Stafford is in danger."

"Phipps, tell my aunt when she rises. I have to leave, and I will return as soon as I can."

"Of course, my lady. Do you need anything else?"

"Food. Please pack a hamper as quickly as you can," Alice said, knowing she'd be hungry soon. Not much put her off her appetite, and she knew that Ezra had a large stomach that was always empty too.

Alice ran as Ezra and Bobby sprinted to the stables in the rain, the ends of her shawl flapping behind the boy as he moved. In seconds she was in her room, pulling out a cloak. After fastening it around her neck, she collected gloves and changed her footwear for sturdy boots. All the while, her mind was whirling. *What should she do?*

Lords Hamilton and Corbyn. Yes, she'd need to find them; they would help. They would know how to find Jamie surely?

Plan made, she went to her desk. Unlocking a drawer, Alice took out money and a pistol. She then hurried back out of the room and downstairs to wait.

"Alice, what is going on?" Her aunt was in the entrance way.

"I need to go out, Aunt Gwen, and I'm n-not sure how long I

will be."

Thankfully, her aunt had slept through last night's commotion, and Alice had hoped she'd not learned about it, but now she wasn't so sure. Her aunt had a very determined expression on her face as she approached.

"Where are you going, Alice? It is pouring with rain out there."

She felt the tears then. Last night's events combined with today's were clearly taking their toll on Alice.

"A-Aunt Gwen." She stepped into the open arms and let them wrap around her briefly. Her aunt's familiar scent settled her.

"Tell me what is going on, Alice. I am stronger than I look, you know. Now speak to me. I've felt like you've been hiding things from me." Her aunt eased back, gripping her arms.

"I need to go and help find Lord Stafford, Aunt. You see, he and I have been searching for someone, and that someone has now kidnapped him." Alice held up a hand when her aunt opened her mouth to speak. "I will tell you the whole of it, I promise, but I must do this first."

"I'm worried for you, Alice."

"I know, but I promise I will be all right. But what I need you to help me with is the address of either Lord Hamilton or Lord Corbyn's townhouse, Aunt Gwen."

She was subjected to a long, studied look, and then her aunt told her the address of Lord and Lady Hamilton.

"Thank you." Alice pressed a kiss to one soft, sweet-smelling cheek. "And I promise to tell you everything when I return. No more secrets."

"I shall hold you to that, child. But first I wish to know one thing before you leave."

"What's that? Alice asked as she heard carriage wheels outside, rolling through the rain.

"Is Lord Stafford important to you because you care for him very much, Alice?"

Shock held her motionless. "Wh-why would you ask me that,

Aunt Gwen?"

"Something Agatha told me had me wondering."

"Ah, well, as to that—" the door behind her opened much to her relief, and Ezra stepped inside, shaking himself like a large dog.

"The carriage is ready, my lady," he said. Then bowed deeply to Aunt Gwen, who all the staff adored. "I will take a moment to retrieve my coat, and one for the boy."

The slap of Ezra's wet boots had him running to the servants' quarters.

"I will return and we will talk about everything, Aunt." Alice kissed her cheek. "I really must go."

"Bring him home safely, my dear, and then you and I are going to talk," Aunt Gwen said.

Alice raised a hand and ran out the door to where Bobby stood, still wrapped in her shawl.

"If you wish to stay, then I understand," she said. The boy had already done so much for her.

"I will come, as you'll need me." The solemn words made her want to weep.

"Right then, where is it we're going?" Ezra said, arriving in his heavy coat with a hamper in his hands. He put that inside the carriage and then handed Bobby the coat he had across his arms.

Alice gave him the address to Lord Hamilton's house, and he helped her climb inside. Bobby climbed up beside Ezra, now dressed in a huge coat that dwarfed him.

"Stay strong, Jamie. We are coming," Alice whispered as the carriage started rolling and rain battered the windows.

She worked through several plans, as was her wont to do when things needed resolving, and she needed something—other than the gripping fear over what Jamie was enduring—to keep her mind busy.

The carriage rolled to a halt minutes later, and she hurried to open the door and step down, straight into an ankle-deep puddle. Shaking her booted foot, she began to walk up to the front door.

Raising the large lion's head knocker, she banged it down twice. It opened and there stood a tall, bald, immaculately clad butler.

"I wish to speak with Lord Hamilton at once. It is extremely urgent. My name is Lady Alice Smythe."

The butler bowed and stepped aside to let Alice enter out of the rain. He then bade her to follow him into a small parlor.

Alice paced the room, seeing but not really noticing the elegant legged furniture and gold paper on the walls.

God, Jamie. She should have told him—what? That she cared for him, that she loved him? No, that would have sent him running, as it would have had he said it to her.

How did Jamie feel about her?

The sound of running feet had her looking to the door. Lord Hamilton appeared in his shirtsleeves.

"Lady Alice, what has happened? Dibley told me that it was extremely urgent."

"Lord Stafford," Alice added quickly. "He has been taken."

"Taken?" The gentle smile he'd entered with disappeared, and in its place was a look so fierce Alice nearly took a step back. Nearly, but not quite.

"Abducted. Please allow me to explain, my lord."

He gave her one curt nod. "However, if, as you say, my friend has been taken against his will, there is not a moment to lose. Dibley!" he then bellowed.

The servant appeared in the doorway. "You called, my lord?"

"Send word at once to Lord Corbyn to come here, and make sure he's armed."

"At once." The butler left, not appearing overly concerned by the order.

"Before you continue, Lady Alice, are you unharmed?"

"Yes, I am, but Lord Stafford is not." Lord Hamilton's lips tightened over that comment.

"Continue," he said.

"It's my fault he was hurt," Alice whispered. Until then, she'd not really acknowledged that. He'd come to find her last night and ended up hurt.

"Tell me everything, my lady, because I know my friend, and know that it's very doubtful anything that happened to Jamie was your fault."

She did, leaving nothing out, the words pouring out of her. Alice felt relief that she had someone to share her fear and concern with. He would help her get Jamie back—he had to.

CHAPTER THIRTY

"WHAT'S GOING ON, Anthony? Your note just said, *come to my house now*, and as your wish is my command, I hurried here immediately, in the rain. In a hackney," Lord Corbyn added what felt like hours—but was possibly only twenty minutes—later.

Alice watched Lord Corbyn move deeper into the room. His eyes found her and widened.

"My lady." He bowed. "The mystery deepens." He then searched, and she thought, looked for Jamie.

"Listen, and don't speak," Lord Hamilton said. "Jamie has been abducted, and we believe Jackson is involved. He had a fight last night when he went to find Lady Alice, who, as it turns out, was watching Jackson's lodgings, because a boy told her that's where he lived."

Lord Corbyn's expression hardened to a mask of anger, like his friend's.

Alice felt guilt lance through her again.

"That bloody fool." Lord Corbyn growled out the words. "He should have told us what he was about."

"He is no fool," Alice said, and then wished she hadn't as they both stared at her. "H-he was coming to find me. To protect me. If anyone is a fool, 'tis I."

"I believe I have already told you, Lady Alice, that my friend does nothing he has no wish to," Anthony said.

"Exactly right. Now what is to be done?"

"The young boy, Bobby, who saw the entire incident, is out-side with my driver," Alice said. "Also, I believe J-Lord Stafford took a book from the Crimson Serpent. Was there anything in there?"

"No, just a few initials and names, which we have been at-tempting to track down with little luck. But Jackson's name was in there," Lord Corbyn said.

"Dibley!" Lord Hamilton roared. When the butler appeared, he said, "Go and ask the young boy somewhere outside my front door in the rain to come inside, please."

"So we know it is likely Jackson is involved in the abduction," Lord Corbyn said.

"Lord Stafford punched him several times, and as Jackson ran away, he vowed to end his life," Alice said.

"I'll just bet he did," Lord Hamilton said, grim-faced.

"And we will be ensuring that does not happen," Lord Cor-byn added.

Bobby arrived then, hair flat to his head, her shawl around his neck and wearing the large jacket. She must see about getting him some new clothes. His face showed no emotion as Alice introduced him to the two lords. She urged him to bow.

"Bobby, can you tell us exactly what you saw last night?" Lord Tobias said.

"He was walking down the street, Lord Stafford was." He shot a look at Alice, who nodded for him to continue. "Then two men came up behind him, and one put a cloth over his face," Bobby continued in his gruff little voice. "His lordship fought hard, but they dragged him into a carriage when he went limp. I was too far away to help."

He went limp. The words slammed into her hard. *Dear God, please be alive, Jamie.*

"I recognized one of them from when his lordship fought with them. The other I'd seen in the Black Dog."

"You didn't tell me that, Bobby."

The boy looked at his toes. "Didn't want you to go there, Lady Alice. It ain't right for you to do so."

Yet another male who thought they knew what was best for her, but Alice knew this was not the time to raise that matter. Now their only focus was Jamie.

"We have few leads, but two that we will start with. One, Jackson's lodgings, and then the Black Dog," Lord Corbyn said. "Get what you need, Anthony, and we'll leave."

"My carriage is outside," Alice said. "Or are you wanting to ride your horses?"

"Your carriage will be quicker," Lord Hamilton said. "Get inside now, and I will be there in a matter of minutes."

Everyone seemed to move at once. Bobby ran, with Lord Corbyn on his heels, and Alice followed, while Lord Hamilton thundered up the stairs, his boots hitting each step with a loud thud.

"Is that a hamper?" Lord Corbyn asked when he was seated across from her in the carriage, and Bobby had once again climbed up beside the still scowling Ezra. Thankfully, the rain had slowed now to a drizzle.

"It is. Would you like something?" It took a great deal for Alice to be put off her food, but suddenly she had no appetite.

"I would indeed. It's early, and I only ate the first plate of my breakfast before Anthony's note arrived." He opened the hamper and unwrapped the first item.

"Shortbread biscuits," he whispered, closing his eyes briefly. "My cook is not the best at making these, although she does try." He bit into one and sighed.

"I shall take some to Bobby and my driver," Alice said. She climbed out with the biscuits and held them up to Bobby. "Eat these, as I have no wish for either of you to faint because you grow lightheaded. I fear the day will be a long one, as we will not be returning to the townhouse until Lord Stafford is found."

"We'll find him," Ezra barked, taking the biscuits Bobby handed him. "Thank you."

She climbed back inside as Lord Hamilton sprinted out the door wearing his great coat and a hat. He climbed inside, and then they were moving.

"Give me one of those," he said, snatching a shortbread out of his friend's hands.

Soon the only noises inside the carriage were of them eating and the slosh of the wheels. Alice felt fear claw at her throat again, now that she was still. Hopeless fear filled her. How would they find Jamie?

"I fear for him." Alice hadn't realized she'd spoken the words out loud until they stopped eating.

"Jamie will look after himself until we reach him, Lady Alice." Lord Hamilton spoke first.

"Alice, please call me that."

"Alice. I am Anthony, and this is Toby."

She nodded for him to continue, needing him to tell her that Jamie would indeed be alive when they reached him—they had to reach him.

"He is possibly the strongest of us all, and perhaps that is why Jackson was hardest on him," Toby said.

"Please allow me to say how sorry I am that you all suffered at Blackwood Hall, as did my brother. It is because of him I am determined to see Kenneth Jackson punished for his sins." Alice knew these two men would understand her need for vengeance.

Toby said solemnly, "He will pay. Anthony, Jamie, and I will make sure of it, Alice."

She had to be content with that as they rolled through the streets of London.

It was just another day for those they passed as they went about their business. Looking out the window, Alice wondered how everything could seem so normal, when it wasn't, not for her. Nothing would be the same again if Jamie didn't survive whatever hell he was suffering.

Her companions asked her to wait in the carriage when they reached Jackson's lodgings, and she reluctantly agreed. Their argument had been that it would be easier to slip in and out with fewer people taking notice, especially if they had to break into the property.

She watched out the window as Bobby led the two noblemen from the carriage until they vanished. Alice gripped the edge of the seat, struggling to sit still. The sudden silence was unbearable.

After a minute, she stood on the seat and shoved open the roof hatch. "If they're gone too long, I shall—"

"You most certainly will not," Ezra cut in. His voice was a low growl, hat lowered so she could see only his eyes. "Let them do what they must. You'll only slow them down."

"I am not a fool," she snapped.

"No," he said, glancing back at her, "but that man's tugged on your heartstrings, and that makes a person rash."

The words hit too close, so instead of answering, she closed the hatch and sat once more.

Minutes crawled past, and Alice wanted to get out of the carriage and pace, at the very least. Every nerve was screaming. Images flashed through her mind of Jamie fighting, Jamie bleeding, Jamie lying still. *No, he's alive.* She forced herself to breathe.

The carriage door opened suddenly. Anthony climbed in, eyes alight with grim purpose. "He's not there," he said. "The room's been stripped clean."

"Completely?"

"Not quite." Toby entered behind him, holding a scrap of paper. "We found this."

Alice leaned forward. "What does it say?"

"The Black Dog."

"Then that's where we go," she said.

Anthony met her gaze. "You're not coming inside that tavern, Alice."

"I am, and I've been there before."

"And Jamie is an idiot for letting you go. We are not."

"You may order your servants about, Lord Hamilton, but not

me. I will not sit idly while he suffers." Her voice shook, but she held his stare.

Tobias studied her for a long moment, then inclined his head. "If we leave her, she'll follow unless we tie her up, Anthony, just as our wives would were they in the same situation."

"I beg your pardon. You had better not be serious," Alice snapped.

Anthony muttered something under his breath that sounded very much like a curse, but gave a brief nod. "Very well, you can come. Stay behind us, speak to no one, and if I say leave, you leave."

Alice bit back the need to say more. To protest that she did not take orders from them, but as they were just as worried as she about Jamie, she didn't. Instead, she sat and looked out the window as the tension inside the carriage rose, and the silence almost choked her.

Anthony was the first to break it. "Do you love him, Alice?"

She could lie, or just not answer, but they were Jamie's friends, and maybe it was time for her to stop being a coward.

"Yes, I think I do."

"Well, now, that's excellent news," Toby said with a gentle smile.

The carriage pulled up outside the Black Dog minutes later, and Alice forgot everything but what they had to do to get Jamie back.

In daylight, the Black Dog looked far worse than it had at night. The shadows that once softened its rough edges were gone, leaving only the stark reality of cracked plaster and filthy windows streaked with grime. The stench of spilled ale, smoke, and something sour clung to the air even out here.

Inside, the tavern was smaller than she remembered, and far dirtier. The weak morning light revealed everything the dark had hidden. Alice found sticky floors, warped tables scarred by years of knife blades, and walls stained with old smoke. The corners where she had once imagined shadows to be now held only piles of refuse and puddles of spilled drink.

A few men dozed over their tankards, slumped in their seats. Others turned to stare at the newcomers, their eyes narrow and assessing. Without the cover of night, there was no mistaking how out of place the three of them were.

Alice was wedged between Anthony and Toby as they moved through the building to the bar.

"Good day, we are looking for some information about the whereabouts of someone," Tobias said to the barman. Thankfully, he was not the same man who had served them last time.

"If he ain't in here, then I don't know his whereabouts."

Anthony pulled a fistful of money out of his pocket and placed it on the counter but did not lift his hand. The barman's eyes focused on it.

"How about we try that again, seeing as I did not even mention his name? I'm looking for a man who goes by the name Jackson. He would have men with him is my guess, because the sniveling weasel is a coward and can't do anything by himself," Anthony said.

The man's eyes flickered up to Anthony's face and then back down at the money. There was a lot there, probably more than he could earn in many months.

"Not overly tall, but solid, and boasts a lot about himself," Tobias said.

The man's eyes were on Toby now, and narrowed. Alice held her breath, sure he was going to say he knew Jackson.

"I know someone who can help."

They all turned to look at the owner of those words. An older man with a grizzled face that Alice thought had seen a lot in his lifetime stared back at them.

"Who?" Anthony demanded.

"Follow me," the man said, walking away from them.

"Stay close, Alice," Anthony said softly, as they followed the man through the alehouse and out the front door. He then led them to the right side of the building and down a narrow lane, which shouldn't feel sinister in daylight hours, and yet did.

Thoughts whirled in Alice's head. Were they being led into a trap? Did the old man really know Jackson?

"Stop here," he said.

Alice caught a flicker of movement in the shadows ahead.

"Who's there?" Toby demanded, his voice sharp.

"She's my daughter," the man said. "But she won't come out. She's bruised because of that bastard. Go on, Lilly. Tell them what you know about Jackson."

Alice strained to see the girl, but she clung to the shadows, as if the light itself might burn her.

"Jackson paid some of us to go to a warehouse," the woman said, her words soft and lisping. "We went, thinking it was work, but he locked us in. Him and others, they hurt us."

Alice closed her eyes briefly, her stomach twisting. *How much more suffering could this man cause?* He had to be stopped.

"I'm sorry for what he did to you," Toby said quietly. "We're looking for him because he's taken a friend of ours. Do you know where he might be?"

"Try the warehouse," she whispered. "Old Fishmarket, by the river. That's where he took me. Fool paid us not to talk, but I'm done keeping quiet."

Anthony's expression hardened. "Then we'll make him pay."

He pressed coins into the man's hand and turned away. Moments later, they were running back toward the carriage.

As Alice climbed inside, her pulse pounded with dread and hope in equal measure. *Please let it be the place*, she prayed silently. Because deep inside, she could feel it—Jamie was running out of time.

❧ ⁕ ❧

CHAPTER THIRTY-ONE

J AMIE WOKE WITH a pounding head and a mouth that tasted as if he'd been chewing old hay. For a moment, all he could do was breathe, shallow inhales of cold, damp air that stung his throat. Then, he heard the slap of water against timber.

He tried to swallow, but his tongue scraped against the dryness of his mouth. Every muscle screamed in protest, each one a reminder of the punishment he'd endured the day before.

It took him a moment to understand why his shoulders burned so fiercely. His wrists were bound above his head, the pull on them relentless, forcing his body to hang so that his toes barely brushed the floor. The strain sent pain shooting down his arms and into his spine like fire.

Blinking against the dim light, Jamie lifted his gaze. His hands were shackled, the iron biting into his raw skin, the chain running upward to a rope looped through a hook fixed to the ceiling.

He forced himself to focus on his surroundings and ignore the stinging pain in his ribs. Warehouse, his foggy mind supplied. He knew the smell assaulting his nostrils. Jamie was near the water.

The place was mostly empty except for a few pieces of furniture hunched in a corner. An old rickety chair, a narrow table, and a trunk. On the far wall, iron rings were bolted into stone, and chains dangled from them with cuffs attached. He understood then where they had brought him. Jackson's place. Not his home, but somewhere he used when he wanted to play his favorite games. A quiet space by the water where there were no neighbors to hear.

Jamie's heart gave a hard, jolting thud. His breath came too quickly. He closed his eyes and counted, forcing calm to replace the rising panic. Then he thought of Alice, and it steadied him. He had to get out of here and back to her. Jamie had to tell her what was in his heart.

The light through the slats told him it was still daytime. He could also hear the patter of rain on water.

"Jackson, you cowardly bastard!" he roared, the sound burning his raw throat. "Fight me like the man you're not!"

No answer came, only silence.

He set his teeth and jerked against the bindings. Jamie was strong, but he'd already been hanging here a while, if the ache in his shoulders was any sign, and yesterday his body had taken a beating. His strength would not last.

"You're not finishing me, Jackson. Not today!" he vowed out loud.

Alice. He saw her as he had last night. Beautiful, passionate, and responsive to his every touch. He wanted more time with her—a lifetime.

Strong and determined. She was being tossed out of the only home she'd ever known by the man who should have protected her, and she had a plan that didn't include Jamie.

He'd do something about that later, he promised himself. After he'd dealt with Jackson.

He pictured his sisters too. Their husbands would care for them if something happened to him. They would mourn him, but they would be all right. But Alice had nobody she could lean on without it costing her pride. She needed him alive.

"I love Lady Alice," he said softly. He had never told a woman that. Not his sisters, Hannah and Briar. Jamie wanted the chance to tell them how much they meant to him, and Alice to her face that she had his heart. Not to these damp boards and empty air.

Jamie grabbed the rope above him and lifted himself, hissing as his shoulders screamed, and tried to change the angle of the rope over the hook. The ceiling beam was old, splintered, and the iron hook hammered into place. If he could saw the rope along the edge of the wood, even one strand at a time, maybe he could free himself.

Moving in small bursts, he swung and sawed, and the rope rasped. Strand by strand, it snapped. Pain sliced through him, but he could do this. Toby and Anthony slid into his head then. His friends, who had been to hell and back with him. Did they know he was missing?

Jamie forced his thoughts anywhere but the pain in his hands and shoulders as he continued to saw on the rope.

He wasn't sure how long he'd been trying to free himself before he heard a door creak somewhere, followed by the thud of boots on wood. Jackson stepped into view. He then took off his gloves, one finger at a time.

"No point in making an entrance here. No one is looking, Jackson," Jamie rasped.

Jackson smiled. An evil one that had once set the fear of God into Jamie, but no more. He was no longer the terrified boy he'd once been, or even the man he'd been before he'd met Alice.

"Lord Stafford," Jackson said lightly. "I told you I'd kill you."

Jamie noted the slight kink in his swollen nose, and the bruise on his jaw, and smiled himself. "I bet those hurt."

Jackson's smile slipped.

"You are at my mercy, Stafford. It would pay you to remember that.

Jamie waited for the fear, but it didn't come. Alice had given him hope and belief. He kept moving slowly, ignoring the pain.

"Once maybe," Jamie said calmly, *but no more*, he vowed silently. "I'm not a child now. But you, you're still the pathetic man you always were. A man who could not get respect from anyone, so had to resort to hurting boys as they were the only ones you could control."

Jackson's face twisted into an angry mask at the taunts, and then smoothed out again.

"I see you've been playing with your toys," Jamie said, nodding to the cuffs hanging from the wall. "Clearly, no woman will come to you willingly."

The face before him turned smug, and Jamie tensed.

"I understand you and Lady Alice Smythe are close." He tsked. "Such a shame about her brother, but then he was a weak man."

"Say her name again, and I'll take your tongue," Jamie growled.

He felt sweat drip down his temple as he flexed his fingers. Above, he felt another strand of rope give. Not enough, but something.

"I will have a little fun with Lady Alice when you're dead. I've never bedded a noblewoman."

He didn't take the lure Jackson had thrown him, even as rage surged through Jamie.

"You're a weaselling little nobody, Jackson, and won't get near her. And if you did, she'd destroy you. Like I said, you're not brave enough to take on anyone stronger than you, and Lady Alice is definitely that." Jamie forced himself to laugh at the man. He wanted his rage. Jackson had a terrible temper and lost control easily. If Jamie could get the man to do that, he'd make a mistake. "In fact, I doubt there are many men you can best without a weapon. You're a coward."

Jackson roared and ran at him.

Jamie threw his weight backward and then swung forward, savage pain ripping through his shoulders as he moved. He pulled his knees up and then lashed out. His boots caught Jackson in the midriff and slammed him backward into the table. It splintered, dropping him to the floor. The sound of keys chimed as they clanged against the wood.

Jackson made an ugly sound, hands clutched to his stomach as he staggered back to his feet. He pulled a blade from his boot.

"I'll gut you!"

Jamie laughed. "You? I'd like to see you try. Even with my hands bound, I'll best you." He threw himself forward again, this time not to kick but to rub the rope hard across the hook. It rasped as more threads broke, and more pain sang through his body.

Jackson lunged, knife out, eyes narrowed to slits of rage. He slashed for Jamie's thigh. Jamie twisted. The blade cut his trousers and the top of his skin. Heat ran down his leg.

"I'll take her, and she'll die in pain!" Jackson hissed.

Jamie jerked his weight again and felt more strands give. He twisted with the last of his strength, and made himself climb, just two handholds, and then drop hard.

The rope gave, and he dropped like a sack of stones onto the floor.

The boards beneath him protested and sent a flash of white pain from his shoulder to his ankle, knocking the breath out of him. Jamie rolled instinctively as Jackson's knife came down where his ribs had been. His roar of anger had Jamie staggering to his feet.

"I'm killing you!" his enemy roared.

Jamie saw the sudden flash of fear on Jackson's face as he brought his bound hands down onto his wrist. The knife dislodged and fell to the floor. Jackson ran at Jamie.

They hit the floor and rolled. He took an elbow to the jaw that made sparks flare at the edge of his vision. Jamie then drove his forehead into Jackson's nose and heard him howl, as he inflicted yet more pain.

Jackson made a noise like a trapped animal. He crawled away from Jamie, searching for the knife, and found it as Jamie regained his feet, searching for a weapon of his own. He found a piece of wood. Picking it up, he braced himself for the next attack.

Jackson charged, slashing the blade from left to right, and he felt it slice through his belly as he brought the bit of wood down with as much force as he could. The nail in the board sank into

Jackson's shoulder. He screamed in pain.

Jamie heard the thunder of feet then, but he did not turn away from the man howling in pain before him.

"Jamie!"

He knew that voice. This time, he did turn, and watched Toby, Anthony, and Alice run through the door. With them was her large, protective footman.

His knees weakened, and suddenly all strength left his body as he fell to his knees. She dropped down before him, as all hell broke loose behind her.

"Alice," he breathed. "My love."

Her hands cupped his face, her lovely eyes filled with tears, and that was the last thing he remembered as he slumped forward into her arms.

CHAPTER THIRTY-TWO

A LICE PACED BACK and forth in one of the upstairs parlors, her skirts sweeping the carpet as she moved. For three long days she had lived like this, pacing back and forth, hearing Jamie whisper, my love to her before going limp in her arms.

It had been Toby and Anthony who carried him from the warehouse, bloodied and bruised, his head lolling against Toby's shoulder, and his coat torn and soaked with sweat and blood.

They'd carried him into his townhouse after an agonizing carriage ride where Jamie's eyes had stayed closed. Toby told her to carry on to her home and promised they would care for him. But Alice didn't give a fig about propriety; she'd just wanted to be there for Jamie. But after a brief argument, they'd insisted this was the right thing to do.

"If you wish a life with my friend, then have it because you both want it, not because it is forced upon you." Anthony had said those words to her, knowing that if society found out she was in Jamie's house caring for him, all hell would break loose.

So she'd gone to her townhouse. Bathed, eaten what her aunt forced upon her, and waited.

The first note had arrived that night, just before she'd retired, and had details of Jamie's progress.

He has seen a doctor, received stitches and care for his injuries, and is now sleeping. Dr. Jones says there is no lasting damage, but he needs to rest.

She wasn't reassured. Alice needed to see him.

"And this is why I should not love another," she muttered, pacing. It was messy and painful, because suddenly Alice's contentment rested entirely on Jamie's health and well-being. She had never wanted this, especially after Charles, someone she loved deeply, had died.

Love, she decided, was an infection of the heart. One moment she had been self-possessed, managing estates and a clinic, battling her father's whims and society's rules. The next, she stiffened at every footstep outside her door because it might bring bad news, or worse, no news at all.

"Would you like tea, Alice?"

Her aunt appeared in the doorway.

"No, thank you, Aunt Gwen. Are you going out?"

"I am," her aunt said with a mild smile. "Lady Hetherington has been reading that dreadful novel about pirates and misplaced virtue. I intend to persuade her that the heroine is entirely to blame for her own misfortunes."

Despite herself, Alice laughed. "I envy you. My own misfortunes seem rather less straightforward."

"Then I shall argue with Lady Hetherington in your stead." Her aunt crossed the room and studied Alice with concern. "Is there any news about Lord Stafford today?"

"No more than yesterday."

"Well, then," Aunt Gwen said with brisk optimism, "no news is good news, as your uncle used to say. You must hold on to that, darling."

"I shall try."

When her aunt departed, the silence pressed in on her again.

Alice had told her everything on the second day she'd returned to the townhouse after Jackson had kidnapped Jamie. She'd answered questions and promised never to hide things from her again. Aunt Gwen had then assured her she would happily live wherever Alice wished to go, after she'd explained what her father wanted.

"I'm sorry, darling, but your father has always been a vile and selfish man," her aunt had said. Alice had agreed wholeheartedly with her assessment.

The problem was, Aunt Gwen might say she was happy to live anywhere, but Alice knew she loved London and her friends here, and she had no wish to take her aunt away from that.

Alice paced to the window. Beyond the glass, the garden stretched green and drowsy in the afternoon light. Bobby was down there with Ezra, listening intently as the man explained something to him. She had hired the boy on Maggie's recommendation, and already his cheeks had gained color and his eyes hope. It pleased her to see some good come from all this chaos.

She heard the sound of footsteps and wondered if Phipps or Maggie was checking on her again, or perhaps another note had arrived about Jamie. However, it was neither of them that stepped into the parlor after the door opened, but her father. Alice's heart sank. She did not have the strength to battle wits with him today.

"Daughter," he snapped.

"Father," she dipped her head.

"Well, what has been done about what we discussed, Alice?"

"You were only here a few days ago, Father. Surely the need to hurl me from my home is not that urgent."

Alice wasn't a nice person to be around when she was worried or tired, or both. She was that now, and her temper was on edge.

"You will marry, daughter, and if you cannot find a suitable candidate, then I will. It is time. Now, I need some money before I leave for France, and when I return, it had better be for your wedding."

"There is no need, as she will be marrying me."

"Jamie," Alice whispered as he walked into the room. A bruise mottled his jaw, and there were dark smudges under his eyes, but other than that, he was as he'd always been. Strong and so handsome.

"Who are you?" her father demanded. He'd not walked in society for many years, so he had lost touch with the names and titles of his peers.

"The Marquess of Stafford." Jamie's tone bordered on pompous as he glared down at Alice's father. "And you, sir, should be begging your daughter's forgiveness for your behavior. What man tosses his family from their home so he can install his mistress there? What man demands his daughter—the daughter who has run his estates and business affairs for years on his behalf—must wed immediately. You, sir, are a disgrace."

She really should intervene, but all she could do was stare at Jamie and smile. He was here, and whole.

"How dare you!" her father blustered. "Are you going to let him speak to me like this, Alice?"

"Yes, because you deserve it. Now leave, Father, and go back to your mistress. I will move out of this townhouse as soon as I find suitable accommodations for my aunt and me."

"You'll be moving in with me," Jamie said, his eyes still on her father. "And I will not treat her as you have. With me, she will be happy and loved."

"My daughter will not move in with you—"

"We will be married first, and to think I am suggesting otherwise speaks more to your nature than mine, sir."

Her father's face looked ready to explode, but he did not speak again, simply turned and left the room without looking at his daughter again.

"Jamie—"

"I love you, Alice." He moved closer, taking her hands as he stopped before her. "I didn't plan to fall in love, or marry a woman that I would worry and care about the remainder of my life. But you are that person."

"Jamie—"

"I knew when I was hanging there in that warehouse—"

"He hung you up!" Alice roared, anger filling her body. "I'll bloody kill him!"

"Jackson is in Newgate Prison, and will stay there, my sweet. But thank you for your anger on my behalf.

"But are you really all right, Jamie? You were stabbed, and that was after taking a beating when those men set upon you." Alice ran her eyes over him, searching for his pain.

His smile was small but reached his lovely green eyes. "I would be lying if I said I was back to full strength. In fact, I'm fairly sure that being run over by a herd of oxen would be less painful. But when I woke this morning, finally clear-headed, my first thought was of you. I rose and dressed with my staff protesting the entire way. My butler told me he would send word to Toby or Anthony if I did not return to bed at once."

"They care for you."

"My hope is that you do too," he said, tugging her hands until her body was closer to his. He then placed Alice's hands on his chest, one of his lifting her chin until their eyes met.

"I do," she whispered. "So very much."

Jamie kissed her then. Gentle and sweet.

"And will you marry me?" He rested his forehead on hers.

"You told my father I would."

"I'm sorry I told him before I asked you, Alice, but I reacted when I heard how he was speaking to you. He's your father, and there is every chance I will have to face him across ballrooms and dinner tables, but—"

"He's a terrible person," Alice filled in for him.

"We will argue, and our life will not always run smoothly, but know that you will always hold my heart, Alice."

"My aunt will need a home also, Jamie."

"Excellent. I've always wanted an aunt like Anthony has. If she has no wish to live with us, then we shall settle her in her own townhouse nearby."

Their words were whispered, faces inches apart.

"We are both strong-willed," Alice said. "It will not be easy."

"There will be give or take, but what I love most about you, Lady Alice, is your strength. You are no vapid miss who doesn't know her mind. Let me share your life, as you will share mine."

Alice had been alone for so long, the thought of sharing her life with another who would want as much control as she did was daunting.

"Let me help you with funding for your clinic, Alice."

"Jamie, I don't want your money."

"It's not mine. It's ours, if you'll have me. You've built something extraordinary, Alice. Let me stand beside you while you continue to do so."

Her eyes softened. "I want that," she whispered. Then, after a beat, "But can you truly move on? From Jackson, from the years he stole from you?"

He cupped her face, thumb brushing away a tear. "There will be nights when the darkness still comes. But I believe now I can face it with you beside me."

She kissed his palm. "Then we'll heal together."

No more words were needed. They had not planned to find each other, and she knew their journey would have many twists and turns, but there was no one else Alice would rather traverse it with.

CHAPTER THIRTY-THREE

JAMIE WAS RUNNING late, and today of all days, that was a terrible thing. He urged his mount forward through the narrow London streets. Sunlight speared between tall buildings, and above them, the sky was a startling, brilliant blue.

He could almost see Alice now. Hands on hips, foot tapping, and those soft lips he'd kissed only last night pursed in that mixture of affection and exasperation that always undid him.

"Make haste, Archie," he muttered, leaning low in the saddle, "or I'll be in a world of trouble."

"It's not his fault," Anthony drawled from his left, "that you were too busy devouring that second slice of cake to notice the time."

"Third slice," Toby corrected cheerfully.

Jamie grunted and ignored them both. They had been teasing him since they left the tea shop. Behind their teasing, though, was a bond forged through years of shared pain and affection. They were the brothers he'd never had.

Above them, church bells rang the hour. He was definitely late.

They were bound for St Giles, a place Jamie rarely visited until recently. It stood two streets shy of the infamous Rookery but close enough to feel its hellish shadow. The district smelled of despair, horse dung, coal smoke, and the tang of gin distilleries.

"Alice will forgive you for being late, Anthony said.

Jamie felt a smile tug at his lips. "My wife may love me, but she'll be sorely vexed if I'm not standing beside her when the first patient walks through that clinic door."

Anthony leaned across his saddle. "Five months wed and still speaking of her as if she's an angel. You'll give us all a bad name."

"Has it passed for you?" Jamie shot back. "You don't still hang on your beloved's every word?"

"Never," Anthony admitted. His wife was due to deliver their first child any day now. Toby's wasn't far behind. They were both equally excited and terrified.

Jamie's smile deepened. "You'll both make excellent fathers."

"And you?" Toby asked quietly.

"I hope to," Jamie said. "Soon."

He hadn't thought he'd ever want such a thing. Not after Blackwood Hall, and the years of darkness that had followed. But Alice had changed that. In the five months since becoming his wife, she'd filled the hollow spaces in him with laughter, warmth, and that fierce sense of purpose that seemed to burn in her like a flame.

"How was she this morning?" Anthony asked.

"Determined and excited," Jamie said. "She left early to see to last-minute details with Maggie, Ezra, and Bobby, but said she had no use for me until the opening. But I was told, in no uncertain terms, to be there on time."

"Ah," Toby said. "So you are in serious trouble."

"Very likely."

They turned onto a broader street, and the building came into view. Even from a distance, it stood out. Three stories of solid brick with tall arched windows, the stone newly scrubbed, and the door painted a deep green. The brass plaque he'd personally had made, gleamed in the sunlight:

The St Giles Medical and Relief House

Jamie felt something swell in his chest. Pride, perhaps. Or disbelief. He shot his friends a look.

A few years ago, they'd all been men clawing their way out of the wreckage of their pasts. Survivors of Blackwood Hall, that hellish school that had taught brutality instead of discipline. Now, they'd built something meant to heal.

All three were now married to women they loved, and with Jackson's incarceration, their need for revenge was complete. They still watched out for any Blackwood boys in need of help, but for the most part, they were at peace.

"There is a crowd," Anthony said as they arrived.

"I can't believe you actually got some of the ton here, Jamie. Not only that, they are standing about outside, in a part of London I daresay they have never frequented," Toby said.

"I am charming and persuasive when required." He took in the elegant carriages and their owners milling about before the clinic.

"Really?" Anthony said. "I have yet to see that side of you, Jamie."

"Very amusing." Jamie dismounted, handing Archie's reins to a boy, whom he handed a coin for his troubles. His friends did the same.

Alice had agreed when Jamie said they needed to get support from other wealthy noblemen. There were good people who walked among them in society, and some he knew would be willing to help fund more clinics in the areas of London that needed it most. Especially after the success of Alice's first clinic.

So, they had worked out with whom they wished to speak, and then had done just that. Alice laid out what she hoped to achieve and explained the requirements. Not everyone they approached had agreed, but most had. They were here today to see what their money had produced.

With his friends, he made his way to the building, nodding to those he knew, and offering smiles and explaining the clinic would be open shortly.

"Jamie!"

Turning, he found his sisters approaching.

"How is it that you are here?" Jamie asked after hugging

them. His friends greeted Hannah and Briar the same, as they'd grown close over the years.

"Alice has been corresponding with us, as she is far more diligent in her letter writing than you are," Hannah said.

He had no answer for that because they were right. Jamie loathed letter writing.

"So we decided to come to London and stay with you for a few nights. The rest of the family will arrive tomorrow," Briar said.

"And when were you to notify me of this?" Jamie asked.

"We're telling you now," Briar said.

"We went to your townhouse first, and your staff are getting things ready as we speak. Plus, your cook is making plum cake, as she's the best at it," Hannah added. "Now go inside and do what you must, and we shall await you out here. I'm sure Alice will speak like she does everything, magnificently, and we shall cheer loudly."

"While you stand at her side basking in her magnificence," Briar added with a cheeky smile, which had Anthony and Toby snorting.

"I'm sure you love my wife more than me," Jamie said.

"Oh, we absolutely do," Hannah said.

Jamie reached for her, but she danced away, eyes twinkling. "Love you, brother."

He looked at his sisters and said, "I love you both too. You two, however," he said, pointing to Anthony and Toby, "I'm not sure why I put up with. But you are right; I must find my wife. You four behave while I do so."

"We shall mingle and make everyone happy until you and Alice make your entrance… or exit, as is the case in this situation," Toby said.

Next to greet him was Aunt Gwen. She was with Anthony's aunts. All insisted on hugging him, and then fixing his necktie, wafting their scent up his nostrils as they did so.

"We have just arrived and will stand with my nephew and

your sisters, Jamie," Lady Petunia said. "But don't keep everyone waiting, as Captain Haleigh has that condition, you know. He can't stand for too long."

"Well, at least if something happens, he's in the right place," Jamie added.

They thought that hilarious and were still giggling as they headed in a gaggle toward the others.

The clinic's entrance hall had been transformed when Jamie entered. High ceilings and walls were whitewashed. The scent of new paint and beeswax mingled with something faintly medicinal. Tables lined one wall, set with pamphlets and ledgers. To the right, doors opened into treatment rooms, where white-aproned attendants stood ready beside polished brass instruments and neat rows of bandages.

And in the midst of it all was his love.

Jamie's heart gave a lurch as he studied her. She was talking to Dr. Hughes, her hands waving as she did when excited.

His fiery wife, who never took a step back when a forward one was offered. Like him, she'd changed. Love and support had helped her to be the woman she was today. Alice smiled more freely and laughed openly and saved all her love for Jamie.

Her dress was lilac, and among the white-clad medical staff stood out, but then to his mind, she always did. *Besotted fool that I am.*

She turned at that moment, and when her eyes met his, the bustle and chatter around them faded to nothing.

There it was again, that steadiness he always felt when she was near. One glance, and the restless, angry boy he'd once been vanished.

Alice's lips twitched as he reached her. "Late," she murmured when he leaned in to kiss her cheek.

"Barely," he murmured back. "Blame Toby."

"Do your friends know you always blame them for your tardiness?"

"Of course, because they do the same." He caught her hand

briefly, just long enough to feel her fingers squeeze his.

"Right then, let's go outside and open this place before there is a riot," Jamie said. "But I must warn you, my sweet, that there are quite a few society members out there."

"Really?" Her lovely eyes widened.

"Really, and that is why we will make haste, as it's not an area many are used to frequenting."

"And as they opened their purse strings to help us get this clinic up and running, we will not leave them standing for too long?"

"Exactly," Jamie said.

Leading Alice through the front door, he stepped back to stand with Anthony and Toby. He and his friends may have provided some of the money, but this was her achievement.

The crowd had grown, he noted. A small line had formed a short distance away, those waiting, careful not to step too close to the clinic's benefactors. They did not wear elegant fashions, but rather threadbare coats and patched skirts. Faces hollowed by worry, shoulders stooped from long days and longer nights.

"Clearly, they know the clinic is opening soon," Anthony whispered into his ear.

"Thank you all for coming," Alice said, stepping forward to look at those assembled before her. "There are many, many people who live within walking distance of us today, who were not born into privilege or can readily seek medical help. It's my hope that for a few, we can change that with this clinic."

She was magnificent, Jamie thought proudly, clapping loudly along with the other guests when Alice had finished talking. Some polite, some genuine. The wealthy smiled as if they'd discovered philanthropy for the first time. But the locals like the mothers clutching their children, and the old men leaning on sticks—their faces told a different story. Wonder, disbelief, and something dangerously close to hope.

Jamie's throat tightened. He'd spent years surrounded by privilege, insulated by power. He'd worn his title like armor. And yet, standing there, watching his wife bridge two worlds with nothing but compassion and determination, he realized how thin that armor was.

When the speeches ended, the crowd began to move inside, curious to see what was beyond the façade.

He turned to Anthony, who stood beside him with Toby. "Did you believe we would ever one day be here? We were unfit for anywhere but hell for a while, but—"

"If you say the love of a good woman again, I will hit you," Toby added.

Jamie laughed. Blackwood Hall had tried to break them and had nearly succeeded. But the scars that had once marked them had now become their strength.

"Do you recall," Toby said, "that miserable classroom where we were locked for days without food?"

"I try not to," Jamie said dryly. Searching inside himself, he felt nothing but pity for the boys they'd been. The anger had gone.

Toby's smile was grim. "I thought then we'd never be free. And now look at us. All married to women far too good for us."

"Speak for yourself," Anthony said, though his grin gave him away. "And now we had better mingle, or Alice will scold, and then tell our wives, as they meet often at the book club my aunts lured them into."

Anthony and Toby drifted off to speak with patrons, leaving Jamie to wander back inside. Alice joined him a few minutes later, her hand light on his arm as they stood to one side of the room and looked at the guests mingling with the clinic staff.

"I'm so proud of you, Alice."

"I'm proud of us," she countered. "Proud of the people we have become together."

"Together," he agreed. "Now, and always."

"Do you ever think of Blackwood Hall? Do Anthony and Toby?"

"Every day," he said. "But it no longer owns us. We can now

speak to each other freely of that time, and there is healing in that too."

Alice rested her head on his shoulder briefly.

"You've done something extraordinary here, Alice," Jamie said.

"We," she insisted.

He turned her toward him and kissed her, brief and over in seconds. Someone gasped. Someone else tittered. But Jamie only smiled against her lips. Let them talk. He was a marquess. More importantly, he was her husband.

"And now that I've disgraced myself, I will mingle," Alice said, her cheeks flushed.

"Disgracing yourself in public again, Stafford?" Toby asked as he arrived with Anthony.

"Tradition," Jamie said. "You'll recall it started at my wedding."

Anthony nodded. "I'd like to make a toast."

"You don't have a drink in your hand," Jamie added.

"To hell with tradition. I'd like to say, to the friendships that kept me sane, and alive, and to the women who saved us from ourselves."

Jamie raised an imaginary glass. "To that."

They clinked the air between them, the gesture simple but weighted with everything they'd endured. The years at Blackwood, the fights, the nightmares, the redemption.

Behind them, the clinic buzzed with life. Soon, the first patients would be seen. The future was not perfect, but it was theirs and so much better than he'd ever thought it would be.

Jamie looked at Alice once more, her face alight with purpose, and realized that the hell inside him had truly gone quiet, and the future dawned clear and bright with the woman he loved.

The End

About the Author

Wendy Vella is a *USA Today* and Amazon bestselling author of historical romances filled with romance, intrigue, unconventional heroines, and dashing heroes.

An incurable romantic, Wendy found writing romance a natural fit. Born and raised in a rural area in the North Island of New Zealand, she shares her life with one adorable husband, two delightful adult children and their partners, four delicious grandchildren, and her pup Tilly.

Wendy also writes small town contemporary romances under the name Lani Blake.

wendyvella.com/index.html

www.ingramcontent.com/pod-product-compliance
Lightning Source LLC
Chambersburg PA
CBHW071611030726
47598CB00001B/238